To Craig & Linda

Thank you for waiting and
for giving me the chance to
put This New venture forward.

I hope you enjoy my Novel.

Thanks Again

Luca D. Matteo

GREEN HAVEN

GREEN HAVEN

A NOVEL

LUCA DIMATTEO

www.mascotbooks.com

Green Haven

For more information, please contact:
Mascot Books
620 Herndon Parkway, Suite 320
Herndon, VA 20170
info@mascotbooks.com

Library of Congress Control Number: 2020905436

CPSIA Code: PRFRE0620A
ISBN-13: 978-1-64543-073-5

Printed in Canada

-words open our world

FOR THEIR LOVE AND GUIDANCE

For Laura, my loving wife, who believes in me no matter what. She makes me laugh when I'm sad. Her strength and courage are contagious. It was through her energy and endless help that my desire to write this novel became a reality. Her love of family, life, and all that makes a person great inspire me. She's more than my partner in life; she is my best friend.

For my children, Quinn, Ariel, Johnathan, Aiden, and Kira, the experiences I have with each of them is a precious moment that I, as a parent, will hold onto forever. I drew on those moments when I felt challenged to write.

For my parents, Idario and Margarita, whose guidance and loving support growing up and still today help me be the man I am. They, with my brothers George and Steven, created a family filled with love, values, and trust. The bond of a family was grown here and passed forward.

For my mother-in-law, Marjaa, I have the utmost gratitude and love. She was one of my biggest supporters for this book. She was the first to read it and make wonderfully constructive criticisms about it. She helped me grow tremendously as a writer and a person.

For my brother-in-law, Mark, who shows me love and compassion. His role here may have been in the background, but without his caring support I could not have moved forward. He is a shining example of passion and drive.

For Maury, a friend and brother, who checks in on me and dares me to be better. His input is always welcome. It's a better world with him in it.

For Ecco, our dog, who lays at my feet as I type away. She is a hairy smile filled with unconditional love.

For Theresa Mackiewicz, a fellow author, who sits with me at coffee shops and pushes me to be better, to go further, and for introducing me to Mascot Books, thank you.

To Mascot Books, who worked with me to make *Green Haven* come alive, thanks.

Finally, to all the rest who helped make this dream real by contributing financially, by editing, publishing, buying this book, I would like to let you know how grateful I am. A mere thank you is written here, but my heart wants to say so much more.

1

"DR. PASSED, DR. PASSED, north wing."

Director of Nursing, Cathy Arden, rose from her 1970s metal desk, annoyed that she was interrupted for the third time this week. Then she thought, just another Tuesday at Green Haven. She stood too quickly and sent the cheap pharmacy cheaters nestled atop her jet-black hair tumbling to the floor. A silent "crap" came from her mouth as she retrieved the glasses. She walked around the aging and dented gray occupant that had been in her tiny windowless office well before she arrived six years ago.

The door to room 103 had been closed. Father Brendan and his spiritual cohort, Sister Diane, were standing outside the room quietly preparing to pray. The newly deceased, eighty-seven-year-old Anna Sparks had been part of Green Haven for the last nine years. When she first came in, she was a vibrant seventy-eight-year-old widow. She and her husband, Thomas, owned a modest but very successful furniture store for over fifty years. Thomas died from a blood clot four years before Anna moved into Green Haven. She never got over his passing. Between Thomas' life insurance and selling the furniture store, Anna didn't have financial worries. She developed memory issues, which led to the start of Alzheimer's and, most likely, her death.

1

Cathy's long, muscular legs from many years of hiking, an activity she hadn't done for some time now, allowed her to move down the hallways at a faster than average pace. As she passed the nursing station on the north wing, she paid no attention to the hushed words coming from behind the desk. She had been working as the director of nursing for long enough to understand that underlings whisper. She would have to occasionally remind herself to ignore it. It was no secret they thought Cathy had been there too long. But her work was good, she was fair, most of the time, and she was prone to letting a lot of the little things go. At times, Cathy also wondered why she stayed. She had been a young, bright star in the beginning, and now she pushed through her days in as much solitude at work as she had at home.

"Okay, you two, let's go." Cathy ordered Father Brendan and Sister Diane to follow her into the room.

Anna Sparks' room was a testimonial to the life that she and Thomas had. Photos of Thomas and their life draped the walls and covered the dresser tops. Anna's body lay in a bed wrapped with a blanket depicting a group of children. Some years earlier, her family had the faces of Anna's grandchildren printed on the blanket so she wouldn't forget them. It's both a joyous and a painful reminder. In Anna's closet hangs a blue dress she wished to be buried in. The dress holds the memory of the day she and Thomas renewed their vows on the fiftieth year of their lifelong bond. Thomas had been buried in the charcoal gray suit from that very same memory. It was a promise they made to each other that same day, while standing at the altar.

"They always look so peaceful," Sister Diane said as she stared at Anna lying in her bed with her hands folded across her waist.

"You can thank the aides or the floor nurse for that. I never really know who sets them up." Cathy's words were as lifeless as poor Anna Sparks.

Cathy had done this so many times in the past six years that she had the death certificates in her desk prefilled with everything but the name, date, and time of death. She pulled over the adjustable tray table and raised it so she wouldn't have to lean over. She chuckled as she recalled the numerous in-services she'd been forced to attend that seemed to always cover: raise the bed, raise the tray table, and lift with your legs: *You only get one back.*

Anna's chart had been labeled "nurse may pronounce." Someone on the Green Haven board thought that allowing the Director of Nursing to pronounce residents deceased would save time and money. The body could then be moved out of the room instead of waiting for a doctor to arrive and make the call. Cathy found it was just one more time-consuming detail that became part of her job description. She used to think to do more meant more respect, or at least more recognition. Those thoughts had long since faded. She now checked in at 6:59 am and left most of the time at 4:01 pm, just for good measure.

Time of death 10:15 am. In the beginning, Cathy always wanted to write the cause of death as a lack of breathing, now she would settle for old, if she could.

"Okay, Father, do your thing," Cathy said as she left the room. She closed the door to give Father Brendan and Sister Diane privacy. The Father and Sister duo had been working at the facility for about two years now. They replaced old Father Timothy, who had been a one-man show at Green Haven since it opened. Rumor has it that he was reluctantly put out to pasture by the local Bishop Anthony, a headstrong progressive Catholic leader who believed in, out with the withering and in with the likeminded. Father Timothy had been set in his ways. A fact that put him at odds with the Bishop more so than not.

Father Brendan asked Sister Diane to stand near the door to keep anyone from coming in. He insisted on privacy and respect for the dead. She leaned against the door, looking back at Anna and Father Brendan. Her thin, frail frame would topple over if the slightest opposing pressure were applied to the opposite side of the door. A fact Father Brendan had reminded her of on numerous occasions. Now, he just hoped it would never happen.

He began to pray for Anna. "Anna, now you can go to a better place. To be with Thomas again. It's our job to help you make that transition. I ask that an angel from Heaven guide you on your journey." Father Brendan's towering six-foot-three-inch frame lumbered over Anna; he explained to her it wasn't just his job to help her, but that it was his and Sister Diane's calling. He spoke quietly and moved his hands over the body, making signs of the cross and looking at the ceiling from time to time. "Go in peace," were his final words, and then he stood there silent, staring at the body of Anna Sparks as if he expected a response from her.

Sister Diane stayed against the door and also prayed quietly. Repeatedly she whispered, "Forgive the sins, wash away the sins, and allow us the entrance to Heaven." It appeared she was given the task of cleansing the soul of the dead.

They covered all the bases in a well-practiced dance. One they had done many times over the last two years. They left Anna Sparks' room, and the process of removing the body, her belongings, and cleaning the space started.

Cathy returned to her cubicle-sized office to add the final touches to Anna Sparks' death certificate. After placing the last letter on the form, she took off her cheaters and pushed back in her chair, hitting the backrest against the wall. She flung her eyewear onto the cluttered desk and muttered, "Is this really the office that the Director of Nursing deserves? Bet Kyle would say yes." A deflated and beaten reality drifted across Cathy's face. One that she had long ago accepted as her fate.

Cathy had graduated from nursing school some years earlier. After a short stint as a floor nurse in a small rural hospital, she found taking orders wasn't for her. She went back and obtained her Bachelor of Science in Nursing. She didn't have the patience or the desire to job hunt, so she took the first offer that came along.

Green Haven Nursing Center was a forty-bed facility that suited her well. It was close to home, and the hours were the same 7:00 am to 4:00 pm week to week. There was little need to stay late or come in early. Besides, Green Haven had agreed to pay for Cathy's advanced degree as long as she agreed to remain at the facility for at least three years. A deal that was as unique as Green Haven itself.

Today was one of those days; the walls of the furnished closet were closing in fast. "I need to take a walk." Cathy left the office and headed for north wing. She took a deep breath before crossing the imaginary line into the "cheap seats." North wing was the wing that housed residents ranging from those needing minimal skilled nursing care to others who'd become bedridden. The rooms were singles and catered to residents with the means to help them along later in life. As far as nursing facilities go, it was a top-shelf wing, but not at Green Haven. South wing was for the lavishly rich senior being hidden away.

Cathy was about to make her round in the north wing when she suddenly stopped, turned, and headed through the lobby, ducking under the window of the administrator's door, then dashing into the open outdoors of Green Haven. "Air, I just need air," she told herself. She placed her hands on the back of her neck and gently rubbed with her fingers. Something was off; she ignored the feeling as she paced the covered outdoor seating area. Cathy exhaled loudly; she was grateful that none of the residents had made their way out to the endless row of rockers sitting and waiting to be occupied.

A few more laps in front of the rockers, some arm stretches, and Cathy was ready to head back in. As she hit the automatic door opener she could see "the holy couple" was preparing to make their exit.

Bishop Anthony had taken Father Brendan right from ordination and placed him in a nearby parish. The Bishop paired him with Sister Diane shortly before removing her from a convent. In their short time at Green Haven, they gained the reputation and nickname "the holy couple." Rumors floated around the facilities very quickly and with a lot of embellishment. Early on it was said the holy couple had a love child and even named it Jesus. It was easy to see how this rumor could start. Father Brendan's squared shoulders and warm deep blue eyes were as inviting as a loving hug hiding the fire of pure lust. Sister Diane's small but innocent blonde, girl-next-door appearance gave the look of needing saving from the evils of the world. Of course, all of it was fodder to perpetuate a good rumor. Like all other rumors, the rumors about Father Brendan and Sister Diane were soon replaced with the next great story, and the holy couple just faded into the walls of every facility they visited.

Father Brendan waived to Cathy as they passed in the doorway. Sister Diane offered an absolutely beaming, large smiling gesture. "Have a great rest of the day, Nurse Cathy."

"Uh, yes, you too, Sister."

Cathy wondered how the Sister could always be smiling. She almost looked back, half wondering if the rumors about them were true. She grinned as she thought, *Good sex could make you smile a lot.*

2

ALL THIS LUXURY DIDN'T transition down to the staff of Green Haven. On her first day, Cathy had everything in her tiny new office removed. The old DON had been a sixty-year-old nursing veteran who'd been at the post for the better part of ten years. She was at the end of her career; she didn't like computers and hated change even more. Cathy saw right away that Green Haven's nursing department needed a significant upgrade. The old, outdated room she called her office would be an excellent place to start. Cathy made a request for a new desk, perhaps something from the current millennium. The lack of an answer set the tone loudly. The nurses had been in their same positions from the day they were hired, and there was no one leading them into today's world. Cathy was new and ambitious. She was determined to move the Green Haven nursing staff into the current century.

During the next few weeks, while trying to learn the ropes, Cathy was taking notes and coming up with creative and overzealous programs to move her nursing team forward. This meant retraining those who were willing and firing those who wished to remain in the dark. She gained a reputation as tough but fair. In the following year, she'd present idea after idea to Green Haven's upper echelon through Kyle, the administrator. Occasionally they approved a watered-down version. Something Cathy would have to learn to live with.

While at a continuing education seminar in Dallas, Cathy wandered into the vendors' area and noticed a small startup company called Pharmatek. They had created software specific to pharmacological concerns in nursing homes. They sold the laptops and software setups for medication carts. This meant that nurses could dispense medication and have it tracked in real time. Hopefully, this would decrease errors.

Pharmatek was new, and the owners were practically begging to make sales. Cathy checked around with similar vendors and discovered that Pharmatek was undercutting their competitors by 35 percent. She returned to Green Haven, convinced Kyle, who then convinced the board to buy four systems. Cathy's pitch weighed heavily on the fact that government regulations were leaning toward making computers mandatory in nursing facilities. Buying them now would be less costly than buying them when they were required. It was only a matter of time before it was law. Green Haven would be ahead of the curve for once. Because the board had a history of declining or diminishing her ideas, Cathy originally persuaded Kyle to request ten systems; she was hoping to get five. The board approved four; she took it as a win. Cathy found out quickly she worked in an industry that was constantly in a state of underfunding and short staffing. The unwritten motto was, "Don't cut corners but don't overspend." This seemed to be true even for the luxury of Green Haven.

Some of the nursing staff were older, and change didn't come without scars. Cathy was a modernized nurse and somewhat computer savvy. She understood the basics and learned quickly. She was forced to stay late and come in early to help train the nurses on the new system. Pharmatek was smaller than Cathy thought. The training person must have been hired minutes after the ink was dry on the contract. She barely knew more than the nurses she was training. Pharmatek's database of medications was greatly underdeveloped. It was definitely a work in process. Eight months later the Green Haven board fired Pharmatek. Then they sued them for breach of contract on the grounds that the company could not produce the technical expertise they promised. Pharmatek settled the suit and closed its doors in fear of being sued by other facilities they had contracted. The Green Haven, Inc. board understood the future possibilities, so as part of the settlement they required Pharmatek to leave behind the laptops. The board hired a consultant who found them a new software company.

A few months later the new software was installed along with desktops at the nursing stations and in the management offices. The program was equipped with every generic medication and had all its brand name counterparts listed under it. Every possible interaction, contraindication, and side effect popped up automatically for each individual resident. It was touted as being able to do everything except give the resident the medication. The new goliath was also fully capable of resident charting. It cost much more, but Green Haven received a hefty settlement from Pharmatek that practically made it free. This all sounded great, but none of that mattered. The nurses were even more terrified of this system. Cathy was relegated to learning the software along with the rest of the nurses with no special consideration for her rank. Even though she could understand the system much faster, she, like the rest of the nurses, was only allowed to go as fast as the slowest learner. The consultant was also charged with hiring a full-time IT person to ensure the system would function consistently, handle updates, and field questions from the staff.

Cathy soon began to feel the repercussions of the Pharmatek failure. Her reviews began to be less than stellar, and rumors started flying that Green Haven was quietly shopping for a DON. Cathy called a meeting with the administrator, Kyle Strong, and Medical Director, Dr. Marissa Oliver.

It was a very one-sided and brief conversation. "Green Haven needs to keep moving forward and stay competitive. I believe that was part of your pitch to me for that Pharma-junk. Wasn't it?" Kyle's bitter tone was not missed by Cathy or Dr. Oliver.

"I believe what Kyle is trying to say is that you were hired to do a job and sometimes overreaching can be disastrous. It might be better to continue within the scope of your position and not stray." Dr. Oliver's words came with a smile but cut to the bone.

"What I'm saying is that you have enough to do, so just worry about doing it right." Kyle's eyes were on fire. His rage was unmistakable.

Cathy said nothing. She was deflated after the meeting. She'd been put in her place. The Director of Nursing whose powerful stride and straight shoulders, that yelled authority, now felt as though they were hobbled and slumped by the weight of her defeat. The hazel glares from Cathy's eyes that the staff could expect to come down the hallway were now focused mainly on the brown speckles that tried to make their escape from the imprisonment of the floor tiles.

The plain but sentimental watch on Cathy's wrist that was given to her by her mother upon nursing school graduation banged against the handrail, pulling her back to the present as though it was trying to remind her the day had ended.

She went home to her two-bedroom condo, uncorked a bottle of red wine, poured a glass, and opened the fridge. She slammed the door closed. Food was not on the menu, at least not at this moment. She sat on the leather couch bought after her three-month probation period at Green Haven was over.

Cathy kicked off the nearly reflective high-gloss black leather shoes she had worn to work today. Green Haven, Inc. "requested" that the DON dress more professionally than the rest of the nursing staff. They were under the impression that the DON would have more contact with family members, thus needing to set a higher standard. Cathy recalled that the heels further increased her already elevated physical status over the nurses. Her five-foot-seven-inch frame ensured most of the nurses would have to look up to speak eye to eye with her now. Deep down Cathy wanted to have a mutual camaraderie with her nurses, but Green Haven, Inc. insisted on a hierarchy. And she was already in enough trouble.

She reached for the remote but threw it down on the couch in disgust. After finishing a large glass of wine, Cathy came to the revelation that Green Haven didn't deserve her genius. No more great ideas. She finally realized what her parents had been trying to tell her for most of her childhood. There are those who have all the power and those who just work for them. Her mother and father didn't have the power, didn't know how to get it, and just gave up trying. She secretly hated her parents for this, but now she thought she understood them more than ever. Green Haven, Inc. gave her the illusion of power, and they could bust that illusion at any time. Today, for instance. From now on, she'd clock in, do her job, and clock out.

Disgusted and filled with wine, Cathy slowly walked into the bedroom, changed for bed, and fell asleep. *Tomorrow will be a better day*, she thought as she closed her eyes. The alarm was already set for 5:45 am, just like it was every day.

3

IT WAS THURSDAY; CATHY had a quiet morning only being belittled by Kyle in the morning report. This was about an hour each day that Kyle took pleasure in showing the Green Haven world how great he was. She returned to her office to continue with her reviews of whatever needed her attention. She enjoyed the solitude after all these years.

11:52 am. Cathy almost cringed hearing "Dr. Passed, Dr. Passed" coming over the intercom. This time it was the south wing. Cathy sighed as she reached into her desk, trying not to mar the nude-colored nail polish, another suggestion from Green Haven, Inc.'s astute professional appearance ideal. She pulled out the form and started down the hallway. South wing was a mirror unit housing twenty residents, all of whom could also afford long-term care with a private aide to assist them. Cathy always thought of it as having a butler or maid in a nursing facility. She figured the rich needed something to spend their money on. The families of these residents paid privately for everything and didn't ask questions. Green Haven residents may have all the amenities, but they're short on family. It's the common link among all of them.

"Okay Padre, it's time to go to work again," Cathy quipped as she passed by the nurses' station.

Cathy pushed back the arm of the hanging twenty-four-inch television so she could get to the resident. Adam James was the managing partner of James, Long, McNeal, and seven other names on the wall of a huge firm of attorneys. Attorney James was ninety-one years old and had not practiced law in over thirty years. He retired early and lived with his entitled four children until they placed him in Green Haven at age eighty-one.

Adam was one of Cathy's oldest residents. She'd known him since her first day. Back then he was lively and spent most of his time at Green Haven giving free legal advice to the residents, as well as the staff. Cathy recalled having a conversation with the scholarly resident many years ago.

"Ever since a bad outcome here at Green Haven. Which I must admit was instigated by me, but I had only good intentions I'll have you know . . ."

"You're talking about the computer snafu. It's not a secret." He gave her a fatherly look.

"Yes. And ever since then Kyle has hated me and has given me subtle beatings on a daily basis." She put her head down slightly.

"Has anyone else been present for any of the 'beatings'?"

"I don't think so."

"I could have a talk with him, or better yet I could come out of retirement and kick his ass." Adam was shaking a fist in the air.

"No. I don't think either is necessary. Please don't say anything." At that moment, Cathy realized she had said too much.

Now Cathy thought this may have been the real reason she lost touch with Mr. James, not the lie that she simply got too busy. She couldn't risk another "snafu," as Adam had put it so many years ago.

"Time of Death: 12:02 pm."

Father Brendan stepped toward the bed, Cathy left the room, and Sister Diane went to the door. Not a word was uttered. The holy couple's religious waltz began.

By 12:30 pm, the holy couple was leaving for the next facility. They covered all the Green Haven, Inc. facilities, just not all in one day. They called it being on tour. They'd worked well as a team ever since Bishop Anthony paired them.

Cathy returned to her desk, took a sip of her cold coffee, and wondered if lunch was on her agenda for today. Dying was a business of paperwork and family notification at any nursing home. None of which Cathy enjoyed or ever wanted to handle. She signed into her computer and looked up Mr. James' next of kin. She called Cleo James and gave her the bad news. There wasn't much of a response. Cathy had long since understood that most families didn't care. She was no longer surprised by the lack of emotion or the performance art of overreacting from family members who barely visited. She had become hardened to it. Thinking of their performance art made her realize that in the two years, since Father Brendan and Sister Diane took over, she had never once stayed in the room to watch the holy couple act out their play. It seemed like an invasion of privacy. Besides, she had enough to do trying to keep the residents alive. The dying part was up to them.

The next morning Cathy walked into the morning meeting and sat down next to Kyle, who gave her his customary, frigid hello. As the administrator, all the successes and failures of Green Haven were his successes and failures. To make things worse, Cathy had done such a good job selling Pharmatek to Kyle that he bypassed researching the company for himself. He sold it even harder to the board. They went on his recommendation of Pharmatek. He'd downplayed Cathy's role in the whole matter. Kyle had seen it as an opportunity to make a name for himself. He was then forced to take all the heat from corporate, nearly getting fired. Kyle has been overlooked for two promotions and the salary hikes that went with them. He was determined to make Cathy feel his pain. For the months that followed the Phamatek fiasco, Cathy apologized to Kyle hundreds of time. She explained that she was duped by the salesman, the fancy demo, and continued personal attention that Pharmatek had promised. She told him she asked the other vendors at the seminar about Pharmatek, and no one had a bad thing to say about them.

Kyle's answer was always the same. "I should have known better. In hindsight, you made it sound too good to be true. You wanted it too much." Fire practically shot from his mouth as he spoke. The veins in his head glowed a dull blue hue, just one step away from bursting.

Cathy would reply, "I was taken . . ."

"No! You don't get to talk. You did enough of that to me when you sold me that damn company!" Kyle shouted in a stroke-inducing rage. It was clear to Cathy; Kyle was never going to get over Pharmatek. She decided to keep her head down and stay clear of him as much as possible. Cathy also vowed that if anything came up again, she was going to make damn sure she examined every detail before even thinking of making a sound. Even after that, she probably wouldn't say a word.

The morning meeting started late with Dr. Oliver sneaking in at the last minute. The medical director occasionally sat in on morning meetings. She rarely said anything and mostly used the time to sign paperwork that Green Haven required. Cathy announced there were two more expirations this week, Anna Sparks, eighty-seven, and Adam James, ninety-one. Causes of death: complications associated with advanced age and failure to thrive. Both residents had "nurse may pronounce" documentation.

Dr. Oliver lifted her head from the stack of papers she was thumbing through and sighed. "Five here, four at Autumn Living, and two at Elite Care this month. That's just more paperwork." Dr. Oliver thought she'd have to negotiate for more money with Oscar when her contract was up. She chuckled, which brought quite a few stares since they were talking about people dying. But her chuckle was regarding whether to negotiate with Oscar before or after their Friday afternoon sex sessions. Either way, he couldn't say no; this made her chuckle more and receive another round of stares. No one dared say anything. It was not a well-kept secret, at least around Green Haven, that Oscar Green and Dr. Oliver were lovers. Perhaps only Dr. Oliver didn't know about the whispers.

4

DR. MARISSA OLIVER WAS in the final year of a substandard medical residency when Oscar's father was admitted to her care. Oscar was immediately taken with Dr. Oliver and not because of her healing ability or even the amount of attention she paid to his father. For Oscar, the attraction was primal. Feelings he hadn't had in a long time. His dad was nearing the end, but Oscar could only think of Dr. Marissa Oliver's shoulder-length blondeness swaying side to side as she walked. He could just make out the perfectly sculpted curves she hid under the perfunctory white lab coat. Neither Oscar nor Marisa would be considered tall, but he stood just above her frame. This was another delight for him since his wife stood a full two inches above him at all times, more if she chose to don heels. Oscar wanted to ask her out, but he was married, and his dying father was her patient. He kept silent while screaming on the inside for her. Dr. Oliver took care of Oscar's father for two weeks before he passed. Oscar made it a point to be at the hospital every day. Dr. Oliver made sure to check in on Mr. Green's father at least twice every shift. Mr. Green, Sr. had a private room, and his only visitors aside from the staff were his son and some clergy. The nursing staff and even Dr. Oliver knew his time was drawing to a close, but Oscar was unwilling to accept this.

Shortly after his father's passing, Oscar was divorced. It had been bitter but quick. Lacey Green, his now ex-wife, was a mother who went back to school to become an attorney. Two years afterward, she filed for divorce, right after accepting a very lucrative position in a large, out-of-state law firm. Oscar didn't have the fight in him and gave her just about everything as long as she left Green Haven, Inc. alone. This was fine with her. She wanted the two children and didn't need any money he might have hidden. Besides, Lacey hated the Green Haven idea from the beginning. Mainly because she thought Oscar was doing it to please his dead father, a man Lacey seemed to dislike for reasons she never made clear. This made Oscar push harder for Green Haven, Inc. to be a success. After Lacey became a successful attorney, she also seemed to despise Oscar, again for reasons she never divulged.

Green Haven was the first and namesake flagship of the Green Haven, Inc. empire that Oscar Green would build. On the lower right corner of each building, Oscar had the inscription "For You, Dad" sandblasted into the stone. He was determined to honor the father he missed. His dad had always been there to help him. If a deal was going south or the city was giving him a hard time, Oscar would call his dad for advice. It was always, always correct. Things worked out just like his dad told him they would.

Before building Green Haven, Oscar was a midsized contractor with little notoriety. He believed in hard work, long hours, and if it worked, keep doing it. His first and only love was work. This was probably why his marriage ended as it did. Oscar's mother died at sixty-eight from dehydration, a complication of severe flu symptoms. His father spent a few years in a sub-par nursing home complaining about the food and always asking his son to build him a nicer place to live. Oscar never had the time or the money. When his father died, Oscar found out he had a significant life insurance policy and a safety deposit box. No one seemed to know about the latter. Oscar discovered the deposit box by accident. He was cleaning out his father's belongings from the basement of his home. He was eventually forced to sell the house as part of the divorce agreement. He found a small stack of letters addressed to his mother. They were in his father's handwriting. Oscar was about to toss them when he felt something bulky in the center of the pile. Among the letters was a single envelope addressed, "For you and only you, Oscar."

Oscar quickly shoved the letter in his pocket. He didn't want to open it with his, not yet, ex-wife and kids present. Later that night he locked himself in the bathroom and quietly read it.

Dearest Oscar,

Since the loss of your mother my will to live is only hanging on because of you, my loving son. Well before your mother passed, we knew that our lives were coming to an end and soon you'd be left alone in this world. We're sorry we never gave you a brother or sister to call family and share memories of growing up with. I knew there would come a time when you would be forced to put me in a nursing home and they would take everything. There is a key here to a safety deposit box in my name and your social security number. Since our names are the same, the box is now yours. Go to my bank and see the bank manager, Lois; she was a lifelong friend of your mother and understands the situation. Please take its contents quietly and make your dreams possible.

Be safe and well, my son. Your loving father.

For a moment, Oscar thought of running away. He would tan himself on beaches and dine in fancy restaurants for the rest of his life. He gave a small chuckle. "I'm chubby enough, my skin would fry, and I don't like to travel. That won't last long."

Between the life insurance money and the secret box, there was enough to buy the land for Green Haven outright and start construction. Two architects and a general contractor later, Green Haven was ready for its first resident.

Oscar planned to create a high-end senior living paradise so the well-off could go toward the afterlife in elegant style. Something he never gave to his father. All the luxuries you could afford for a set yearly price, for life. This was Oscar Green's master plan. He didn't know or care about the rules and regulations of running a nursing home. Oscar left that to the board, with one caveat; Dr. Marissa Oliver was to be hired as medical director.

As Green Haven's construction continued, Oscar leaned on those professionals whom he had come across in his past to help him form the Green Haven, Inc. board. Oscar may not be a super cranium, but he had enough sense to know what he didn't know. The board agreed to his caveat, and Oscar pushed the issue further. He demanded that he make the offer to Dr. Oliver and had the right to make whatever offer it took to get her to say yes. The board was puzzled by the request since Oscar had little interest, if any at all, in the actual running of the place. He explained that she tried to save his father and she should be rewarded for her efforts. Secretly, Oscar delighted in the chance to reunite with the woman who implanted herself in his heart with surgical precision. Oscar knew this was his own doing and she had made no indication of feelings towards him. "We all have to have dreams," Oscar told himself aloud.

After the board's weak approval of letting Oscar handle Dr. Oliver, he set out to find her. Her residency had ended, and she'd moved on. After several failed attempts to find out where she'd gone, he decided to just Google her name. It worked. She had opened up a small office two towns away. He left a voicemail for her that night, and she returned the call the next morning.

Oscar re-introduced himself and explained that she'd taken care of his father at his passing. He told her that he found her using the internet. Marissa pretended to remember. He realized how this must have sounded; he didn't want to seem like a stalker or some internet psychopath, so he quickly jumped to offering her a position as medical director of Green Haven.

Marisa did vaguely remember the situation, but she was unable to place a face to the voice on the other end of the phone. Holding the phone with her left hand, she reached into the bottom drawer of her desk and removed an old logbook from her last year of residency. Every resident kept a log of their patients just in case something came up.

"Can I put you on hold for a moment, Mr. Green?"

"Yes. And it's Oscar. Please."

Marissa needed both hands to thumb through the pocket-sized book and she didn't want the strange caller on the other end of the phone to hear the rustling of the pages. There it was, the name Oscar Green, seventy-nine-year male, heart failure, frail, unwilling to thrive . . . Marissa stopped reading; she didn't need to go over the rest of the details. She recalled the tired old man who wanted to join his wife, and now she could place the grief-stricken kind face of his son who silently cried for her to save his father.

As Oscar waited for Dr. Oliver to return to the phone, he thought that he didn't want to meet at her office, giving her home court advantage. He didn't want to meet at his office because it was cluttered and unkempt. He did want to make a good impression. Oscar would ask if they could meet over lunch soon since the facility was about to open.

"Sorry for the delay, Mr. Green. Uh, Oscar." She wanted to make him believe she had only a faint recall of the entire matter.

"That's okay. I'd like to get back to why I called. Like I was saying . . ."

"Yes, of course. You want to discuss me taking a position as medical director of something called Green Haven."

"That's right. Can we set an appointment?" Oscar rubbed his eyebrow with his pointer finger. He wanted this badly.

"I'd need to know a lot more about the position and the details of a contract before even considering it." Marissa smiled as she looked around her sparse office. Maybe this was her ticket out of here.

"I understand. As I was saying, I'd like to set a lunch meeting with you to discuss the position in more detail. Time . . ."

"That's fine, but I'll have to check my schedule."

"Would you like to do that now?"

"I did as you were talking. How about this Friday?"

"That works. I'll make a reservation at Andre's Café on Friday the 23rd for 12:30. Does . . ."

"That's fine. See you then." Dr. Oliver placed the receiver down quickly to give the impression that his call was somewhat of an intrusion to her busy day. It worked.

Oscar grinned at the thought of seeing Marissa Oliver again then frowned as he played back the conversation. He smiled again as he thought they would have plenty of time to work on their conversation skills.

5

TUESDAY MORNING 8:45 AM. Cathy was at her desk reviewing the events from the previous evening when she heard the call for Dr. Passed. She headed out the door, a certificate in hand. When she reached the room of Miss Samantha Whitehall, the holy couple was already perched and awaiting her signal. Cathy smiled and entered the room with the two in tow. She went over to the bed and called out Samantha's name three times. She then briskly ran her knuckles over the center of the resident's chest. Cathy put on her stethoscope, listened for breath sounds, and turned to look at the clock.

"Time of death 8:53 am."

The prefilled paper only needed the resident's name, date of birth, and cause of death. Cathy could do this in seconds and probably with her eyes closed. She turned her attention to the tall priestly man and his plainly dressed but attractive female sidekick, who were looming in the shadows awaiting their cue. Without the slightest bit of emotion, Cathy summoned them into action as she walked past them. "Okay, do that thing you guys do."

Father Brendan looked at Sister Diane. "I know. We've had this conversation many times. The result is always the same."

Sister Diane placed her hands on her narrow hips. "But, shouldn't we talk to her? She can't be that callous to it?"

"We both agreed. We cannot judge her. And perhaps, she should be hardened to death. Nurse Cathy's lack of emotion is how she deals with death." Father Brendan made a sign of the cross as though he was blessing Cathy.

"But it's all bottled up inside of her. I can . . ." She was almost pleading with him.

Father Brendan interrupted her, an action neither of them was used to, and then he pulled rank on her. "You are a sister and my title as the priest trumps yours. So, with all the compassion I can give you, please let it go and don't say a word to Nurse Cathy about it. Don't we have enough work consoling the residents? You what to start on the staff too?"

Sister Diane had not ever seen Father Brendan pull rank on her. It was understood that he was in charge, but it was never an issue before. The rest of the Green Haven visit was a series of short conversations between the two. Sister Diane was licking her wounds while Father Brendan carried an oversized backpack filled with guilt. Guilt was not a stranger to the priest, but it had been two years since he was afflicted with it.

Father Brendan's given name was Brendan M. Pierce. He was the only child of Alicia Martin-Pierce and Connor Pierce. Brendan's mother, Alicia, was a financial advisor who was making a name for herself in the financial industry. She always had meetings, lectures, or speeches to give, and awards to receive. Alicia Martin-Pierce maintained a slender, attractive figure with youthful hands and a lack of any creases on her face that might relinquish her age. Despite her allure, she wasn't approachable; her reputation for being a ruthless financial shark was well known. The words *sophisticated* and *intelligent* were always added before *shark* because of the fear of a backlash from Alicia. She had been recruited countless times and could choose her own destiny.

Brendan's father was a tenured history professor who spent more time with his students than his family. Connor Pierce, while not as famous as his wife, did manage to gain moderate notoriety from publishing articles and authoring a book. His book on the history of documenting history was an academic bestseller for almost a year. He was well liked by his students. He thought of himself as a scholar among scholars. Connor Pierce was a cliché in the academic dress world. He preferred to wear a tweed jacket with elbow patches, carry a shoulder-slung satchel, and tote an Indiana-Jones-type hat, which he carried in his hand most of the time because his head would get too hot.

It was never clear to Brendan if his parents had him out of a sense of parental duty or purely by mistake. Either way, he didn't really want to know. Brendan's childhood was spent growing up mostly at the hands of nannies and grandparents. His parents made all the behind-the-scenes decisions and gave the appearance of "a happy family" for special occasions.

Both parents were too busy and too absorbed in their own worlds to care much about anything else. This was quite evident as Brendan, as a young child, overheard numerous conversations between the nannies and one parent or another regarding his dress.

"Mrs. Pierce, Brendan's clothes are getting too small. He is a fast-growing boy. He needs new clothes."

"Okay. I'll place money in his account today, and you can take him tomorrow."

"Me? Mrs. Pierce, don't you want to pick out your boy's clothes?"

"Use your better judgment, then go one step higher, and we should be fine." She walked away before the nanny had another chance to object.

At ten years of age, Brendan felt the pain of being an unnecessary burden to his parents. Brendan could recall countless stories of this nature throughout his childhood, each one producing a pang of remorse and loneliness.

When Brendan was twenty-one, his parents told him via email they were getting divorced. They explained his education would still be paid for and he'd be fine. There was no follow-up, no phone call, nor in-person contact. It was merely a matter of fact. The email continued to say this was a mutual agreement on a long-overdue formality. Brendan couldn't deal with the situation and had no other family members to ask for help. His only family comfort in life was that his parents had managed to stay happily together even with all the time apart. Now that was a lie too, just like showing up at holidays as a cheerful, close family. Brendan felt the childhood pangs return.

Days after receiving the email, Brendan was wandering along the streets talking to himself. He asked himself why they couldn't include him, why they couldn't be honest with him, and why they even had him. He vowed he wouldn't allow himself to feel this much pain again, ever. Unknowingly, Brendan had stopped to contemplate his life directly in front of St. Michael's, a large but simple Catholic church. Looking at the angelic structure, he was surprised by the almost God-like calling he felt to enter the church. Since he wasn't Catholic and hadn't been to any church in forever, this was even more puzzling. Brendan's parents only prayed to their careers; the idea of visiting a church wasn't a blip on the proverbial radar.

There were stained-glass windows, many long wooden pews, marble floors, columns, and painted ceilings, but everything seemed simple and not ornate. Brendan walked up to about the fourth row and sat down, unsure why he was there. He wasn't even sure he believed in God. But he was drawn to this church today. He sat for what felt like hours and then looked at the watch his parents had given him for his high school graduation. It shined like real gold and had a Swiss name that his dad said was famous. It kept time and that was good enough. He laughed quietly as he realized he'd only been sitting there for five minutes. It was a peaceful space with gentle, non-threatening whispers. Not from the patrons that currently occupied the church, but from something else. Something he just couldn't place his finger on. Then a thought came to mind. Brendan wondered about the watch. Was it real or as fake as everything else in his life?

A middle-aged priest named Father Matthew came over to ask if he needed help. Brendan replied with a polite no and then continued to explain that he didn't even know why he was there. Father Matthew smiled;

he knew the young man's slumped over posture and convoluted response were a cry for help.

"The Lord will call us when He needs us, or we need Him." Father Matthew looked at the ceiling while pointing his right index finger up and placing his left hand on his heart.

"Today, Father, I think it might be the latter. I don't really see what your God could need from me." The priest noted no change in Brendan's posture, but at least he was communicating.

"It has been my experience that it's not one or the other but more of a middle of the road calling." He held both his hands in the air evenly like a balanced scale.

"Honestly, Father, and I don't mean any disrespect, but this may be one of those exceptions."

"Well, um." Father Matthew looked at Brendan as if to ask for his name.

"Brendan, Brendan Pierce."

"Well, Brendan, why don't we sit here for a few minutes and see what the Lord has in store for us? Or perhaps what you have in store for the Lord and me."

Brendan laughed quite loudly, causing heads to turn and see what the commotion was about. Brendan noted it felt good to laugh or even to just smile. Father Matthew knew he was doing his job well.

Over the next few months he strolled into the church looking forward to chats with Father Matthew. The priest never seemed to disappoint. This was something Brendan often noticed and even came to cherish. He once told the Father he wasn't Catholic and wondered why God would call him.

There are plenty of Catholics out there," Father Matthew explained. "God doesn't really play favorites. It's us who plays favorites in God's name."

Brendan was again amazed at the wisdom of the father. He told Brendan that the Lord asks of us many things that we don't understand, but if we have faith enough to follow, the Lord shows us the way. Brendan never forgot this.

In his next to last visit to the church, Brendan found Father Matthew standing at the front of the church speaking with a handful of people. They were thanking him for his service to their parish. Brendan was puzzled and terrified at the same time. He greeted the priest with a concerned look. Father Matthew began to explain that his stay at St. Michael's was temporary and it was time for him to return to the seminary. He informed Brendan that his true calling was teaching young men to be the best priests they could be. He told Brendan that he'd make a great priest. Brendan smiled, said thank you, and then reminded Father Matthew that he wasn't Catholic. The priest laughed and suggested to Brendan that God doesn't mind what you were born into. To the Lord, it's more important to become the best version of you possible. He asked Brendan to think about it and offered to help if he wanted to convert and then he would recommend Brendan to the seminary. They spoke for a while as they had many times before and said their goodbyes. Father Matthew gave Brendan a card with his personal number on it and told him to call if he needed to talk.

In the weeks to come, Brendan mourned the loss of his mentor and the only real father figure he'd ever had. He received an email from his mother that merely said, "It's done, and both of us are happier. Let's set a time to talk. Love, Mom."

Brendan was shocked. His conversations with Father Matthew had allowed him to completely forget about the divorce. He also realized the lack of emotion and sensitivity that his parents had toward each other and him regarding this whole matter. This was true of most of his childhood now that he thought about it. Both his parents were numb to their family life. He wondered if this would happen to him. Brendan returned to the church one last time. He sat in the church for hours that day contemplating how his life might play out, the genetics that were handed down to him, and if he'd pass them on to his children one day. That night Brendan M. Pierce called Father Matthew and asked for help getting into the seminary. Secretly, he thought he wasn't going to turn into his parents or pass on those genes to a child. Brendan told the priest the only happiness he felt was in the church and working with him. This was only a partial truth, Brendan knew that he was afraid of becoming his parents, but he couldn't tell Father Matthew this. It was still the truth, just not the whole truth. The rest was just as he had stated. Father Matthew set up an appointment to thoroughly discuss what this commitment truly meant. Brendan agreed.

6

LUNCH WAS LIKE ANY other lunch. Cathy sat at her desk pouring over the reports of medication errors, various complaints, and the occasional letter of gratitude from a distant family member who felt compelled to write about a recently passed resident. She used to wonder why she didn't get more of these letters. After all, they were supposed to be a high-end facility that took only the financially able and treated them like royalty. Cathy soon realized the family members were the empowered rich and the residents were unimportant memories. *Damn, it's Mom and Dad's view of the world all over again*, she thought as she sighed.

Rich, busy adult children placed their mother or father here to be comfortable and quietly unseen. With the emphasis on unseen. Most of the letters were complaints about the amenities: the sheets are too hard, the water isn't cold enough or hot enough, or some other squeaky wheel initiative. Cathy just thought these spoiled, rich child-adults were trying to get some little trinket for mom or dad to quiet their guilt. The truth is Green Haven is pretty good to its residents. Although she didn't know the actual numbers, Cathy surmised that each resident's family paid a small yearly fortune for that luxury.

She was just taking her last bite of a rather tasty pasta dish from the dining room when the call came over the intercom again. She hit the south wing running, peered over at the holy couple, and told them, "It's a twofer day, let's go."

After Cathy pronounced, she looked at the holy couple and told them they were here late today. Sister Diane smiled. "God's work doesn't punch a time card."

Cathy thought she must have practiced that line hundreds of time and was dying to use it. Cathy laughed and Sister Diane smiled, thinking Cathy was giving her an accolade.

Father Brendan placed his hand on Sister Diane's arm. "We should get to work."

Cathy left the room, once again wondering about the old rumor. She decided it was their business and she didn't need the headache.

Cathy returned to her desk, completed the death certificate, and walked out to place it in Dr. Oliver's box when something caught her eye. At the top of the form stamped in blue ink were the words "NURSE MAY PRONOUNCE." She wondered how many times she'd made that call. It seemed like a lot lately. She placed the form in the medical director's box and went on about the day.

The rest of the day was fairly routine except for the minor fender bender between Father Brendan and a family member at the entrance of the facility. Father Brendan was in a bit of a hurry and overshot the bend in the driveway, nudging the back edge of the oncoming car. No real damage was done, just some light paint scratches, and Father Brendan's car took the brunt of it. "I would be most appreciative if we didn't involve the police or insurance companies. It's my second minor accident this year. The Lord must be trying to tell me something. Anyway, I think you can trust that I am an honest person and . . ."

Father Brendan stopped speaking suddenly; both he and the family member turned abruptly to look at Sister Diane, who was fighting hard to hold back her laughter. "I'm terribly sorry. Obviously, the good Father is honest. It just struck me funny that he said it."

They exchanged information as they joined in the humor of the earlier statement. Sister Diane could see the annoyed look that Father Brendan was hiding, but she was not going to call attention to it. Father Brendan gave Sister Diane a look of concern as they re-entered his car. The screeching of tires could be heard as the holy couple left Green Haven.

Later that night, while watching the newest, hottest detective show based on recent headlines, a death certificate was flashed on the screen, and Cathy recalled the words atop the Green Haven forms. She realized that recently she had seen the bold blue lettering much more often. Why hadn't she noticed how many times she was pronouncing people dead and why didn't it register with her that this number was on the rise? Cathy had been working in a nursing facility long enough to understand that residents die, but her intuition was sounding alarms. Cathy had a history of her insight triggering alarms in her body, and when she didn't listen, she would regret it later.

Her grandmother said, in a Russian-laden broken English accent, "If your belly is calling you and it is not for dinner, then you better listen to it. If you don't, there's going to be trouble one way or another."

Being a nurse, Cathy knew what trouble belly pain could bring. She also knew that wasn't what her grandmother was trying to tell her. A smile peeked out of Cathy's face as she poked fun at her grandmother by repeating the statement over and over, each time with a more profound Russian flair.

Cathy thought of the Pharmatek mishap and convinced herself she didn't need to create a new problem. Besides, Kyle was still on the hunt for her head. The detectives got their man, the show ended, and Cathy went to bed.

After three hours of restless sleep and images of those damn blue words in her mind, she made an agreement with herself to take a peek at the actual number of deaths she called versus the number called by Dr. Oliver. The rest of the night didn't go any better. Cathy kept seeing the Green Haven administrator telling the board that Nurse Cathy Arden was a troublemaker and she was creating a problem where none existed. And then there was Grandma repeating, "You must listen . . ."

By 4:00 am she'd had enough. Cathy got out of bed, made a pot of coffee, and tried to figure out what was more important to her. She liked her job; she loved the pay and even the illusion of power. She unexpectedly decided she disliked the complacency that plagued her. A thought of when did she become the old DON that she replaced, was followed by the question, is it time for her to be replaced?

Cathy decided if Kyle wanted to get rid of her, she wasn't going down without a fight. Tomorrow she'd start her own detective work. She'd figure it out; that is, if there was something to figure out. In the shower, Cathy relaxed. She reminded herself she's a nurse and not a TV detective. "Thanks, Grandma, for a lively evening. Now I don't have a choice." Cathy felt an almost fetal-like twitch in her stomach. "Sorry, Grandma."

7

ANDRE'S CAFÉ WAS AN unassuming and elegant little spot Oscar had eaten in many times, but not enough for him to be known by name. He arrived early and chose a window table away from the door. The tables had white tablecloths that added a bit of sophistication without reaching snobbish. The room was well lit; Oscar didn't want it to seem like a date, although in his mind, it was the first of many dates they'd have.

Marissa was ten minutes late and quipped that doctors don't do well with staying on time. Oscar greeted her with a pleasant handshake; he was just relieved she showed. He could feel his heart racing as their hands touched. He wondered if there was any chance she felt anything for him. He was keeping it professional. For now.

"We'd like a bottle of the Syrah, please," Oscar told the waitress as she reached the table. He was being bold and in charge. He figured Marissa would prefer a take-charge kind of guy. Especially in a boss and later on. He thought Dr. Oliver was a woman of power, and Oscar felt he needed to match that power and perhaps exceed it.

"No. Please give us a moment." Marissa spoke directly to the waitress, bypassing any looks from her future boss.

"Is there a problem? Do you not like red wine?" Oscar's inquisitive but puzzled look hid the terror that now consumed him.

"No. That's not it. I have patients this afternoon, so I'm not drinking alcohol beforehand." Her conviction was stern. Now she was looking directly at Oscar.

In Oscar's world of meetings with potential business partners, drinks lightened the setting. He hadn't thought of the implications for Marissa. Oscar realized he'd have to think more deeply about his actions around her. He needed to up his game. "I apologize, Marissa. May I call you Marissa?"

"Marissa is fine. And don't apologize. It's a question of being coherent and of protecting my reputation. If my patients started smelling alcohol on me in the middle of the day, then word would spread, and I would be done," Dr. Oliver explained with a smile. Oscar knew it was forced.

As they ordered lunch, Oscar made small talk by asking about what she'd been doing since they last saw each other in the hospital. He was cautious not to go into too much detail about his father's death while under her care. Oscar was trying to keep the mood light. He wasn't sure how doctors dealt with the death of their patients.

Oscar toyed with complimenting her on the green A-line dress she was wearing but thought better of it. He wondered if she wore it to work today or had changed for their meeting. Oscar bought a new white dress shirt and had his shoes polished. The navy suit he wore was only a few months old. He assumed it was still this year's fashion. The tie was red. Oscar chose it because red symbolized power, strength, and romantic relationships.

While Dr. Oliver was enjoying the small talk, she was secretly anxious to hear the offer Oscar had mentioned. "Oscar, I'm enjoying our lunch, but I do have to get back to the office soon, or I'll walk into an angry bee's nest for keeping my patients waiting." The truth was Dr. Oliver had a new practice, and the patient load was thin at best. She recalled looking at the schedule and seeing that only three patients were booked. The first patient was not until 2:30 pm. Marissa actually had plenty of time but wanted to give the impression of being very successful. She needed Oscar to feel that he was forced to offer a better deal than he'd intended.

The green dress she wore was borrowed from an expensive store. Marissa planned to return it tonight on her way home. She was extra careful not to lift her left arm up too high and expose the sales tag still attached. The rest of the ensemble was owned and kept very safe for special occasions such as this.

Oscar felt a wave of anxiety come over him. What if his feelings for Marissa were not returned? He decided to keep the rest of the lunch business-like. There'd be plenty of time to win her over after she took the job.

Oscar started in about building Green Haven as a legacy for his father. How he wanted it to be a place of luxury and excellent care so family members didn't have to feel guilty about placing loved ones in a facility, as he did. He pulled up a photo on his phone of the almost completed exterior front of the building. Then some renderings of the interior. Oscar laid out his entire dream of Green Haven.

Marissa was intrigued, not by the Green Haven plan, but for Oscar's passion. She remembered that wide-eyed ambitious drive in herself as a young first-year medical resident. Now all she felt was the weight of a new practice and enormous amounts of student loans. She'd spend the next twenty or more years trying to repay them if this deal didn't work.

After Oscar explained his Green Haven dream, she asked how she fit in. He began his pitch slowly and methodically, elaborating on his goal to find a compassionate and caring doctor. A doctor who wasn't jaded by the pitfalls of the medical industry or beaten up by the insurance bullies. Oscar knew that even as a new doctor Marissa would have the same concerns as most of her seasoned colleagues. He told Marissa that Green Haven's financial model was entirely different. It wouldn't accept insurance, and all payments would be determined at the time of occupancy and due yearly.

This ensured the facility would receive large amounts of income monthly. Oscar told her that the initial residents' fees were determined by him, but going forward the board would handle any changes in the yearly fees. He assured her he had it all figured out. The board would take into consideration wages, supplies, cost of living, tax increases, and whatever else to set the fee for the following years.

"Honestly, I don't understand or even care to understand most of the tiny details. My job is to make sure I build the best, most appealing place possible." Oscar was proud of not sweating the little things.

"And hiring me helps you make this dream come true?" Marissa wondered how much he missed not looking at the tiny details.

"Yes, you might say it's a key piece of the puzzle. I, we, need someone like you."

"What does that mean?" Marissa took offense if he was talking about her looks and not her doctoring skills.

"It's all good. It means we need a compassionate, honest, caring, and smart doctor like you." His face had a tinge of redness to it. He hadn't realized the double meaning. "I assure you that this offer is one hundred percent on the up and up." Oscar said the words before his mind had a chance to register the lie.

Oscar was now pitching hard and fast and trying not to fumble over his feelings at the same time. Marissa, on the other hand, was desperately trying to be officious while remaining lackadaisical. The dance they played had moved from a waltz to a salsa.

Oscar told Marissa he was already thinking about the next building and that her salary would be no problem to cover with this model.

Marissa may have just started her own private practice, but she wasn't dumb. She asked a question now and then, keeping Oscar on his toes. After all, he was the one chasing her. Dr. Oliver actually had hundreds of questions; those would have to wait for the next meeting. First, she had to make him really want her to take the offer.

Lunch was coming to an end, and Oscar was getting tired trying to keep such a high level of energy and enthusiasm while not overstepping boundaries. Marissa was enjoying all the attention. The prospect of making money and not having to hunt for her food was very appealing. This was made more so by the man delivering it. Dr. Oliver looked at her watch. Oscar took this as a sign that the meeting was over and paid the check. He handed Marissa his business card and asked her to think about the offer. For good measure, and because he wanted to see her again as soon as possible, he told her she needed to decide in the next two days.

Dr. Oliver played it cool, saying she'd call him in the next few days to set up a follow-up meeting if she was interested. She was interested, very interested. The money could be useful, and the add-ons could be better if she were stern and patient.

They shook hands while thanking each other for the meeting. Oscar held the door open as she walked out. He waited in front of the café for a moment to see if she would turn back to wave goodbye. She didn't.

Marissa was smarter than that. She knew he'd be waiting for confirmation of a good meeting. She also knew that she needed the upper hand during negotiations.

Oscar walked back to his car trying to decide if she'd take the job or not. His mind was overtaken by the sound of her voice and the movement of her hands as she spoke. He reminded himself that the board only agreed to offer her the position after they had vetted her.

The board was comprised of people with varying backgrounds and many different talents and connections. Checking on Dr. Marissa Oliver was a rather simple task when they combined their efforts. The board concluded she wasn't the best or worst possibility. They thought this made her easy to control and just as easy to get rid of if necessary. The board had already suspected Oscar's motive for hiring Dr. Oliver, and they also knew they could keep Oscar in line if it became an issue. Their final decision to allow Oscar to retain Dr. Oliver came with the notion that if he were busy with her, he wouldn't bother them. Oscar may have been the major money behind Green Haven, but he had no idea what he was doing. He'd offer lots of guidance and little real input.

The cell phone rang just as she got into her car.

"I trust all was a success?"

"Yes." She looked around but saw no one.

"Then all is agreed upon?"

"Yes." Her response was filled with astonishment. She thought to herself, *Was he following me?*

"Okay, I look forward to a very amicable relationship."

The line went silent. A feeling of fear penetrated her midsection, and with great effort, she chose to ignore it.

8

CATHY RUSHED INTO HER office still yawning from the previous all-nighter she unwillingly pulled. The entire drive to work all she could think of were all the bad things that could be happening at Green Haven and how she could be unknowingly wrapped up in them. Her belly alarm was blaring. She sat and forced herself to take some deep breaths. Cathy told herself she was letting her imagination get too wild and she had to stop watching detective shows.

Nurse Cathy wasn't in the right frame of mind to just start snooping around. First, she had to calm down, and then she needed a plan. Pulling old death certificates for no reason would raise flags. Especially since everything was now entered into that damn mega computer system she helped get here. During the training, Cathy was told that every entry, query, and move within the system was recorded by date, time, and user. She didn't have the expertise to hide within the system, so she was basically signing her name to every keystroke. Cathy sarcastically wondered if the old DON knew how much freedom she really had. She could do just about anything without a single trail left behind. Cathy caught herself wishing Pharmatek was still here and let out an ironic laugh. She needed to become the old DON she'd replaced. Now nurse Cathy Arden had to think like that old DON. Cathy thought, *Where would she go to look for those older death cer-*

tificates? By law, all paper charts were kept for ten years, and they were in the basement storage room. It was locked, but as the DON, Cathy had a master key. She wondered if it opened the storage room door. The sublevel of the building also housed the laundry, maintenance, and a small storage unit for each resident that came at an additional cost. These storage units were not a part of Oscar's original design for the building. Someone on the board saw an opportunity to turn a significant profit with space that was underutilized. The board instructed the sales team to tell family members that they didn't want it to get out that their family member was the resident who couldn't afford to have a personal storage unit. In fact, every unit had been rented and only about a third actually contained anything in them. Cathy had never been down to see the storage units, but rumor has it that staff members use the empty units to store their personal junk or that the vacant units are used for discrete trysts between staff members. One wild rumor purported that owner of Green Haven and the medical director have been seen leaving one of the units every now and again. As far as Cathy knew, none of these rumors had ever been confirmed.

After the morning meeting and her third cup of coffee, Cathy returned to her desk. She was feeling better except for a slight lack-of-sleep head-ache. The last week of death certificates were probably not yet filed. Those would be easy to get. She called Sally Grimes, the unit clerk, and asked her to bring last week's residents' reports, including death certificates, to her office. This wasn't an unusual request, especially with the quarterly meeting coming up. Sally dropped off the reports and left. The unit clerk of a facility is always overworked and has no time to chat even with her boss. Cathy counted on this.

She started by looking at the nursing error reports because they were on top. She thought it would appear less conspicuous if she didn't bypass what was on top of the pile. Cathy shook her head as she realized she was paranoid. No one is watching her. No one even thought there might be a problem. She quickly thumbed through the pile to last week's death certificates.

Six deaths had occurred. Cathy looked over each certificate, noting four of them had blue lettering at the top. All six residents were quite old. She smirked as she thought, *That's a given. I must be getting as senile as the residents if I thought that would be a clue.*

The other two were pronounced by Dr. Oliver. And all six had been signed off by the doctor. Cathy thought, *It's vacation time for Nurse Cathy.* Since she didn't have much of a life outside work, Cathy didn't usually take her vacation or sick time. Every year, Green Haven, Inc. was forced to pay her for her unused time. But that was going to stop this year. The board had decided that any remaining paid time off would be forfeited. Since most everyone took advantage of their time off, no one was going to complain. The board knew this. Cathy thought this might be the work of the administrator, Kyle. Just another vengeful attack on her for the Pharmatek mishap.

Cathy noted today was moving smoothly. This was good, considering she had no sleep last night and her mind was tired from the conspiracy sprints it had been running. Cathy thought it was quite a day: no staff issues, no resident issues, and the holy couple wasn't prancing around the building stirring up righteousness with the residents. She decided to take a chance and sneak down to the locked records room. The PA system ran throughout the building; surely it was also installed down there for the workers' safety. Cathy looked around before punching in the three-digit code that opened all the stairwell doors. The code was changed monthly. The new code appeared as three digits at the bottom of each employee's paystub. A clever game thought up by Lenny, the IT guy.

Cathy hit the lower platform and opened the door, peeking in to see if anyone was in the hallway. It was empty. She followed the hallway, passed doors marked maintenance, restroom, storage, and finally reached the door marked records. There was no fancy security lock on it like with the stairwell doors. The door was metal and had a simple door-handle lock. Cathy was about to insert the key, when she grabbed the handle and it turned. The door was unlocked. As Cathy started to open the door, a maintenance man came out from behind a door and into the hallway.

"I don't think I've ever seen the director of nursing come down here." There was a proud smile on his face as he walked towards her.

"Well, I thought that it's high time I see the whole place." Cathy returned the smile and extended a hand.

"Can I offer you a tour?" the older portly gentleman said, still beaming with pride.

"No, I'm kind of a do-it-yourself gal. I was going to start here at the end of the hallway and work my way back. I thought I would open each door, stick my head in, and say hello. Kind of a surprise from above." Cathy pointed to the ceiling.

The gentleman gave a giggle that made both of them laugh. Cathy's was more to hide her fear. "You know, we do get up there."

"As I said it, it sounded strange to me too. Say, can you tell me what's behind each door? I don't want to look like more of a fool than I just did."

"Sure, Director."

"Cathy is fine."

"Okay, Cathy, that door you're in front of just holds old resident records, but it's always locked. The next one down leads to the resident storage area. The last door is mine. I'm in charge of maintenance around here. Martin, Marty for short, at your service." The man was beaming more with the news he just relayed.

"Well, Marty, I'll take you up on the tour. We just have to make it quick; I have to get upstairs. I'm kind of in charge up there." Cathy let a smile slip out as she again pointed to the ceiling.

After a tour of Green Haven's catacombs and no success with the records room, Cathy returned to her office. By 3:00 pm, Cathy was starting to wind down. Exhausted, mentally and physically, she was thinking of leaving early. It was quiet, Kyle was in his office, and the nurses would call if they needed something. She grabbed her bag, pulled out her keys, and headed for her car. The thoughts of a conspiracy were fading quickly.

"Cathy," Kyle called to her as she was locking her door.

"Crap, this can't be good." She turned with a giant but labored smile on her face. "Hi, Kyle."

Kyle didn't return her greeting. "Do you still have last week's reports? I'd like to review them. All of them."

She didn't know that Kyle ever looked at reports. Not even the ones he was supposed to. She figured if it didn't have to do with firing her or making her work more aggravating, he didn't care. She unlocked her door and handed the pile of papers to him.

Kyle turned to walk away, then turned back. "I notice you're leaving an hour early."

Cathy didn't smile. Under her breath, she murmured, "Take it off my built-up sick time."

"Enjoy it. Last year for that," Kyle retorted as he turned again and walked away. He got the last word. The administrator perfected this skill. Not that anyone would really challenge him.

Cathy quickly made her way to her car. The seat of the four-year-old blue sedan was inviting. Cathy thudded into it, banging her head on the way in. Inside, the leather seats hugged her as she massaged the pain away from the back of her head. The tired nurse was tempted to fall asleep right there. Instead, she started the engine, drove to the nearest liquor store, and bought a bottle of red wine. It had been a long two days, a glass of wine and a mindless sitcom was exactly what Cathy needed. She could barely drive home and had no energy to make dinner.

She remembered the leftover pasta in the fridge. She took out the food to nuke it. Ah, the microwave, BFF of a person living alone. She opened the wine.

Many of Cathy's evenings started with her standing in front of the microwave. She wasn't a cook and never wanted to be one. Her mother was a fantastic cook. She could make a gourmet dinner out of whatever was hiding in the back of the pantry or buried deep in the freezer. Her mom tried to teach Cathy several times, always telling her that to catch a good man, you have to know how to feed one. Cathy didn't want a man she had to feed to keep.

She turned on the television and found the first mind-numbing rerun she hadn't seen. The microwave's come and get it bell chimed; Cathy retrieved her food, the glass of wine, and settled in. After eating the leftovers and two glasses of wine, the Green Haven world and any thoughts of conspiracy catapulted out of her mind. Cathy's head began to feel heavy as she drifted off to sleep on the couch.

9

ABOUT A WEEK AFTER calling him, Brendan met with Father Matthew at his office in the seminary. The look on the priest's face was one of concern as he hugged Brendan then ushered him to a chair.

"You seem a bit rough around the edges if you don't mind me saying so."

"I recently received an email from my mother telling me their divorce was final. Can you imagine telling your child in a one-line email that you got a divorce?" Brendan showed him the email.

Father Matthew viewed the email then returned the phone to him. "I must admit, I can't. However, people deal with difficult situations in all kinds of ways. Most of them don't fall into the good category."

"My parents weren't present for me as a child. I grew to understand that. I was able to handle that because I thought that at least we were some kind of a family; now that's gone. Father Matthew, my parents cared more about their work than they did about me." His body was tense, and his hands were clasped together tight enough to demonstrate the white discoloring of a lack of circulation to his fingers.

The priest could see that Brendan needed to talk. He reached over and tapped his hands so Brendan would let go of the stranglehold. He then sat back and allowed the distressed young man to release the angst he had been holding back for years. He gave the occasional nod or hand gesture to affirm that his attention didn't wander off.

"If I'm honest and sincere, the only time I feel like I belong is when I'm talking to you at St. Michael's and that's gone too. It's the only time I felt loved and appreciated," Brendan told his mentor.

"Brendan, why do you feel you need to have God as a replacement family? He's already part of your family. Just let him in. His love is additional, not instead of."

Brendan sat back defiantly, amazed at the priest's comment. He wanted to ask if the Church was too busy with business to love a willing soul. Father Matthew caught the dismay in Brendan's face and quickly continued.

"There's enough room for everyone in the Lord's world, and each of us is loved unconditionally. Brendan, do you wish to join the priesthood to help others, or to escape the pain of your family dynamic?"

Brendan hated that the priest could see right through him. He thought this must be a talent they teach at the seminary; one Brendan would make great effort to master. Lie detecting 101; he snorted slightly.

"I thought that at first too. I realized that it might have been the initial reason, but the picture of you saying goodbye to the parishioners at St. Michael and the looks of gratitude on their faces keeps playing in my mind like an omen. You truly helped them. That's a calling. And since that vision won't leave me alone, I have to follow it." Brendan found himself feeling more at ease with each word he spoke.

Father Matthew gave a pleased smile. They sat in his office for over two hours going over many possibilities: what would need to be done, the process of conversion, and finally about becoming a priest. Father Matthew explained in detail what he'd given up for this work. He asked Brendan to go home and think about it deeply.

Brendan returned to his apartment tired and overwhelmed with the massive amount of information Father Matthew gave him. He reached into the small wooden cabinet that was struggling to hold a television way too heavy for it. Brendan remembered he'd meant to replace it with a much more formidable opponent. It just wasn't high on his priority list. He took out a bottle of cheap vodka and poured himself a glass. The first one went down smooth. A second followed, then a third.

He remembered a voicemail from his mother three hours after the raw text about the divorce being final. He thought about how odd it was not seeing the word "Mom" on the caller ID. Brendan always found it strange that she only called when there's a crisis in her life. He recalled pushing the phone to his side as he thought twice about answering the call. He had started to listen to the voicemail but stopped quickly at the sound of his mother's voice. Now Brendan held the phone at arm's length. It was as if he was forcefully willing himself to listen to the voicemail.

His mother's attitude was sullen, which was not uncommon, but her usual monotone voice had a little shakiness to it. She was painfully upset. "Brendan, dear, please call me back. I, I need to speak with you. It's important, very important."

He replayed every word of the conversation twice. He stood, wondering what had changed. Maybe his mother was having second thoughts about the divorce and was finally calling to share her heartfelt feelings with him. He couldn't believe this. Brian had played this game many times before; it always ended the same way: in utter disappointment.

Brendan sat rigidly straight as if to show no signs of weakness. He was determined not to allow any crackling or lowering of volume in his voice. He would not be submissive just because she wore the title of mother. He wondered what bombshell his parents would drop on him now, most likely in a matter-of-fact manner. He hit the call back icon on his phone.

Alicia Martin was shaken for the first time in her life. She battled back and forth whether she should show her only son her frailty or maintain the rigid outer core that was her reputation. Another first in her life. She answered the phone.

"What is it, Mother?" Brendan was intentionally cold in his delivery.

"It's your father. He's had a heart attack."

"Where is he? Which hospital?" Concern replaced the coldness.

Brendan's muscles were at full attention, not to battle his mother but out of fear for his father. He could feel his mouth go dry, and his words were starting to speed up.

"He's not in a hospital, Brendan." Alicia's words were slow as she struggled to deliver the blow as gently as possible. A sign her son missed.

"Where, Mom, where is he? Stop playing games!" Brendan's tone loudened.

She waited for a moment, trying to figure out how to say it. "Brendan, he's gone."

A long silence was broken by a sniffle. "When, where . . ." Brendan couldn't speak. The news had left him unable to breathe. He felt his chest gasping for its next breath.

"We signed the divorce papers and decided that we'd have one last dinner together tonight. He called me just before the ambulance got there. I saw the call and thought he was calling to cancel the dinner. I was busy; I didn't pick up. I let it go to voicemail. I listened to it an hour later just before leaving the office. I was making sure he was still coming to dinner. I'm sorry, Brendan."

"You let him die alone! You let him live alone!" Brendan slammed the phone down on the counter as he hung up on his mother. Tears continued to flow.

The alcohol hadn't numbed his pain. He thought about pouring the last of the bottle's contents into the glass, but he drank it straight from the bottle instead. He looked at the stressed cabinet, trying to decide what to drink next. He stood too quickly and fell back onto the couch. His mind was blurred by the news as his body fell prey to the effects of the alcohol.

Brendan's eyes closed as the last of his tears ran down his face. Thankfully, the drinks had pulled him into a coma-like sleep.

Brendan explained to Father Matthew that he had not spoken with his mother since the funeral. Not because he despised her, which he did, but because he still felt the pain of her words cutting through him. Father Matthew told him he needed to clean up his messes before he could do the Lord's work. In reality, his words were much kinder. Father Matthew explained that he had to be clear of conscience and heart.

Brendan returned home; once again he took confidence from the straining cabinet. He called his mother. As the phone rang, Brendan finished the last of a second bottle of vodka, again straight from the bottle. By the third ring, he was ready to hang up. He didn't want to leave a voicemail. The alcohol had clouded his mind, and Brendan didn't think that she'd see he'd called either way.

Suddenly, someone answered. It wasn't his mother's voice. The voice was younger and softer. Brendan asked for Alicia Martin-Pierce. The young woman told him this wasn't her phone anymore, and now her name was Alicia Morgan.

Brendan's vodka-drenched brain couldn't register this information. The girl said Alicia had gotten a new phone and gave this one to her for her birthday. Brendan stumbled through the words but managed to ask whom he was talking to. The girl answered that she was Emily, Alicia's stepdaughter. She then asked who he was—drunk or not, those words sunk into his brain hard. Brendan flung himself against the cushion of the couch then muttered back that he was an old work friend looking for advice and he'd call her office. He quickly hung up.

Brendan sat on his couch, crazy with thoughts of betrayal. Betrayal of him and his father, betrayal of their whole family. His body was shaking and thrashing in anger. How could she do this? Did Dad know? Did Dad care? Was this the real reason for the divorce?

His phone rang. Brendan stared at the buzzing phone on the coffee table. He picked it up. It was a phone number he didn't recognize. He answered it.

"Brendan, it's your . . ."

Brendan hung up as fast as he could. He knew that voice. Why was she calling? Had she no shame? The phone started to ring again. It was the same number. Whether it was the vodka or his curiosity, he answered the phone. Once again trying to stay in a rigid pose.

"Brendan! Don't hang up."

The sternness of his mother's voice was in full swing. Brendan could feel himself falling back into the childhood obedience that he hated. He stood abruptly, almost falling over from the effects of the vodka. He grabbed onto the arm of the couch to steady himself and lofted an equally stern volley back at his mother. "Wow! How could you call me now? Is your new family busy?"

"Brendan, whatever you're thinking now, you don't know the truth. And don't talk to me like that. I'm still your mother." Her tone was more commanding than before.

"Okay, tell me the truth, Mother." His voice matched hers.

"I've never sugar-coated anything with you, and I'm not going to start now. Your father and I grew apart many years before our divorce. We were smart enough to see this and agreed if either of us found someone else the other would not stand in the way."

"Stop! How do I know this is true? Dad isn't here to co-ob, co-ober . . . verify the facts."

Brendan was now fully leaning on the outer wall of his apartment with one hand clasped to the wooden windowsill. His words were slow and less deliberate. The alcohol was outflanking him as his mother took the head-on approach.

"Are you drunk? Maybe this isn't a good time to do this."

"It's the only time you're going to get." Another volley, only with much less power.

"Very well. Connor, your dad, and I met other people at about the same time. He was dating a grad student, not one of his, and fell in love with her. I met Robert, a colleague, and fell in love. You father and I were always practical with each other. It was time for a divorce. We weren't going to hurt each other. We were both happy about it."

"What about me? What about hurting me, my happiness?" Sorrow had taken over.

"Brendan, you were grown and living your life. You didn't need us anymore."

"Dad had a heart attack because of the divorce!" The tears ran freely from him.

"No Brendan, your dad had a heart attack, his second, because his heart was failing and had been for about two years. He was seeing doctors and looking for a new heart. It just didn't happen in time. He was happy at the time he died. We were both happy. I didn't want him to die either." Alicia's words seemed so matter of fact to Brendan.

Brendan hung up the phone, stunned. The truth was too much in this altered state of mind. He ran to the bathroom and threw up, several times. Luckily, he made it to the toilet. While trying to get into bed, Brendan knocked over a photo of him and his parents that stood on the night-stand. The last thing Brendan heard before passing out was the sound of breaking glass.

10

CATHY WOKE UP THE next morning looking for aspirin. She had to get to work. She didn't drink much, and hangovers were not a state she was familiar with. After three aspirin, a shower, and a challenging time getting dressed, she managed to get into her car. She sat behind the steering wheel, contemplating calling in sick. Cathy had tons of sick days she was going to lose. Unfortunately, she hadn't shaken the death certificate issue. The headache only made it harder to think clearly about her next move.

Cathy hit the first drive-through and ordered two large black coffees, one for her and one for the hangover that wanted to become her new best friend. Cathy thought these were the times living with someone would've come in handy. Someone who would've told her she was being stupid and not just with the wine. After the first large cup of coffee, Cathy began to feel better. Now she could turn without wanting to pull over and vomit.

By the time Cathy reached Green Haven, the thought of food was starting to sit okay. The dining room always had pastries. She seized her third coffee and some plain type of donut thing, deciding not to take chances with something covered or filled with sweetness.

Cathy reached her office managing to avoid contact with anyone who wanted to engage in a lengthy discussion about whatever. She closed the door, sipped her coffee, and slowly ate the donut while pretending to read a report just in case anyone walked in. Halfway through the donut, she felt better and could focus again. The basement record room was too risky at this time. Besides, two visits to the lower level in two days would raise several eyebrows. That would need a better plan, one her brain couldn't formulate just yet. She started to create a list of what to look for and how to go about getting the information. Suddenly she wondered if Green Haven, Inc.'s other facilities were having the same issue. That would be the last thing she'd tackle. Cathy had to be sure something was going on before going companywide.

"Dr. Passed, Dr. Passed, north wing."

"Not now!" The mild protest sounded like a police siren in her head, but she had to keep up appearances, so she reached for the form, cautiously got up, and mustered the energy to get to the north wing. Cathy knocked the cheaters off her head again. She decided that she didn't need them right now. Picking them up would be far too painful. The walk seemed twice as long as the days before and the effort even more difficult. The hangover was not gone yet; it was fighting to stay with her. As she reached the north wing, she felt a wave of nausea come over her. There was no time to stop; she had to fight through it. Cathy could feel the beads of cold sweat forming on her forehead. She momentarily stopped in front of the air conditioning vent, allowing the cool air to bathe her pounding forehead. She pretended to be analyzing the form in her hand. The nausea passed.

She arrived at Mrs. Grace Harding's room with the floor nurse now on her heels. Cathy was about to walk into the room when she stopped abruptly, her brows raised in surprise. Even the hair of her eyebrows hurt to move. Grace Harding, eighty-eight years old and a resident at Green Haven for the better part of ten years, was sitting up in bed. Red-faced and flustered, Grace had moderate dementia with bouts of delusion. Her children had placed her in Green Haven years ago when she became too much for them. Honestly, they just couldn't be bothered with her. Mrs. Harding had been the dean of a prestigious and wealthy private boarding school. They paid her well, and her children took advantage of the situation as soon as they could.

Cathy looked at the floor nurse, who looked as confused as she did. "What happened? Why the intercom call?" Cathy could no longer bring herself to utter the words "Dr. Passed." The pain from her drinking was now mixing with the rage of incompetence she felt for the nurse.

"One of the CNAs ran over and told me she was gone. I checked; she wasn't breathing, then I put out the code." The young and much smaller floor nurse was fighting hard not to panic.

Cathy walked over to Mrs. Harding, letting out a sigh of disgust. "Grace, are you okay?"

"I am now." Grace was glaring at the floor nurse, like she was mentally yelling, "Where the *hell* were you?"

Giving the floor nurse a despising glare then turning back to Grace, Cathy continued. "Do you know what happened?"

"I was almost asleep when someone put a pillow over my face. I couldn't breathe, so I decided to play dead. You know, like you do when a bear attacks you."

Another evil glare was fired off in the floor nurse's direction by both of them.

"Then what happened?" Cathy knew Grace's account would be 100 percent fabrication. She also knew that Grace would believe every word of it. She showed Grace compassion; the disease was making itself known more each day. Grace had no control over it, nor did she even know she had it.

"I held my breath as long as I could. Then I peeked out of one eye, my right eye, I think. I could see a man standing at the door, so I continued to play dead until I heard the aide's voice.

"When did this all happen?"

"I don't know! I wasn't watching the darn clock! I was trying to save my life!"

Agitating Grace was something Cathy was trying to avoid. "Okay, Grace, you're safe now. And we'll keep an eye on your room to make sure the . . . person doesn't come back."

Everyone knew Grace's history, and Cathy could see the floor nurse was thinking the same thing. She asked the floor nurse to take Grace's vitals as she turned to leave the room.

Cathy stopped at the nurses' station and waited for the nurse to return with the vitals. They were normal, as Cathy suspected they would be. The nurse asked if the police should be called.

Cathy widened her eyes. "You know Grace is loony, right? She's had these hallucinations for years. Truthfully, they're getting closer together, and she's getting out of bed less and less. That's the way it goes around here."

The floor nurse said she was glad it was a false alarm. Cathy sternly reminded her to use the code only when it was needed. The floor nurse understood the not-so-subtle advice. Cathy headed back to the sanctity of her office. She'd try to hide in there as long as possible and hope she'd seen the last of the nausea.

Back in her office, Cathy became panicked. She had left the list she was compiling on her desk for anyone to see. After a stern silent self-reprimand, she got back to the task at hand.

1. Check certificates for the last year to see if they're marked "nurse may pronounce."

2. What did the resident die of?

3. . . .

Cathy was out of ideas. She quickly realized this wasn't like a detective show. She decided to start with step one and see where that led her. Only this time she'd look closer at each certificate. If something was going on, she had to be smart. At least smarter than whoever was doing whatever. With each minute the hangover was losing its hold on her. Last night's pathetic escapade was being reduced to a slight pain behind her eyes until it happened again: The call over the intercom, grabbing the form, racing down the hall. It all seemed like a bad movie she couldn't remember the name of.

Cathy got to the room, her headache in full swing. Of course, the good father and sister were already there waiting to usher off the dead to their new home. Cathy didn't have the energy to acknowledge their presence. She walked right past them to the bed of Regina Thompson, old money, old age, and out of time. Regina hadn't gotten out of bed for about two months. The orders to turn her every half hour had kept her from getting bedsores but did nothing to wake her.

Cathy pulled over the tray table, looked at the clock, and called the time of death. Under her breath, she whispered, "About time." She was about to fill out the certificate when the floor nurse rushed in to stop her. Regina Thompson didn't have a "nurse may pronounce" on her chart.

Father Brendan shot a glimpse over to Sister Diane, who stood paralyzed. Sister Diane sensed there was a change in Cathy's demeanor.

They all understood that Dr. Oliver would have to pronounce the death. Cathy looked up at the ceiling wondering when she'd stopped doing a good job and started just going through the motions. She looked at the holy couple, who were still frozen in place. "Okay, have at it."

As she walked out, she looked at the door with Regina's name on it. There was no small blue star in the left corner of the nameplate. The blue star told the staff that the resident could be pronounced by the nurse, by her. Cathy was again stunned by the lack of presence she had. She promised herself she'd pay closer attention to her job, especially now that she was snooping around. Then she felt a pain deep in her belly as she recalled the phrase "Have at it. When did I become so jaded?"

Back at her desk, she decided to make a copy of all death certificates from now on. She'd keep them in a file at home for safekeeping. Cathy knew this was a severe Green Haven, Inc. and HIPPA violation. Taking resident's personal information without permission and then storing it in an unsecured location would definitely get her in trouble. She told herself she'd bring back the copies to shred them as soon as she was done doing whatever she was doing. It occurred to her that she didn't have a clue as to what she was doing. The one thing she was sure of was she had to be all in. It felt good to take a stance again. It felt good to be alive.

11

It had been a little less than three days when Marissa called Oscar to set up their next "business" meeting. This time she'd choose the location. She'd control the playing field. Dr. Oliver hated to admit it, but she enjoyed the games they were playing. She wanted the job, and she found Oscar more intriguing than she was willing to acknowledge.

They would meet at Scappio's, an Italian restaurant she had eaten at a few times. She had become sort of friends with one of the waitresses. While making the reservation, she asked to be seated at one of her tables.

Truth is Dr. Oliver was an adequate doctor but not a shining star, a fact she hoped she was keeping to herself. The job offer was a lifesaver. She was drowning in student debt and had an office she couldn't afford. She paid her employees more than she paid herself. The rent, along with most of the other office bills, was at least one month behind. Sometimes weeks would go by before Dr. Oliver could take a paycheck. She had to be smart in handling Oscar. She could use his undeniable attraction to her as a tool, but she didn't want to push too far and blow the whole deal. She also didn't want Oscar to feel that he was being played.

They met at 7:00 pm. This time Marissa made sure to get there early. She was seated at the table when Oscar walked in. She had ordered a glass of wine, an observation Oscar made immediately.

"Not expecting any late-night office appointments or emergencies?"

"I'm not on call tonight. I have covering doctors who answer the calls."

There were no covering doctors, not that she needed them anyway. Dr. Marissa Oliver was finding it hard to become associated with her colleagues. She had a few outbursts as a resident and gained a reputation for being difficult. A reputation that was not based on fact but nevertheless carried weight in a small club.

Oscar called the waitress. "Please bring us a bottle of whatever she's drinking." He looked at Marissa. "How much catching up do I have to do?"

Marissa smiled into the rim of the glass and took another sip. The game that amused her was well into swing now. She would let him think he had the upper hand for a while.

"Have you eaten here before? Oscar looked at Marissa; she seemed overly comfortable. He knew that her answer might be a white lie, but he didn't really care. His pulse had skyrocketed in anticipation of this meeting, and nothing was going to ruin it. Marissa intentionally squirmed in her chair so that Oscar would definitely know her answer would be a stretch of the truth. She was testing him. "Once or twice, a while ago, but I don't remember the menu."

"I'm not too picky. Since you've been here before I'll just have whatever you have. I'll order the wine; you order the food."

"Just because I'm off duty doesn't mean I'm planning an assault on my liver."

"I'm sorry. I was just trying to lighten the mood. Look, we don't know anything about each other, and we're trying to decide if we should work together. So how about we forgo the business talk tonight and learn a little bit about each other, professionally."

"Okay, but there are ground rules, and you have to agree to abide by them, or it's back to business."

"So, what are the rules?"

"No deep personal questions, no date-like questions, and absolutely no politics."

"So, it's clever small talk. Okay, I've got it."

Marissa thought he was smart and a quick learner. Clearly, she was enjoying the chess match, but in time she would show him that he was just a pawn on the board.

After a three-hour dinner consisting of a bottle of wine and conversation, little of it about the job, Oscar ordered a Scotch and Marissa bourbon. He thought this was an excellent closing to a brilliant start. Oscar asked for the check. He paid the bill, leaving a hefty tip. He was shrewd enough to see that Marissa knew the waitress. He realized they'd discuss the tip amount at some point later on.

They walked out of the restaurant together; Marissa held out her hand just like last time and Oscar obliged. As they were walking away from one another, Oscar asked when they should meet again. Marissa asked if the job was real or if he had other plans in mind. Secretly, she hoped the deal was real. She already had the plans. Oscar looked at her sheepishly; he knew she had seen through him. His yes was quick and deliberate, trying desperately to make the save. She told him to come by her office tomorrow at noon to actually discuss the details. Trying to bounce back from the last question, he was caught off guard and agreed without thinking it through. Oscar didn't want to meet in Dr. Oliver's office, but now he had no choice.

At noon the next day, in an expensive suit and a new leather satchel over his shoulder, Oscar showed up at Dr. Oliver's office. The receptionist told him the doctor was too busy to meet with a drug rep today, but if he wanted to reschedule for another day, that would be fine. He was about to tell her that he wasn't a drug rep when Marissa appeared from behind a door. She greeted him with a big smile and asked him into her office. The receptionist looked at her. Marissa told her he was a business associate.

She then asked the receptionist to buzz her ten minutes before the next patient was scheduled to arrive. There was no next patient today.

She sat down behind her desk and asked Oscar to take a seat. She was setting the tone. It was going to be all business today, and she was in charge. Oddly, Oscar found himself liking her take-charge attitude. Dr. Oliver pulled out a pad from inside the top drawer of her desk. She had made notes; actually, they were demands of what she wanted from the Green Haven, Inc. board to make the deal work. Honestly, it was more what she needed than what she wanted.

Dr. Oliver started in. She had decided to overextend her demands and settle on what she was really going for in the end. Negotiations 101.

Oscar had done many business deals regarding construction, and he knew she'd shoot for the moon and settle for clouds in the end. He let her ramble off item after item. When she was done, he opened his satchel and removed a contract the board had already prepared. Oscar had the contract in his possession for about two weeks. He was just prolonging its presentation to spend more time with her.

Marissa tried to hide the look of amazement on her face. She didn't expect to see a contract today. She imagined Oscar would leave her office with his tail between his legs. He'd head back to the board with a list of her demands, and they'd cave on almost all of them. Now she was caught off guard. She listened as Oscar covered the subtler points of the contract. He occasionally stopped to let her catch up. She tried to ask questions but was still amazed. Dr. Oliver thought she was playing him, but now felt she'd been played. She was slightly angry and impressed all at the same time.

When he was done going over the contract, Oscar placed it on the desk in front of her. He stood and told her to review it, edit it, then get it back to him sooner than later. He shook her hand goodbye and left.

Marissa could feel the power of his essence still in the room. She was intrigued. She placed the contract in the top drawer of her desk. She was in no frame of mind to review it now. She had just seen the power of a seasoned negotiator at work, and it left her dazzled. Oscar's net worth increased drastically today.

Driving back to Green Haven, Oscar wondered if he was too aggressive. The board's contract was fair and there was some wiggle room, but did he dismiss her negotiations too quickly? The last thing he wanted to do was offend Dr. Marissa Oliver. She did take the meeting off neutral ground by making it at her office. She was all business today. He wanted her to take the position, and it was his company. Ultimately, she had to understand who called the shots. He decided he had played it just right. He was looking forward to the next meeting.

Not wanting to alarm her staff to the impending end of their employment, Marissa forced herself not to look at the contract until she was at home tonight. She couldn't have her staff looking for work and then have the deal fall through.

After work Marissa picked up a quick bite and headed back to her apartment with the contract in hand. She was curious to see what it said. She realized she had only heard about half of what Oscar had covered. As she pulled out the contract, a rage came over her. The date at the top of the agreement told her Oscar had held onto it for two weeks. He was trying to soften her up. She put the contract down and took a shower. She needed time to calm down. Marissa told herself this deal was too important; this wasn't the time to let emotions rule. She needed to make this work. It could change her life.

The shower worked. Marissa calmed down and started to read the contract. It was fair, and the pay was better than she thought it would be. Of course, she'd try to squeeze a few more thousand a year out of them. She saw quickly that the Green Haven corporation wasn't following the usual rules. They wanted her to be an employee and not a consultant. She'd be required to cover Green Haven and up to two other facilities in the surrounding area should they be built. There was mention of a pay increase for additional facilities but no actual figure. This would have to be remedied immediately.

The benefits were okay, but there was no mention of her student loan payments being made by Green Haven. She'd stressed that with Oscar today. Then she recalled the contract was drafted two weeks ago. She could feel the anger start to brew again. She also wanted a five-year contract with sizable increases each year. She made all the necessary edits to the contract and put it away for the night.

Her phone rang. It was the answering service. She was told it wasn't an emergency, but Oscar Green was trying to get hold of her. She took down the number the voice from the service rattled off. Again, she was angry, now Marissa was also curious. She finally picked up her phone and dialed.

"I'm sorry to bother you," Oscar answered.

Marissa stayed silent. Oscar could sense the tension but continued. "If you've looked at the contract, you would notice it's dated about two weeks ago. Yes, I've had it that long. I had to make sure you were the right doctor, the right person for the job. This is my legacy we're talking about."

Marissa didn't speak, but she was softening. Oscar's words seemed sincere and authentic.

"I'm also sorry for today at your office. I'd really like you to be the medical director of Green Haven. So how do we make this work?"

Marissa smiled. She had him! "I did notice the date on the contract, and honestly, I almost tore it up!" She paused to let that sink in. "It's fair, but it needs a few large edits."

She thought about telling him that she was simply too tired from a hectic day at the office and they would have to review the contract another day, but she enjoyed his company, so she remained on the call. They covered the edits Marissa spoke of one item at a time. Oscar was slow and methodical. Marissa suspected he was just trying to prolong the call. She was taken by his desire for her. It had been a while since a man tried to woo her. Marissa found him easy to work with. By the time they hung up, she knew she would take the job and maybe Oscar too.

12

GREEN HAVEN WAS NEARLY complete when the tours started. Family members were impressed; some signed contracts the same day as their tour. Oscar's idea was working. Giving rich children a luxurious place to tuck away their elderly parents and absolve them of their guilt turned out to be the golden ticket. Even the board couldn't deny it.

Most residents at Green Haven were visited by their families regularly in the beginning, but as time passed the visits became less and less frequent. A majority of the long-term residents like Anna Sparks and Adam James barely saw their families, even during the holidays. Oscar had created a haven for the rich and forgotten.

The board had enough policies in place to ensure Green Haven met most state requirements. Since it didn't take insurance of any kind, they didn't concern themselves with such matters. The yearly payments by family members, or lawyers who assumed power of attorney over the resident, were staggered so that every month had someone's annual fee collected. Green Haven was up and running, the money was coming in, and Dr. Marissa Oliver was working out well. Oscar and Marissa had agreed to meet once a month on Friday afternoons to discuss any concerns either might have. The mediocre construction owner had moved to the next level. Oscar's bank account grew nicely, and he enjoyed his new condo.

There was no other facility of its kind around. Green Haven wasn't bogged down with governmental red tape, and families were happy to see their loved ones living so lavishly. Oscar paid back the investors ahead of schedule. They were so pleased they re-invested in two more facilities, Autumn Living and Elite Care.

Both facilities were very similar to Green Haven. Oscar always believed that if it works, keep doing it. Riding on the reputation of Green Haven, the two new facilities had waiting lists even before their completion. All three facilities thrived for the next five years. As the economy took a downturn, so did Green Haven, Inc.'s posh popularity. Even the rich felt the crunch. The census for all three facilities dropped by 5 percent. Under the current financial plan, this meant soon there might be times when the monthly receivables might not be enough. The board was concerned with the future of Green Haven, Inc. Their impression of Oscar also started to fall short. They decided to make substantial increases in the new resident contracts to offset the shortsightedness of Oscar Green.

The board had trusted in Oscar's vision to build two facilities at the same time, and now they were worried. In the months to come, Green Haven, Inc. would lower its financial standards slightly, taking in the well off in addition to the rich. Since the amounts of all yearly payments were confidential, neither the families nor the board could discuss the actual value of other contracts with potential clients or just about anyone else. The contracts were long and very specific. Knowing that no one would actually read them, the board built in miscellaneous fees and harsh penalties. Two of the residents were family members of lottery winners. A deal had been struck to admit these residents with an escrow account set up to make yearly payments to Green Haven. If the resident out-lived the fund, the family member would be required to replenish the fund in its entirety or move the resident out of Green Haven with payment of a stiff penalty. All of these measures barely offset Green Haven's growing costs.

The board secured an anonymous private investor. His investment was made through two levels of lawyers so that none of the board knew his identity. The board's financial concerns heightened the anxiety, pressuring them into accepting such a precarious alliance. Oscar was not informed. The board knew he'd never agree to risk so much on an unknown. He also didn't bother showing up to most of the meetings, so Oscar didn't know about the financial crisis his company was going through.

"We're glad you could join us today, Oscar. Some of what you'll hear at today's meeting may be new to you, but I assure you that we have been handling the current financial crisis for some time now and, rest assured, while our concerns are serious, we're making every effort to rectify the shortcomings." Lorraine Carter shifted in her chair as she looked at Oscar then at the other board members. No one on the board enjoyed the few meetings that Oscar would attend. Lorraine was the current chairperson of the board and only by default. Dealing with Oscar had become cumbersome and time-consuming, and Lorraine retired last year from an executive position at a local investment firm. She originally joined the board as a way to build a reputation in hopes of being asked to hold positions on larger, more lucrative boards—a decision she now regretted.

"Much to your surprise, I have read the minutes, and I can assure you that the 'shortcomings' you're worried about are temporary and insignificant." Oscar smiled; he felt he was now one up on the chairperson.

"I, we the board, don't think you have a firm grasp on the situation, respectfully."

"I've been in the construction world for a long time, and I've seen the ups and downs of the marketplace, and this is no different. I believe that if we just ride it out for a few months, we'll be fine. My father was always great at predicting an upswing whenever I went to him with this type of concern. He was always right. I think he passed that ability onto me."

The board members looked at each other with grave concern. Then they turned to Mr. Perkins, the board treasurer, almost begging him to explain the painstaking details of Green Haven, Inc.'s financial forecast again. They hoped that during the second explanation he might accidentally tell Oscar about the secret benefactor who invested a large sum of money to keep Green Haven, Inc. afloat. Mr. Perkins sat there silently, defying his fellow board members' pleas. He shot them anger-filled silent orders to stay quiet and let Oscar dig his own grave.

Green Haven, Inc. was stable financially for now, but balloon payments were coming due in the next ten years for the two new facilities. Even with the secret investor, there wouldn't be enough to cover the payments as they came due.

Oscar continued. "When I was building modest homes, I didn't worry about the money. People always need a place to call home. The same principle applies here; we have a bed that needs filling, and they have a wealthy family member needing a beautiful and safe place. What's it called? Ah, yes, supply and demand."

"Oscar, there will be two large balloon payments to be made for the new facilities. We need to start planning better for them now." Mr. Perkins was now staring at the younger board members with hatred flaming from his otherwise calm brown eyes.

Oscar rose to his feet to pace around the back of the board members, placing a reassuring hand on the shoulder of the occasional board member as he passed them. Oscar may not know much about finance or corporations, but he did know how to work a room. He spoke slowly, choosing his words carefully to give an air of as much confidence as he could.

"The balloon payments for Autumn Life and Elite Living are ten years off, and a lot can happen in ten years. I can predict with great certainty that we will be absolutely fine." The board listened to Oscar's closing argument quietly and with as much respect as they could muster. They didn't believe him. The meeting ended with no real progress. Oscar left the meeting confident that he had silenced the board's concerns and the Green Haven, Inc. ship was righted again.

The board members began talking about Oscar's participation in Green Haven, Inc. Perhaps he was too much of a dreamer. Maybe he put too much trust in fate. A few of the members loyal to Oscar told him of the board's concerns. Oscar may not have gone to college or taken business courses, but he was street smart and scrappy. He concentrated his efforts to determine which board members were loyal and which were plotting against him.

Oscar wasn't about to let anyone take his dream from him. Green Haven, Inc. was his and always would be. He found that four board members planned to oust him, and the rest were loyal but afraid to speak up. Oscar's influence in the world of executives was limited, but he prided himself on his street connections. Two of the four board members resigned shortly after a conversation with "peers" about the choices they were making and how it might affect their lives. Another member was told about a delicate matter that might not play out favorably for him if he didn't play along.

The last board member presented more of a challenge. Oscar couldn't find any flaws to exploit or points to apply pressure. John Perkins was a sixty-eight-year-old widower with no children. He didn't drink excessively, didn't gamble, and had enough of his own money. Oscar thought the man had no bad habits except for numbers. His expertise on the board was finance, so Oscar knew he couldn't go toe to toe with him there. Breaking this man was impossible.

Oscar set up a meeting with Mr. Perkins to discuss the financial future of Green Haven, Inc. Perkins thought this was odd because Oscar had never taken an interest in board matters other than making demands to further his own whims. Perkins was further surprised when Oscar said he wanted to get a better handle on how the corporation was doing. Especially after the last meeting where Oscar gave a blatant display of his unwillingness to see the financial reality that Green Haven, Inc. was facing. Oscar stated that he wanted to be able to talk to investors more intelligently if the need arose. Perkins decided to give Oscar the benefit of the doubt.

Oscar wanted to meet at John's house. He needed to see if there were any hidden skeletons he could use. He was sure the man couldn't be as squeaky clean as he appeared to be.

The home of John Perkins was clean, tidy, and had no visible skeletons, much to Oscar's dismay. Oscar found the meeting boring. The relentless bombardment of numbers and projections made Oscar want to scream. The hour-long meeting seemed like days, and Oscar had his fill of finance for a lifetime. He decided that he'd have to take his chances with John Perkins. Oscar calculated that one vote couldn't remove him from the board.

Something must have actually gotten through during the meeting because Oscar stopped thinking about the board members and started to concentrate on the numbers, not the actual numbers John Perkins was spouting off. He realized when the board felt the numbers were good, the board members were good, and when the board members were good Oscar was good. The key wasn't getting the board on his side; it was getting the numbers on his side. If he could increase the profit margins of Green Haven, Inc., the board couldn't complain. How could he do that? He needed to figure it out and fast. While listening to John Perkins drone on made Oscar want to rip his own ears off, he had to admit that it somehow gave him insight on how to work with the board. He now understood he couldn't be a one-man show barking orders; he had to learn how to work the system. More precisely how to manipulate the board members one at a time.

A few days later, Perkins called Oscar.

"Hello, John. I didn't expect to hear from you so soon. Might I add that our meeting the other day was very enlightening."

"Thank you, I guess. Anyway, I'm calling you to let you know that after our meeting I felt very uneasy. There was something off about the meeting." John's voice now carried outright defiance.

"Really?" Oscar ran a hand through his hair. A look of "how dare you" came across his face.

"Oh, don't get me wrong. It wasn't actually about the calling of the meeting. Although, I must admit it did seem a little out of character for you."

"Should I be offended?" Oscar's voice was now angrily sarcastic.

"No, again I apologize. I'm a bit disturbed. Our conversation got me thinking about the figures and the projections, so I went back and recalculated all the numbers. I was wrong, and you were wrong."

"You're not making any sense. How could we both be wrong?" Oscar's anger turned into confusion as he made his way over to a chair.

"Let me explain it in more detail."

Oscar was glad they were speaking on the phone so Perkins couldn't see him roll his eyes as he slumped back in his chair. Oscar braced himself for a second numerical beating.

"The numbers don't lie. Green Haven, Inc.'s choice to expand . . ."

"You mean my choice to expand." Oscar felt the anger starting to well deep in his chest again. He was now standing and waiting for the next insult to be hurled at him.

"Well, yes. Please let me finish. Your choice to expand and the downturn of the economy have created too large of a financial gap. Do you follow me so far?"

"Please try not to offend me on multiple levels at one time," Oscar interrupted.

The truth was that Oscar's interest was quickly waning as he fiddled with an app on his phone, trying not to have Mr. Perkins hear the clicking sounds emanating from fingering the keys.

"Sorry. Anyway, what we take in each month is not enough to cover what we have to pay out. Having said that, as the older residents die off, their antiquated fees are replaced with more realistic ones."

Oscar's stillness turned into angry pacing as Perkins laid out his plan. Long gone from Oscar's mind was the joy of victory at the last board meeting. Pretending to throw his phone across the room as though it was Perkins created a safety valve so he could return to a calmer place before speaking.

"Mr. Perkins, I'm not trying to invalidate your feelings, but as I stated in the last board meeting, Green Haven, Inc. always has new families asking about the facilities, and tours are always going on. This means the money will always be coming in. You have to trust in the process. The numbers don't always give the full picture."

It was now John Perkins' turn to find a safety valve. As a corporate numbers guy, he knew his research and forecasts were true. His mind was structured to see figures and make assumptions with consistent reliability. He could not and would not be a dreamer. Perkins paused for a long moment and then revealed the real purpose of his phone call.

"Frankly, I think that your predictions for the future and your continued shortsightedness won't be good for the corporation. I'm calling an emergency board meeting to discuss new information and to ask formally for your removal from the board."

Oscar's anger began to boil again, this time no amount of pacing, no safety valve could prepare him for what came next.

"Furthermore, I will strongly recommend, no ensure, that Green Haven, Inc. abandon the ludicrous practice of a yearly stipend. I will see that the board approves taking insurance payments immediately." The accountant decided to move full steam ahead. He held nothing back.

Oscar could take no more. Rage sped through him like a swarm of bees rebelling against an attack on their queen. He flung the phone across the room, smashing it into hundreds of pieces. The conversation was over. His fury prevented the functioning of his fine motor skills. He could barely unclench his fists as he reached for the bottle of Scotch on the bar. He tried to pour himself a shot but managed only a mouthful straight from the bottle.

Hours later, Oscar was able to regain his emotions and start thinking more clearly. The thoughts were now flowing smoothly again. There was only a slight feeling of being incensed by Perkins's unwillingness to see Oscar's vision of the future.

He knew the rage could return at any moment. Oscar walked over to the gold-framed mirror in the foyer. He not only needed to hear himself, but he also needed to see the force he believed he possessed. "One of the only things more powerful than money is the fear of not having it. If Perkins got to the board and scared them, they'd panic and look for a quick solution. The board is already volatile, and Chicken Little Perkins will run in and light that fuse. Those idiots will aim that blast right at me. I'll need a plan."

13

CATHY BOOTED UP THE computer in her office. She logged into the facility's mega system and asked for a report on all residents that had expired since the beginning of the year. As she sat and waited for the data to be compiled, she wondered if she was making something of nothing. Pharmatek was still an open wound, and she didn't want to create a second one. Kyle would surely fire her if she wasn't right. Then she thought there might not be a job to be fired from if she was right.

Thirty-seven names appeared on the screen. Cathy sat back in her chair, removed the cheaters from her face, and inhaled slowly. Thirty-seven was a lot in four months. She took a sip of her cold coffee, deep in thought. How could thirty-seven people die in four months and no one see it? There had to be someone somewhere whose job was to check on things like this. Cathy's mind could not turn off; she assigned blame to every department within Green Haven, to the local law enforcement agencies, and even the federal government agencies.

Cathy printed all the death certificates. First, she separated them by month; this confirmed her thought of an average of nine residents passing per month. That's about two or three a week. Lay that out over a year, and you've got over a hundred residents. Something's definitely wrong. She gasped as she thought that the entire facility would turn over in a year if this continued.

Now Cathy focused on the number each month and in total that had the designation "nurse may pronounce." In both cases, more than 75 percent carried the label. *How did I miss this? How long has this been going on? Am I being set up?* The thoughts were running wild, and she couldn't stop them.

Two hours later, Kyle knocked on her door then quickly opened it. He didn't even look in Cathy's direction. He merely snapped the orders at her. "You're needed on north wing, two aides arguing or something. Handle this or I will."

For once Cathy was happy that Kyle hated her so much; he couldn't stand to even look at her. If he had, he would have seen the piles of death certificates strewn over the entire surface of her desk. Cathy thought to herself it would have looked like she was planning the next murder, her next murder.

At least it's not another dying resident. Cathy shoved the copies in her desk drawer and walked over to the north wing. Two of the CNAs were in dispute over coverage because the third CNA called out sick. Cathy looked at the floor nurse, who just put her hands up and walked away. "I tried," she whispered as she passed Cathy.

Cathy took both CNAs to a small supply room behind the nurse's station and gave them each a chance to explain the situation. Apparently, neither wanted to care for old Dr. Thorne. Dr. Thorne lived up to his name. He was a pain in the side of all the caregivers. He was loud, rude, and very free with his hands. Both Dr. Thorne and his family had been warned many times about him grabbing the staff. It never went any further than a verbal reprimand. Rumors started that the Thorne family had agreed to pay a yearly nuisance fee to keep him there. Of course, this could never be confirmed. Dr. Thorne was in his nineties and had been a resident of Green Haven for over ten years. His mental health was deteriorating quickly while his physical health remained that of a seventy-five-year-old, or a teenaged boy if you listened to the CNAs.

The impromptu scolding by Kyle had given Cathy an army captain's sternness in her voice. Cathy ordered the CNAs to split the time so that each would take care of him for half of their shift. Both nodded in military-like obedience without uttering a word. As she walked to Kyle's office, Cathy knew she was headed for some kind of verbal attack again. She knocked on Kyle's door. He could see her through the glass and let her wait a long moment before waving her in. Cathy started to tell him the matter had been handled when he cut her off mid-sentence.

"You need to control your staff, or I'll find someone who can." A look of utter disdain shot from his face.

Cathy thought to herself, *Yeah, an email would have been better.* She tried not to smile.

Kyle asked her if there was anything else. She shook her head and left his office. She should have been angry, but her expectations were right on. That gave her satisfaction beyond any anger Kyle could stir up in her after all this time.

She returned to her desk and placed the copies in her purse so she could review them at home. It would be safer that way. Inadvertently, Cathy reached for the simple but elegant designer watch that had shifted on her right wrist, remembering that many years ago, her mother had "requested" she wear the watch on her left wrist. Her mother told her it was customary for a watch to be worn on the left wrist. To comply with her mother's wishes, Cathy wore the watch on the left, but it always hindered her writing. She chuckled now as she adjusted the right-handed watch. She saw the time and realized that except for settling a staff dispute, she hadn't been on the units the entire morning. She made her rounds and spoke with some of the more coherent residents like she always did. Now she was wondering who was next, who was doing it, and why. Thoughts ran wild in her head. Some of the staff repeated questions and conversations twice to her because she wasn't present. Cathy headed back to her office quickly. She had to get control. She knew how fast the rumors flew around Green Haven. She didn't need to be the focus of anything while trying to uncover a conspiracy.

Getting control was out of the question. Cathy had to continue with her research. She pulled out the death certificates again and looked at the age and the sex of each resident. There was no pattern. There were more women than men, but that couldn't be a factor. There are far more women than men in nursing facilities because women live longer. There was no age pattern, either. The expired residents ranged from their seventies to almost one hundred. What was she missing? The copies weren't the answer. If they were, they were doing an excellent job of hiding it. Her frustration grew at a sprinter's pace. She wanted a clear-cut answer, and she wanted it now. Cathy made herself laugh as she said aloud, "This is why I'm a nurse and not a detective."

In her mind, she started playing back old detective shows. What would they do? How would they flush out the criminal? Whoa, stop right there! Researching this is one thing. Confronting a killer is another; let the police handle that part. "Trying to be a hero is what got you in trouble with Kyle all those years ago," Cathy said this aloud so she could hear it. "Let's stick to the fact-finding behind the scenes. Deal? Deal." Cathy shook her right hand with the left and chuckled.

Cathy's phone rang. The receptionist told her Father Brendan called to say he and Sister Diane weren't coming in. His car was being repaired following last week's fender bender. She said they'd be back on their scheduled days as usual.

Cathy thanked the receptionist and hung up. She thought, *Well, if someone dies today, it's just me, no holy couple dance for act two.*

Cathy placed the copies in her purse. She removed the cheaters from her face and leaned back on her chair, rubbing her tired eyes. She closed her them for only a second, and the faces of Anna Sparks and Adam James came flooding into the darkness. Cathy nearly fell from her old metal chair as she jumped to her feet in a panic. "Okay, no more of this for today."

She spent the rest of the shift performing her typical routine; the conspiracy was never far from her thoughts. "This is going to keep me up all night," she whispered a bit too loudly.

The nurse at the north wing station replied, "Sorry, what was that?"

"Nothing, just making a mental note." Cathy smiled and headed back to her office.

At 4:00 pm, with no death certificates to sign, Cathy grabbed her purse, placed the death certificate copies in it, and headed for the door. As she reached the glass doors to the outside, Cathy could see the reflection of part of the death certificates peeking out from atop her purse. The blue writing was not legible, but it was unmistakable. A bead of sweat formed on her forehead as she wondered if anyone may have noticed the blue lettering. With great care, Cathy stopped and pretended to reach inside her purse to retrieve her car keys. In that same motion, she shoved the papers deeper into the darkness. Cathy exited Green Haven quietly, forcing herself not look around to see if anyone was watching. She remembered from the detective shows that suspicious people do suspicious things, such as always trying to see who's watching them.

She was about to get into her car when she looked down at her purse; the temptation to study the copies while driving was too much. She didn't need a car accident on top of a conspiracy. Or worse, getting into an accident and someone finding out she had the papers. Cathy placed the purse in the trunk and drove away from Green Haven.

14

BRENDAN'S CONVERSION WENT SMOOTHLY. He found that when motivated, he could learn quickly and easily. With Father Matthew's help, he was accepted into the seminary school. Brendan never contacted his mother to let her know he'd chosen the priesthood. He didn't want the backlash or shame she'd undoubtedly levy onto him. Besides, they never consulted him about the divorce or even his father's sickness. On the surface, Brendan told himself that he didn't owe her anything, but, deep down, he still wanted her approval. He wanted his father's approval just as much, but that would never happen now. Alice Pierce, now Morgan, left several voicemails for her son, none of which he ever returned. Finally, she tearfully gave up.

Father Matthew was the man the Brendan wanted to become; his father-like mentoring filled the emptiness inside soon to be young priest. The seminary gave Brendan a sense of belonging, and his work there was exemplary, so much so that when the local Bishop Anthony visited, he always made time to sit with Brendan. The bishop told Brendan that Father Matthew had picked well. Brendan explained that Father Matthew helped him turn his life around. The visits with the bishop became longer and more frequent. Bishop Anthony told Brendan that he too saw something special in him, and when he was ordained, he wanted to take him under his wing. Bishop Anthony said that as Father Brendan, he could do great work. Brendan believed the bishop. He saw the kindness of Father Matthew and his own father's strength in the bishop.

After his studies were complete and he was ordained, Father Brendan took a position in a small parish at the request of the bishop. The new priest was disappointed at his placement. He'd expected a more grandiose start, but the New Testament taught him there's a higher purpose for each of us and only the Lord knows the end game.

His meetings with Bishop Anthony became almost a welcomed weekly event. Their discussions covered Catholic doctrine to philosophic theory. Sensing the young priest's discouragement, Bishop Anthony would assure him that his position at this small parish was deliberate and meaningful. Father Brendan did excellent work at the parish, but his heart wasn't in it. He wanted something else. The older priests treated him well, but he knew they considered him as young and that he needed to pay his dues. While Father Brendan was disappointed, he put all his trust in the bishop. He followed every directive and completed every task in hopes that Bishop Anthony would soon make good on the many promises of greatness he suggested were in Brendan's future. Brendon, the man, thought he would be groomed to replace the bishop when the time was right; Father Brendan knew better and fought these desires but lost most of the time.

Three months into the posting, Father Brendan was asked by Bishop Anthony to accompany Father Timothy to nursing facilities to help treat those unable to come to church. Father Brendan was told that he needed field experience in giving last rites to those moving on. He tried not to dwell on further disappointment. Brendan thought, by now, he'd be sitting at the bishop's side on a daily basis. The young priest had no clue that politics played a role in the Church.

A few weeks of tagging along with Father Timothy gave him a new appreciation for the work he was doing. Father Brendan could see the joy on the faces of the residents at Green Haven's three facilities when they saw Father Timothy. He felt the love that both the residents and Father

Timothy shared. Father Timothy introduced him as the new Father Brendan and asked the residents to welcome him into their hearts.

Father Brendan began to recognize that the old priest had no malice even if he thought he might be replaced. There was a peaceful calm about Father Timothy. At every visit, those residents that were coherent would confess what sins they thought they'd committed, and Father Timothy would show mercy by relieving them of their burdens. Two weeks into Father Brendan's trips to Green Haven, a resident passed away and they were called in to give last rites. Father Brendan was nervous. He'd never actually performed the last rites ritual on a person.

"Have you done a lot of this, considering who we help and where we work?" He was hoping Father Timothy would say it was only a tiny part of their job.

Father Timothy looked up as he replied, "Thank God it only happens once or twice a month per facility." He could see Father Brendan was nervous and began to walk the new priest through the ritual.

After the last rites were completed, Father Timothy placed his hands together and looked at Father Brendan. "Death is a part of the Lord's greater plan, and as servants of His will, it is our duty to get His flock ready to see Him."

He told Father Brendan he had performed the ceremony flawlessly. The young priest thanked Father Timothy and felt more at ease. Father Brendan thought since God had continued to place him in the hands of caring and kind people after such a rocky start, he must have made the right choice. He trusted the men who looked after him and vowed that he would one day do the same for them and others.

As time passed, Father Timothy was able to get the residents to trust and believe in Father Brendan. They eventually accepted him. Soon Father Brendan was hearing the confessions of new residents and absolving them. The older, established residents were more resistant to change and stayed with Father Timothy. Months had gone by, and Father Brendan was feeling more comfortable working at the facilities. He preferred the nursing home work over the parish work. He sensed the people who met with him in the facilities did so out of joy. This filled the hole left from his childhood. He wanted to help the residents any way he could.

Bishop Anthony checked in with him regularly. "Father Timothy tells me you have taken to your new life quite well."

Father Brendan smiled. "Father Timothy is a wonderful mentor and more. I love what I do." The smile left his face as he continued, "I have to admit it was difficult in the beginning, seeing some of the residents who just lie in bed and have no clue that I, we, are in the room."

Bishop Anthony now leaned in close to him. "Remember, in those cases you are tending to their souls. Their physical body is truly a husk waiting to have the fruit burst out and flourish in a whole new way."

"I'd never thought of it that way. So, you're saying that we're like the farmers of the soul tending to the plant." Father Brendan felt like it was reaching, but he wanted to show the bishop he understood the metaphor.

The bishop made the sign of the cross and grinned widely. "Exactly."

"You think Father Timothy sees it that way?"

The grin left the bishop's face as he slightly debated his answer. "I'm guessing he believes some version of it."

"This reminds me of when I was about sixteen; I took a part-time job at a veterinarian's office. People would bring their dying pets in to be put down. They were sad and crying; Dr. Gene always found a way to comfort them. I wanted to be Dr. Gene."

Bishop Anthony was grinning again. "I'm sure you're doing that to a degree."

Father Brendan nodded in agreement with the bishop. "I guess you're right. I just think that at times there's more I could do. Especially for the residents who don't even know where they are."

While Father Brendan adored the bishop, he still wondered when he'd reveal the plan for him to take over as the new bishop or some other role tied to working more directly with him. Those thoughts became less and less as he enjoyed working with the residents of Green Haven, Inc. During one visit, the bishop asked if he was comfortable with the residents and confident about working with them alone.

Father Brendan was surprised. He enjoyed the residents but didn't want to push Father Timothy out; the old priest had opened his world to him. Father Brendan was terrified to give a truthful answer. He wanted the position. But he couldn't do this to a man who was so gentle and kind, a man who had given everything to his faith and freely shared with him.

"I love what I do, but it's really a two-person job. There are too many residents to be served by just a single priest."

Bishop Anthony leaned back in his chair. "Mmm, I do admire your loyalty, and I hope that I also will benefit from it for a long time. The truth is that Father Timothy asked that you take over from him. He said he was tired and needed to retire. I couldn't deny his request, and I know you're up to the task."

Father Brendon stood; a look of utter amazement blanketed his face. "But, he didn't say anything to me. I want to discuss it with him. Maybe I could take on more so he could slow down."

Seeing the apparent panic and frenzy taking over the young priest, Bishop Anthony stood and placed a hand on Father Brendan's shoulder. "He's already left for a quiet place to live a peaceful life. Don't worry; the Church has provided well for him. The man was a good priest and he's paid his dues. Let him go."

"Why didn't he say goodbye?" His eyes welled, but Father Brendan fought back the tears.

"I'm not sure, but I suspect he knew how hard it would have been on both of you." The bishop placed a hand on the Father Brendan's hand to console him.

The young priest, now the sole heir to the Green Haven, Inc. spiritual empire, felt the pain of his familial abandonment all over again. Father

Timothy was another in a long line of father figures to leave him without so much as a goodbye. Just Bishop Anthony remained, and Brendan feared that at some point he would leave too.

Father Brendan's next few weeks were filled with giving explanations as to the whereabouts of the sweet older priest. For Brendan, it was like a flower desperately trying to hold onto its last petal, only to watch it fall to the ground time and time again with each explanation, reliving the sudden departure without any say in the matter.

The bishop did take Father Brendan's advice regarding the need for two people to serve the residents of the three facilities. Bishop Anthony handpicked a young woman named Sister Diane. She was raised by very religious foster parents and entered into her training at the request of those foster parents. She knew nothing of her birth parents.

15

CATHY PULLED INTO HER garage, closed the door, and for some reason looked around before opening the trunk. She let out a sarcastic smirk as she realized she had closed the garage door. She went right to the kitchen table and took out the death certificate copies. The drive home felt like it took hours. She kept seeing the words "nurse may pronounce" in bold blue letters on each copy. Again, she asked herself, *How did I miss this?* As she sat at the table, Cathy began to replay the last six years of her life. When did she fall asleep? When did she start to give up? She realized that when she now walked around Green Haven, she had stopped making contact with the residents and the staff, only interacting when necessary. She had let go of her humanity to become an android devoid of caring. "Damn you, Pharmatek. Damn you, Kyle. Damn me!" Cathy nearly screamed as the realization sank in.

Cathy knew she had unconsciously allowed herself to become plain and unseen. She realized she had taken her dreams of nursing excellence, traveling to faraway grains of sand and the joyful sunshine of life, and replaced it with fear and smallness. Cathy removed her cheaters to wipe away the tears now freely flowing from each eye. She glanced around the apartment, only to see the life of singledom she had chosen. The sorrow intensified as she saw there were no family photos, no remnants of past couple's vacations, no his stuff, no their stuff, only her stuff. The Cathy that existed now was not who she imagined herself to be. Cathy got up from the table to storm around the living room for a minute. She knew she needed to calm down. The painful inner rage fought hard to remain, but Cathy could feel its flux as she tried to regain control in order to think more clearly. She had let the Pharmatek snafu, then Kyle's repeated torture over it, beat her down. She'd stuck her head in the sand, and now something was telling her to wake up. This would be her ticket back to the Cathy she had buried all those years ago.

The emotional intensity created a physical call by her body that now required food. Cathy needed food and some sugar. She'd have to keep her energy level high and her enthusiasm higher. Cathy headed back into the kitchen, glancing at the copies on her way to the small pullout pantry. She recalled that marathon runners ate carbs before a race for long-term energy. She removed some pasta and a jar of tomato sauce, started the water boiling, and then poured herself the largest glass of soda she could find.

While the water was heating, she sat back down to make a quick review of the copies. Still, nothing stood out. Cathy fought hard to keep the last few minutes of her life in the background so she could concentrate on the task at hand. She felt a new and different vibe about the challenge. She rearranged the data by sex, and again nothing; then by age, nothing. The only thing most of them had in common was that damn "nurse may pronounce" label. Cathy removed all the certificates that didn't have the bold blue lettering at the top. She thought those might just be random deaths. The unlabeled certificates were adding confusion. Still, nothing jumped out at her. She put the papers down.

"Who could know about the 'nurse may pronounce,' and why were they setting me up? Who did I piss off so much that they would want to send me to prison? Kyle! I won't let you get away with this. This is way too far. I will put you away forever, you *bastard*!" Cathy slammed her fist on the table. The hatred she now felt for Kyle was undeniable. As she sat at the kitchen table, Cathy became consumed by the emotion. Her anger was broken by the sound of the boiling water on the stove. Cathy's need for food returned.

She calmed herself down again, finished cooking the pasta, and ate her dinner in front of the news. There was a story about a local man, John Perkins, who died in a car crash. Alcohol was thought to have been the cause. Cathy thought she knew the name but couldn't place it. She finished her dinner and poured a second glass of soda.

Back at the table, Cathy stared at the copies once again, getting nowhere. She decided to go line by line to find anything that matched. She reached into her purse to pull out a pen and saw her paycheck. She forgot to stop at the bank to deposit it. Cathy had the option for direct deposit but never took it. She needed to hold the check in her hand every two weeks to feel the satisfaction of having worked. Specifically, she needed a good reason to keep working for Kyle. She thought just for one day she'd like to be his boss and torture him, or better yet, she wished Green Haven, Inc. would get rid of him. She realized that now she would get rid of him, an act of revenge long overdue.

She pulled out the check to sign it and gasped when she saw the stamped signature of John Perkins, Treasurer, at the bottom of it. She didn't know him personally but had seen his name on her checks for as long as she could remember. She wondered if the board knew the man controlling the money had a drinking problem.

She went back to the task at hand, but she couldn't stop thinking about John Perkins. Cathy was in detective mode and according to the shows they never stopped detecting.

How long was he drinking? What else was he into? Did he do drugs? Did he gamble? Did he gamble with Green Haven's money? Did he use Green Haven's money for anything? Was Green Haven in financial trouble? Was her retirement in trouble?

Cathy told herself to stop; she could only handle one alleged conspiracy at a time. It was now almost 10:00 pm. She was tired, and it was too late for more sugar. She had learned nothing from the copies, but she'd still keep them at home. If something was going on, which she was sure of, those copies were not the answer.

As she readied herself for bed, she saw a news update. Mr. Perkins' blood alcohol level was well below 0.08 percent for driving under the influence. According to the reporter, the police were checking Mr. Perkins' car for mechanical failure and an autopsy was scheduled for some time in the next few days.

Cathy lay in bed trying not to tie the treasurer's and the patients' deaths together. "What if Mr. Perkins found out something and was killed for it? No more detective shows. From now on just sitcoms with phony laugh tracks." She turned off the television and tried to go to sleep. Between the soda and the news, Cathy was restless. After forty-five minutes of tossing and turning, she got up.

She went into the living room trying to not to look around and set off another round of tears; she sat on the couch. She needed a different approach, a new way to look at the information. Cathy started from the beginning. She asked herself what every person has when they become a resident.

Cathy jotted notes on a pad. She'd decided not to use a computer because it could be hacked and left a trail she didn't know how to hide. She tore off the sheet she had been scribbling on earlier that night.

1. Contract signed
2. Contacts, POA(s)
3. Release page(s)
4. Admission form
5. Medications list with allergies
6. List of belongings
7. Illnesses
8. Doctors

This list was longer than the one from the morning. Cathy thought this would be a good place to start. Green Haven, Inc. made it a practice not to allow resident contracts in the charts. They were housed at the corporate office. Only the board and the owner had access to them. Cathy wondered if the administrator had access or even copies. Each contract contained personal financial information detailing the yearly amount to be paid by the family or Power of Attorney. The board had each resident and financially responsible party sign strict non-disclosure agreements about the yearly amount paid. It was a longstanding rumor around all three facilities that the fee was set on a sliding scale in the corporation's favor. If a resident had more, Green Haven, Inc. wanted more. Getting the contracts would be difficult and would raise too many flags. Cathy had never shown any interest in them before, and they were definitely above her clearance. She'd have to move further down the list.

It was now well into the next morning, and she was getting sleepy. Her mind was losing the battle. She'd have to be at work if she wanted to gather more information. Cathy hid the copies and her notepad in the back of her closet inside a box containing an old pair of cowboy boots she hadn't worn in over two decades. Cathy didn't want to look at the alarm clock as she climbed into bed; better that she didn't know what time it was. Tomorrow she'd compile a list of what each resident's form includes upon their death or leaving the facility. She wondered how many residents ever really left. Most just stayed until they were carried out. Within minutes of being prone, Cathy's thoughts were fading, and she fell asleep.

16

SINCE GREEN HAVEN WAS growing to full capacity, Dr. Oliver was being kept extremely busy. She called Oscar and postponed their very first Friday afternoon meeting until the following week. Something she thought long about before doing. She still denied her attraction to him. The whole contract negotiation caused her to look at the possibility of a love life again. Marissa knew there would be complications, both now and possibly in the future. She rolled her eyes as she thought about maybe having some Friday afternoon fun. She'd put her personal life on hold for so long; now she was beginning to doubt she'd remember how to have fun.

Green Haven was accepting residents faster than the medical director could keep up. Like the rest of the staff, Dr. Oliver was new. The staff and doctors didn't know how to work together or even trust each other. Marissa Oliver, MD, was not about to put her new medical license on the line for anyone. She double-checked everything that was her responsibility. This took a great deal of time. It was like being back in her residency.

Except for her brief stint in private practice, Dr. Marissa Oliver was not used to being on her own. It was a scary thought. There was no safety net. No Attending was looking over her shoulder, preventing her from making a career-ending mistake. Now the mistakes would be dealt with after the fact. She'd planned to fly under the radar as long as possible. She was being paid an excellent salary, didn't have to deal with insurance companies, and her student loans had vanished. She was left alone as long as she didn't call attention to herself. It was a sweet deal. She wasn't going to let a nurse or anyone else ruin it for her.

The only attention Marissa would try to attract was from Oscar Green, and even that had to be secret. She didn't need rumors starting that she got the job by sleeping with the owner. First, it was not true, yet. Second, it would destroy any credibility she'd have with the staff. She needed to be apart from the staff. In her eyes, Dr. Oliver was above them. Inside she was terrified that someone might see every decision was made with painstaking detail to avoid an error. She was a new doctor, and maybe she should have worked for someone a few years before becoming a medical director. Too late. You're the medical director. Put that mask on and wear it well.

She convinced herself it was on-the-job training. Make them respect— no, make them fear the name Dr. Marissa Oliver. She recalled the fear of tangling with an Attending during her residency. Marissa wanted to feel that power for once. In reality, she'd wanted to feel that power for a long, long time.

Marissa had now been at Green Haven for about nine hours. She was getting tired. Dozens of charts, too many resident reviews, thousands of questions answered, and she was done. It was time to stop. She drifted over to the nurse on duty and said goodbye. The nurse looked puzzled. Dr. Oliver told her, in a rather stern and somewhat condescending voice, "All the necessary meds and treatments were done. The rest can wait until tomorrow." She didn't give the nurse a chance to respond. Marissa walked away. Inside she trembled, wondering what she would say if the nurse replied. The now open-mouthed nurse didn't. Dr. Oliver smiled as she hit the exit button.

Marissa drove away, hoping no one followed her into the parking lot for one last signature. As she pulled out of the newly-paved Green Haven driveway, it was a drink she craved. She didn't want to be alone, or with anyone for that matter. She wanted to be in the presence of people but not with them. She stopped at the first bar she saw. It was a run-of-the-mill, small-town bar with a few locals. The barstools were practically held together with duct tape. The heavily marred surface of the wooden bar appeared like an old man's calloused and withered hands from years of hard work. The low wattage bulbs making their feeble attempts at creating an atmosphere were probably a blessing. Marissa noted the sickly smell of old beer rising from the depths of the dark floor. Thankfully Marissa didn't recognize anyone she might have treated as a resident or in her former practice. She laughed. She only had a handful of patients in her office in those long six months. Thank God for your father, Oscar.

Before sitting at the bar, Marissa checked the stool for any remnants of its previous master, then she ordered a glass of white wine. As the bartender began to turn away, she changed her order. "Make that bourbon. It was too long a day." She decided she needed to really unwind before a second round tomorrow. Wine was just not going to cut it.

The man sitting next to her looked her way.

Marissa gave a low and gravelly response, "What? It's been a grueling day. And don't ask me about it, okay."

"Okay, I didn't . . . never mind."

The man stood up and moved to the other side of the bar. Sitting there alone, she began to wonder, *When did I forget how to be human? He said nothing and I cut him to shreds*. Marissa looked at the bartender.

"Can you send him another of whatever he's drinking and tell him I'm sorry?"

Without looking up, the bartender replied, "He's already gone. You okay?"

"Yeah, just stressed. Actually, everything is pretty good right now."

He stopped fumbling with the ice and now looked directly at Marissa. "You sure have a funny way of reacting to pretty good."

Marissa resisted the urge to flip him the finger and settled for, "Well, it may just be who I am."

The bartender gave her a look telling her the conversation was over and no other would be needed as he worked his way down the bar pretending to wipe it clean.

Marissa sat on the barstool, quietly sipping her bourbon and listening to the senseless chatter in the background. It was just what she needed: to be on the outside while being in the middle, no pressure to participate but still in the thick of things if she wanted to join in. Marissa admitted she might want to get some therapy later. Today therapy came in a glass and slid down her slender throat to warm her belly. When she finished the bourbon, Marissa held the empty glass in the air, defiantly ordering the barkeep to do his job. All without uttering a word. He reached for a clean glass, poured the spirit in, and placed it on the bar with a thudding force that seemed to make the other patrons stop and shutter. He never looked at her, and she never thanked him.

Her thoughts floated to Oscar. What was he doing now? She wanted to call him, but that would be totally unprofessional. She didn't want to let him know that she was becoming infatuated with him. She preferred he do the chasing. She was in control. Marissa wondered what the home of a high-end nursing facility owner looked like. She lived in a small one-bedroom apartment where the rent had always been two months in arrears until she received the five-thousand-dollar signing bonus. The electric company made daily calls that she avoided. Soon she'd be able to afford furniture that she was the first to purchase. She had big dreams now that Green Haven, Inc. had come to save the day. Her student loans were not going to be a mortgage she'd be saddled with for eternity. One day soon she'd purchase a house of her own. The bourbon was doing its job. Marissa was feeling relaxed. She took the final sip from the second glass, speechlessly summoned the check and paid. "I'm never coming back to this dump," she barked just loud enough for the bartender to hear as she left.

Marissa had every intention of driving home, but she couldn't get the thought of Oscar Green's home out of her mind. She pulled to the side of the road, slumped over towards the passenger seat, and struggled to reach her cell phone. Her slight stature was no competition for the top-shelf bourbon served her by the vengeful bartender. Marissa tried to press the buttons on the phone with less than cooperative fingers. She heard the clicking of the buttons through the car's audio system and remembered that the phone's Bluetooth auto-synced with the vehicle. She managed to press the call button on the steering wheel with little effort. "Call, um, Oscar Green mobile."

Oscar recognized the number and rose to his feet with the excitement of a faithful sporting fan continuing the wave. He picked up quickly.

"Hello, Dr. Oliver? Is everything okay? Do I need to come down to Green Haven?"

"Uh, no, no. Uh, I was just wondering. This is a terrible idea."

"No, it's okay. Do we need to talk in person? Where are you? I can come meet you."

"No, that's, uh, okay. I'm already in my car." Marissa was now grasping the steering wheel tightly with both hands, trying to keep calm.

"I'm at home. Do you want to come here? I'm sorry. Is that too forward or inappropriate?" Oscar could feel his face flush.

"No, um, that's fine. What's the address?"

Oscar gave her the address, and she quickly hung up. She smiled, and then the fear of her boldness took over. She had been drinking too much and let her guard down. The bourbon worked too well. Now she was committed. A second phone call would just make things much worse. She decided to go to his home. Marissa sat parked at the curb for a few more moments realizing she also needed to gain more control over her motor skills if she was going to make it to Oscar's. She fumbled with the air conditioning knob until she was slapped in the face with an Arctic blast hard enough to shake the spirited demon from her mind, at least for now. *Damn bartender, probably drugged me just because, well just because.*

On the drive there, the alcohol's bite had lessened, and Marissa came up with some story of a problem with Green Haven's forms, something small and easy to fix. When she pulled up to the house, Marissa reached for the metal tin sitting in the center console. She placed a breath mint in her mouth, thought a moment then added a second just for good measure. As she sat there chewing on the hard mints paying close attention to make sure that all areas of her mouth were introduced to the new sent, all the previous story planning went out the window. She was like a schoolgirl on her first date. Marissa was excited and terrified at the same time. She'd made the first move. Her mind whirled. What if Oscar didn't feel the same? What if she'd misread the signals? What if she ended up looking like a fool and losing her job? Marissa suddenly feared the future of her financial security. She was about to turn around when Oscar opened the door. Marissa made a motion like she was locking her car door with the remote. Her car didn't have a remote lock button. She turned back to Oscar, who waved her in.

Oscar's home was modest and not at all what Marissa's bourbon-soaked brain had imagined. No central spiraling staircase, no large chandelier hanging in an enormous foyer. The condo was quite simple and ordinary. It was like any other upper-middle-class home you'd find in America. She looked disappointed.

Oscar caught her expression and asked her to come into the living room where he'd opened a bottle of red wine. He told her that it was after work and she wouldn't be seeing any more patients today. A reference she understood instantly. She accepted the glass of wine and was determined to sip it as slowly as possible. Her nerves were at full alert, as full as two glasses of bourbon would allow. What had she done? She planned to remember the story she made up, to tell Oscar she would handle it but wanted him to know about it first, and then she'd leave.

"What was it you wanted to discuss?" Oscar felt the long awkward silence after his question but didn't comment on it.

"Oh. Yes. Some of the Green Haven medical forms are multiple pages and don't have a space for the resident's name or any identifying information at the top. If the first page is lost or removed, then it's questionable if the remaining pages are for that particular resident. I think I can ask the IT guy to go into the system and correct the forms electronically. Then the staff can review the new forms, well you get the idea." Marissa was babbling and she knew it.

"Ah, okay, sure. I, uh, will let you handle it then. I'm glad you brought it to my attention." Oscar could smell the faint scent of alcohol already on her breath but said nothing.

Marissa's nervousness, and perhaps the bourbon, made her lose track of how much wine she was consuming. Oscar was trying to keep pace, but he too was losing control. After an hour of small talk and an entire bottle of wine, they were snuggled on the couch together asleep. Early the next morning, Oscar's wrist alarm sounded, waking both of them. Neither would look at the other. Oscar finally broke the ice and asked if she wanted coffee. Marissa nodded, which her head made her pay for dearly. She decided to take the coffee to go, leaving as quickly as possible. Marissa stared at the ground as she made the "walk of shame" to her car. She got into her car, making sure not to look back. Oscar watched as she drove away. Both were uncomfortable with the events of last night. Oscar didn't want their relationship to start this way. Marissa quietly, very quietly, spoke to herself, trying to convince herself that everything was okay. "But I didn't do anything. We fell asleep." The concern of messing up her deal weighed heavily on Marissa, and then she wondered about Oscar. What was he thinking of her actions, her boldness, her stupidity?

17

AT 6:45 AM, CATHY arrived at Green Haven; she wanted to get in early but not early enough to attract any attention. She reached her office and fired up the computer. On the drive in, she had concluded that creating a blank spreadsheet using a program on the computer would be okay. It wouldn't mean anything to anybody, thank you detective TV. She created the blank grid in Word because she didn't know how to use Excel well enough to hide anything. Cathy printed out the form, then filled it in with the information she thought could help make ties between all the expired Green Haven residents. "A manual spreadsheet, just like the old DON would have done." She laughed. "If only that old nurse knew how good she had it." Cathy laughed again.

The spreadsheet covered the entire page when printed out. The boxes were big enough so she could write in them, and the columns and rows were numerous enough to include whatever she thought might be important. Cathy printed out five sheets, just to be on the safe side. She left a copy on the computer in case she needed more of them later.

The whole time she was creating the spreadsheet she kept thinking about Mr. Perkins. What really happened to him? If someone found out what she was up to, would she have an accident? This time she thought, *Too many detective shows.*

Cathy signed into the charting portion of the mega system and pulled up the name of the resident on the earliest death certificate. She wrote the name down on her spreadsheet. She scanned the form on the screen looking for anything that stood out. Nothing did. She kept filling in the spreadsheet with data hoping that by the end she would see the information she needed. Name, date of admission, age at admission, sex, life-threatening diseases, date and time of death, weekday of the death, age at death, cause of death, and finally, the number of years at Green Haven. There was a box to mark if the "nurse may pronounce" stamp was on the chart, but she later decided to abandon this box as every resident she was looking into would get this box checked.

Cathy had entered in the first ten residents on her spreadsheet. She looked up living residents in between the expired ones so the name searches would look random to anyone who might be watching. For a moment, she thought she might make an excellent criminal. After entering in ten of the thirty-seven residents on her spreadsheet, Cathy decided to stop before her login time was not too much over any typical day. She would return this afternoon to retrieve information on five more.

Cathy logged out and was heading to south wing when the floor nurse told her she was just about to call her on the intercom. A chill ran down Cathy's spine. *It's happening again.* She turned to head back to her office for the form and walked right into Father Brendan, who was heading to the north wing. Sister Diane was right on his heels and ran into him from behind when he abruptly stopped. The floor nurse called over Cathy's shoulder to Father Brendan telling him to return to south wing, that he wasn't done there. Cathy sidestepped the father and headed for the form.

Tammy Grey was a ninety-six-year-old woman who was bedridden for the last three months and failing quickly. Her chart was marked "nurse may pronounce." Cathy whispered, "Crap." Father Brendan looked at her in surprise. She apologized and continued to fill out the form. She looked up at the father and sister duo after she was done and whispered to them, "This routine is becoming way too popular around here lately."

The moment she said it Cathy regretted it. She hoped that she didn't open Pandora's box. Would the holy couple start to suspect foul play and go to the police? Cathy wasn't ready. She knew all the evidence pointed at her. This would not be a good thing. Not yet.

"Life has a strange way of ending in death, and we all get there in good time." Sister Diane's response was a welcome relief to Cathy. She just needed the good father to feel the same way. But he kept silent and started his work with Tammy Grey. Cathy touched Sister Diane's shoulder as she left the room. The sister stood at the closed door as she did every time. Cathy let out a large exhale and headed back to her office, taking a split second to subtly glance over, first at the door and then at the blue star on the nameplate. "Crap," quietly leaped from her lips again.

Once back in the office, she closed the door, finished the form, quickly made a copy, and then shoved the copy into her purse. Cathy told herself she had to remain calm about this; acting out would draw attention. She felt like her mother scolding her for something she did when she was a child. She could hear the harsh tone coming from her mother. "I've told you many times. You're not in charge! Listen and follow; that's all there is!"

Cathy leaned back in her chair and felt the wave of exhaustion come over her. She hadn't slept well again, and she'd been burning an incredible amount of mental energy in the last forty-eight hours. Cathy needed a break, so she closed her eyes. A loud knock at the door startled her. By the sheer anger of the rap, she knew it was Kyle. He opened the door smiling. She thought she must be asleep.

"I'm taking a few personal days, so you're 'in charge.'" Kyle made air quotes with his fingers, letting Cathy know that the truth was far from his last statement.

"Okay. Going . . . ?"

"Don't worry about where I'm going. No major decisions." There was a long pause before he delivered the last blow. "Oh, and don't buy anything!"

So much for being asleep, Cathy thought. She nodded, thinking better of any kind of a verbal reply. Kyle was about to close the door when his head reappeared.

"You are to use my office while I'm gone. We need to have it look like someone important is up front. Don't break anything. Oh yeah, please."

Yep, not asleep, Cathy told herself again. She nodded once more, but was thinking, *What an ass!* This time Kyle closed the door and left. Cathy had been put in charge before, but she knew she had no real power. Kyle would never give her any real control. She was sure that spies were also put in place. They were just waiting to report any little mishap to curry favor with the big bad boss man. Like all the other times, it would be business as usual. Except for this time, she was the secret spy looking to solve a series of murders.

Use of Kyle's office was the perfect cover. Kyle had a reputation of burning someone at the stake first then asking questions later. No one would ever snoop around in his office. Even she would move around that office with great caution. But this time, Cathy was on a mission. She could sign in using Kyle's computer with administrator access. Kyle changed his passwords monthly but couldn't remember them, so he would write them down on the backside of his blotter. He would cross out the old one and write the new one in succession. Cathy overheard him telling the IT guy this one day while they were standing outside his office discussing something about Kyle's computer. Kyle was a mean person who was proud of his self-proclaimed genius. And he liked to tell this to anyone who would listen. He would always start his bragging with "It's on a need-to-know basis." Cathy thought again, *What an ass.*

Cathy saw Kyle leave the parking lot and headed to his office. She was going to set up shop immediately. She closed his doors, realizing they had glass window sections and no blinds. The man was too cocky to hide from anyone. He wanted everyone to see when he was hard at work or when he chose to take a break. After all, he was the boss. Cathy smiled as she almost repeated the phrase for a third time. She made sure no one was looking, then she lifted the blotter on the desk to retrieve the password for Kyle's computer. There were two passwords not crossed out. This was odd. Kyle always crossed out the old one so he knew which one to use. Cathy could see the sequence running down the left side of the blotter. She could see that Kyle started using two passwords just a short time ago. She wrote both passwords down on a sticky note, replaced the blotter, and typed in the first password. It worked. She had too much on her mind to go snooping. She smirked as she thought Kyle might be using the second password for a dating service or maybe porn. She would circle back to that later. It would be good to finally have something to hold over his head for a while.

She looked up five more deceased residents on Kyle's computer. The oversized screen made her nervous. She wondered if others could read it from the parking lot or maybe the next town over. It reminded her of the electronic billboard on her way home. It's a monster of a sign displaying everything from diapers to fireworks, creating light pollution for miles. The people living around it never knew what hit them until it was too late. One day it was just there. They fought it for months, using every tactic their attorneys knew. In the end, the sign stayed, and most of the people moved.

It was nearing 4:00 pm, so Cathy shut down the computer. She walked back to her office to pick up her jacket. The floor nurse from south wing passed by her on her way home, and Cathy waved goodbye. Dr. Oliver was seated at the desk signing charts. Cathy walked over to her to say hello. She really wanted to ask her if she had noticed an increase in deaths recently. But one close call was enough for today. Dr. Oliver looked up, and Cathy couldn't resist.

"Excuse me, Dr. Oliver. Have you noticed that we are getting a lot of new residents recently?" Cathy was trying not to let her voice crack.

"Cathy, in my line of work there's always a point when my patient dies. Someone new is bound to take their place. I've stopped counting comings and goings a long time ago. You should be used to it by now." Dr. Oliver waved her hand in the air as if to dismiss the entire conversation.

"Oh, I am. Just a long day and a lot of forms filled out. Guess I'm just tired. Have a good night." Cathy let out a silent sigh of relief as she let the thoughts of exposure drift from her mind. She wondered, *How many smug asses could be hired to work in the same place at the same time?*

Cathy concluded that Dr. Oliver was either clueless or a damn good liar. Either way, she had learned nothing from the conversation. She turned and walked toward the front exit of the building. She was eager to get home to see if she could find any patterns from the fifteen residents on her spreadsheet. She made an agreement with herself to get a good night's sleep tonight, even if it killed her. She thought about her words but let it go. She could use a break today.

18

DIANE LORETTO'S CHILDHOOD WAS nothing spectacular or especially cruel. Actually, it was quite ordinary except for having foster parents. She was not poorly treated or alienated. She chose to be isolated from the family. She had no real friends in school and didn't care. Her grades were at best average. She didn't go to her high school prom, again by choice. A couple of boys did ask her, but she had no interest. As a foster child, Diane always kept one foot on the outside. She never wholly engaged in anything. There was always the possibility that she might get discarded again, so why give it her all? This self-imposed rule would follow her throughout most of her life. During high school, she took a couple of meaningless jobs that required little more than showing up on time. Eventually, she would quit or lose enough interest to get fired.

This isolation coupled with no money for college was what made her foster parents suggest she become a nun. They were religious people who took her to church every Sunday.

"Diane, your father and I have been thinking about what your next move should look like. We prayed to the Lord for help, and He answered us. We think it would be a good idea if you become a nun."

"I guess. I haven't given it much thought."

"We're here to help you. What are some of the other kids in school doing after graduation?"

"I don't know. I didn't want to ask them."

Her foster parents thought a life of service and solitude would fit her mindset. Diane was not opposed to the idea. She wasn't sure she liked people, and she was used to being alone. She had no desire to have a family of her own. Being a nun also seemed like a good fit to her.

Her foster parents helped her research what steps were needed. First, she had to start a discernment program, which entailed speaking with nuns, visiting convents, attending retreats, and praying, all to determine if she would become a nun and what order she would join.

Diane started her discernment working with a mentoring nun named Rosanna. Diane shadowed the little but feisty nun throughout each day. Through conversations with other nuns, attending retreats and visiting one religious building after another, Diane found she didn't have the commitment to make her solemn vows.

Diane understood that even though she preferred some isolation, she couldn't be cloistered in a monastery in prayer for eternity. She had done the research and determined that becoming a sister still meant a life of obedience, poverty, and celibacy, but her simple vows afforded the privilege to be an active sister. She would have the choice to remain in the world to spread God's word, if she wanted to. Six months into her two-year discernment program, Diane Loretto took her simple vows and became Sister Diane.

Deep down, Diane's rule still would not allow her to step in all the way. Being a sister kept her options open. After her simple vows were completed, Sister Diane took a position as an assistant to the Mother Superior of the local convent. She had no money and nowhere to live, so the nuns allowed her to stay in a room at the rear of the convent. Disappointed she didn't become a nun, her foster parents practically disowned her. Diane felt that she had been discarded like the trash, again.

She did her job well but kept to herself. She had no need to make friends or get to know any of the nuns or other sisters. When her work hours ended each day, Diane retreated to her room, much like she did growing up with her foster parents. She knew that someday the nuns would ask her to leave and she would still be alone, so she had no desire to become attached to anyone or anything. Diane did make it a point to venture to the outside world to keep up. She found that she enjoyed the strolls down streets with people to whom she could say hello or even engage in light conversation as long as she didn't have to get too deeply involved.

Sister Diane met Bishop Anthony on one of his routine visits to the convent. He liked to visit the convents regularly to search for the next up and coming religious star. Bishop Anthony was known for picking the right person for the right job. He liked to joke that God had bestowed that honor on him. He would always make the sign of the cross after every recital of the phrase. Sister Diane found him to be a force. For the first time in her life she looked forward to interacting with someone. The young sister would do anything to keep her friendship with the bishop. She invented ways to be around when she knew he was coming. The bishop also noticed Sister Diane and made it a point to engage in conversation with her during his visits. Her small frame and ginger walk gave the appearance that the harsh stone walls of the convent might swallow her whole at any minute. Bishop Anthony could not resist the urge to help the poor childlike woman. She seemed lost, yet she had a comfort about her that was soothing. At each visit he'd inquire a little more about her past and what her views of the world were. He would intentionally plant seeds for thought and discuss them at the next encounter. Bishop Anthony treated her with respect. He listened to what Sister Diane had to say with genuine interest. The Bishop was older but didn't treat her like the lost child she always saw herself to be. With each conversation she trusted him more and more. He was opening her up to a world of possibilities. The young sister started to feel like there might be a place she belonged. There were people, at least one person, who would not throw her away. Sister Diane found their conversations left her with a sense of hope.

After about four months of meetings, Bishop Anthony asked her if she had ever thought of leaving the convent to serve in other ways.

Sister Diane adjusted herself in her chair. "Truthfully, it was a concern when I chose to become a sister and not a nun. But I had forgotten about it until we had our first conversation. Why do you ask?"

"Where would you go? What would you do?" the bishop's hands were folded in front of him. His eyes fixed on her.

"I . . . I have no idea. I only started thinking about it since we met. That's even a big step for me. I haven't even gotten to the where or what stage."

Bishop Anthony smiled. "I believe that you have a calling you haven't reached yet. Service to others that might be as fulfilling for you as it is for them."

"But you barely know me." Sister Diane felt a nervous tension building in her body.

The bishop raised his eyes skyward. "God has bestowed on me a great honor. He has given me the ability to recognize a flickering star in the darkness."

"I'm not sure I know exactly what you mean." Diane looked down.

"You hiding here, in this convent, is a disservice. There are many ways to serve and many who need your service. Just think about it. We can talk more about it on our next visit."

Sister Diane's head became filled with ideas, for what seemed the first time, of giving fully to something. The bishop had awakened feelings of wanting to trust and wanting to be part of something. Mother Superior asked on one occasion if she had been drinking because her nature seemed so lighthearted. Sister Diane was still frightened, but she was willing to deal with the fear this time. Bishop Anthony had made her feel safe with trusting someone besides herself. Diane felt the grip of her isolation loosen.

The bishop spoke with a soft and inviting voice that she couldn't get out of her mind.

Bishop Anthony returned a few weeks earlier than scheduled. This caught Sister Diane pleasantly off guard. He didn't want to discuss her past or future. This time, he asked her to join him on an outing to a small parish. He wanted her to meet a young priest who was doing good work. She was reluctant, but the bishop told her that he had already cleared it with the Mother Superior. Sister Diane was skeptical. She had never been asked to leave the convent with anyone. And now, it was not just anyone; it was the bishop. She realized refusing wouldn't look good. All eyes were on her already. Bishop Anthony never took such an interest in anyone else in the convent. There were no rumors, but the nuns did make it a point to give her long, concerned looks. Sister Diane never confronted the nuns. She just continued to keep to herself. Bishop Anthony asked a second time, and she agreed.

19

THE SPREADSHEETS WERE LAID out on the kitchen counter. They were longer than the table, and Cathy aligned them vertically so she could match up the columns on successive pages. The four pages of organized information looked impressive but overwhelming. She got ready to settle in for a long evening of super sleuthing when her phone rang. It was Green Haven. She had forgotten that Kyle was out, making her the person to call. A quick frustrating look at the ceiling followed by the forceful shoveling of the cheaters from her face to her jet-black hair, and Cathy was ready to answer the call.

Cathy answered her cell phone, trying not to sound bothered by the caller.

"Hi, Cathy. Sorry to bother you. It's Wendy, the nurse on north wing."

"Yes, Wendy. Hi, what's wrong?"

"It's Grace Harding. She's insisting that a man tried to kill her again today."

"Today? When today? I was there up until an hour ago."

"She says it was earlier today, sometime this morning, but she too was afraid to say anything until she was sure he was gone."

"Who was gone?" Cathy rolled her eyes.

"She doesn't know. Should I call the police?"

"No! God no! Grace, as you already know, has a history of hallucinations. Did she get her second dose of Ativan? If not, please give it to her, and I'll speak with her in the morning. Call me back if there's a problem."

Cathy kiddingly slapped her face thinking that she actually missed Kyle. He'd get these calls, and he'd have to make the decisions or decide who to call for help. She went back to the kitchen counter, untangled the cheaters she hastily pushed into her hair, reapplied them to her eyes, and started looking at the columns one by one. Just for good measure, she decided to start from the beginning. The names didn't mean anything. She was sure of this. The dates of birth didn't seem to form any pattern; all of them had lived long lives. The diseases they had were all over the place. The dates they died were scattered over time. The arrival dates ranged from eight to ten years except for two of them. One had been there for about a month, but he came in very sick. Another was a resident with a long history of heart disease, and she was waiting for her third heart attack. She had been at Green Haven about two and a half years. Both were just distractions, so Cathy crossed them off of the spreadsheet. She needed more data. She would collect the remaining expired residents' information tomorrow while working from Kyle's office.

After she was sure she had finished entering all the information on the spreadsheets, Cathy placed the copied certificates back into a drawer in the kitchen. She told herself that no one would be searching her home, so the boot box was overkill. Cathy smiled as she thought that it was a very detective-show-like hiding spot, but getting to it was a pain. She put the two certificates that didn't fit the criteria back into her purse. She planned to cross-reference the names on the certificates with the dates of admission that she would get from Kyle's computer in the morning. Any of the remaining residents that didn't fit the criteria would be shredded with the two in her purse. Cathy thought if she got caught with copies, the fewer she had, the less harmful it might look. She wasn't even sure the amount mattered, but why take the chance?

Cathy knew she only had tomorrow to look further. Kyle would be back on Monday, and going in on the weekend would definitely call attention to her. Cathy was putting the spreadsheets away when she came across the sticky note. She had to get dirt on that ass. She realized that she had no choice; she had to manage both tasks quickly. "Kyle, you're going down," Cathy said aloud as she placed the sticky note safely back into her purse.

Once again, Cathy had ignored the basic needs of her body, causing an echoing growl from her stomach. Cathy hadn't eaten since lunch, and it was now 7:30 pm. She opened the refrigerator door and found nothing that was appealing. She reached for the phone and called the Chinese restaurant around the corner that delivered. Cathy had them on speed dial. They were fast, and the food was excellent. Fifteen minutes later a young delivery boy knocked on the door. Cathy was halfway through her cashew chicken dinner when it came to her. She pushed away the plate and pulled out the spreadsheets again. The admission dates, they were the key. Every resident on the spreadsheet had been there for almost a decade. What's going on? Why are long-time residents suddenly dying? It's too much of a coincidence. She stared at the dates on the spreadsheet for a long time, only to reach the same conclusion. She didn't have all the information she needed. She would start with the date of admission for every resident on her list.

Cathy had a game plan. The frustration that built up was giving way to satisfaction; she now had a direction in which to proceed. Kyle would be next. What dirty little game was he playing? Knowing that for the first time in a long, long while she might have the upper hand on the ruthless administrator was even more gratifying.

Sitting on the couch with the television on in the background, all Cathy could think of was the hundreds of ways that she would make Kyle pay for the years of torture that she endured. First, she imagined making him give her a big raise, then an office with a window. She wondered if she could get a company car. Cathy stopped suddenly; she understood that she was not thinking rationally. When she had enough proof on Kyle, she would start by dropping clues that she knew his secret. Then she would make it clear that she would use the information to her advantage every chance she could. She would make him grovel just the way she was forced to do. Revenge wouldn't come close for the man who made her practically bow at every encounter. Slumping against the back of the couch, Cathy felt a sense of what it would be like wielding power. She gave a sinister snicker and thought how this sounded like a movie cliché. Cathy realized she didn't care how it sounded; she would have her revenge.

Cathy's thoughts of retribution came to a sudden stop when she remembered that people might be getting murdered right in front of her. It became apparent that her personal vendetta would have to wait; this was much more important. But if she didn't try to find out about Kyle tomorrow, she might miss her opportunity. Cathy found herself sitting on the edge of the couch again as the dilemma grew larger in her mind. Her hatred for Kyle was too great to let it wait. Again, she came to the same conclusion. This time Cathy justified it as a dual obligation—one to the residents and the other to herself.

She turned off the television and went to take a shower. As the warm water rained over her body, she could feel the stench of being under Kyle's foot washing away. Cathy felt her muscles starting to relax. It was the first time she could remember her body feeling at ease. At the thought of his name, a wave of anger flooded back in. How could she let someone put so much misery onto her? The warmth and relaxation of the water running over her returned her to the calm. She was utterly relaxed by the time she turned off the water. She dried off, noticing that every soft fiber of the towel felt comforting. She became acutely aware of every sensation her body was feeling. Cathy decided to climb into bed naked. She hadn't slept naked in about two years. And that was only because of a brief sexual interlude she had with an old friend. It lasted only a short time, but it was fun. She wanted to feel the sheets against her skin. She wondered if this was what it felt like to be alive and to care. The feeling of the sheets against her naked body made her tingle. Cathy had thoughts she hadn't had for quite some time. Two years to be exact. She turned out the lights. Green Haven, Kyle, the death certificates, and the conspiracy had faded into the background. For now.

20

OSCAR WAS SITTING AT his desk, wanting to call Marissa. *This is her mess*, he thought. *She called me and wanted to come over. We didn't do anything. Could that be a problem too?* He looked at the papers on the desk, then he turned to look at the phone, hoping it would ring.

"Marissa Oliver, MD, how stupid could you be? He's your employer," Marissa spoke to herself as she drove to work. "Would he be there? After all, he did own the place." She turned into a coffee shop parking lot and sat there panicking with a death grip on the cell phone in her hand. She needed to handle this on the phone, not in person. She didn't want to talk to Oscar where others who knew them could hear. She turned the phone over, staring at the darkened glass face then threw it down on the seat next to her, only to start another round of chastising herself. After ten more minutes of flogging, she was ready to make the call.

She dialed Oscar's number. He picked up on the first ring. She hesitated then said, "Hello," in the most secure-sounding voice she could muster.

"Hello, I wasn't expecting you to call."

"Oscar, can we stop this game?" Marissa pushed her hair out of her eyes.

"Yes, I'm tired of it too. Look, I like you, and I didn't want last night to go as it did." Oscar's palms were wet from the fear of virtually standing naked in front of her now. He had spoken his real feelings.

"It was not my intention either. Well, to be honest . . ." The car's Bluetooth engaged, and Oscar missed the rest of what she said.

"Hello, Marissa, are you there?" Oscar was at full fear alert now. Why did she hang up mid-sentence?

"Oscar, I'm still here. The damn Bluetooth. I was saying that I wanted to see you. I had some bourbon after work that gave me the courage to be stupid.

"Yes, alcohol can make all of us very brave. Why don't we leave the stupid off? How about we have a redo tonight?" Oscar raised his brows hoping to get the response he wanted. His fear was replaced by the playback loop running in his head: *She wanted to see you. She wanted to see you.*

"That would be great."

This snapped Oscar back to reality, and through a smile a mile wide he replied, "One condition: we start drinking at the same time."

Marissa laughed. "Agreed."

"Since you already know where I live, meet me at my home at seven. I'll make a reservation."

"See you then." Marissa hung up the phone and let out a deep, relieved sigh, feeling her shoulders drop as the tension dissipated. She put the car back into drive and headed towards Green Haven. Now she was hoping Oscar would be there. Dr. Oliver entered the building looking for Oscar; there was no sign of him. She felt the disappointment hit her hard. All this emotional back and forth had made her exhausted. She stopped in the dining room and poured a large cup of coffee, black. She hoped it was leaded. Marissa walked over to the north wing and started reviewing charts. Even though she had been the medical director of a new senior facility for a short time, Dr. Oliver had a routine down. She would handle the "need immediate attention" charts on each wing, then go back to see residents, then review and sign orders. Marissa ended with the new admissions that needed her attention. Dr. Oliver was getting good at managing her time. Most of the rooms were filled, and the residents seemed to be the cream of the crop. They didn't have many severe ailments and took a minimal number of medications. Most were pleasant and coherent. Dr. Oliver thought she had a cake job with great pay, though it was a rocky start with lots of long days. She added great benefits, thinking of her date with Oscar tonight. She smiled but quickly hid it with her hand.

Marissa's thoughts about her date with Oscar moved in and out of the forefront of her mind throughout the day. She tried desperately not to show excitement, but the nurses were already beginning to read her body language. They knew when she was in a good mood and when they should keep their distance. Today was a good day. Some of the staff had made codes with hand signals to give each other the heads up. One finger held behind the back meant it was a good day. Two fingers behind the back meant tread lightly. Three fingers behind the back meant dash into the nearest resident room that Dr. Oliver wasn't in. As time went on, the hand signals were utilized less as Dr. Oliver's body betrayed the secret of her mood. Dr. Oliver didn't seem to acknowledge the signals, or if she did, she didn't care about them.

After work, Marissa drove home and showered. She slipped into a blue dress with a mid-cut neckline; this one she could now afford and did own. She wanted to spark Oscar's interest but didn't want all his attention focused in one direction. Marissa saw herself as a respectable woman who now had time to attend to the needs she postponed during her training. Getting the wrong reputation was not good for most careers. Marissa finished dressing by putting on a slender silver necklace with a coral stone that accentuated the lines of her long neck and matching earrings tastefully dangling from each ear.

Oscar wore a casual white shirt with some indistinguishable thin navy print on it. The shirt was neatly tucked into a pair of dark gray pants, and he wore casual but expensive-looking shoes. This was his attempt at looking younger and hip. It was the fifth wardrobe change for his date with Dr. Marissa Oliver. He was showered and completely dressed by 6:15. He failed miserably at trying to wait patiently for Marissa's arrival. He continually paced from the front door to a street-facing window. He poured himself a Scotch and was about to take a sip, to take the edge off, but then realized they had agreed to start drinking together. He poured the Scotch back into the bottle. This date had to be perfect to make up for last night's fiasco. The pacing resumed, as did the peering out of the window, now followed by glances at his watch.

Marissa rang the doorbell at 7:04 pm. They were both acutely aware of the precise time. While Oscar checked his watch, Marissa checked the time on the clock in the car as she drove over. She didn't want to get there early or exactly on time. She didn't want to appear overly eager for their first real date. Oscar saw her pull up, but this time he waited until she rang the bell twice. Apparently, the games were still being played.

He opened the door and asked her in. He explained that the reservation was for 8:00 pm. He asked if she wanted a drink and then joking added, "Just one." She gave him an embarrassed smile and agreed. He was about to reach for bourbon and thought better of it. Instead, he opened a chardonnay and gave each of them a modest, non-threatening pour.

Marissa was happy to see Oscar had kept his word. They were starting over and taking it at a respectable pace. She liked that he was conscious of her feelings. The dating scene had not been kind to Marissa. In the past two years, she had gone on a few dates. All had been self-absorbed wannabes of one kind or another. She had given up on dating until Oscar came along. Their chess matches intrigued her. She liked the back and forth infused with the tension of unspoken sexual energy. Oscar was dashing in an old-fashioned kind of way. It made her feel comfortable yet desired.

As they sat on Oscar's leather couch, Oscar broke the ice. "Marissa, how about we agree not to talk about work tonight?"

"That would be great. About last night . . ."

"There was no last night. I want to get to know Marissa from today forward. I already know Dr. Oliver and have great regard for her. Is that okay?" He leaned forward slightly.

Marissa sat back with her arms folded across her breasts. She knew Oscar would undoubtedly take note of this. "Oscar, that would be fine, but I was hoping you had great respect for Dr. Oliver."

Oscar nodded and held both hands in her direction, "I do. I thought that was obvious."

Marissa relaxed her arms slowly but didn't take his hands. She wanted him to wait just a bit longer. "That's nice of you to say."

Marissa gave little detail about her life. Oscar thought it rude to press too hard. He wondered what was in her past that she was afraid to talk about, but he didn't want to upset her, and he certainly didn't want to ruin their evening. Oscar believed there'd be other dates and when they were more comfortable with each other socially, she'd open up.

Oscar looked at his watch, the first time since her arrival. It was 7:45 pm. He called the restaurant. "It's Mr. Oscar Green. Unfortunately, we're stuck in traffic and will be delayed. Would you be so kind as to move our reservation to 8:30?"

Marissa gave a loud laugh accompanied by light clapping.

He got up and told Marissa they would take his car since he knew where they were going. As they walked to the car, Oscar held her hand for the first time. Marissa allowed it. She liked feeling the warmth of his hand. Holding her hand was all Oscar could concentrate on doing at this moment.

"Do you make a habit of lying?" Marissa asked.

"Only to restaurants with great food and when a beautiful woman is involved."

She thoroughly enjoyed the answer. The delightful small talk continued throughout the drive. Once at Cocina del Dios, Oscar became worried. What if she didn't like Mexican food? He was about to ask when Marissa

129

told him she heard this place had great food. Oscar decided not to tell her he had eaten here several times. He didn't want to field a question about taking other dates here. The truth was Oscar hardly ever dated. He usually ate alone or with business associates. He also didn't want to look like a lonely loser. He also kept to himself that he had built the building some years back for a French restaurateur that failed shortly afterward. It wasn't the building that failed. But why brag?

Oscar parked the car. He would have used the valet service if the restaurant had one, just to impress her. Marissa waited for Oscar to come around the car and open the door. She wanted to be respected but also expected good manners from Oscar. She had to make up for her extremely bold moves the night before. She wanted Oscar to chase after her a bit. Oscar's mother made sure he grew up to be a respectful gentleman. He opened the door for her and extended a hand to help her out of the car. She accepted and smiled just enough to assure him. She gently squeezed his hand, giving him the acknowledgment he hoped for.

They walked in and were seated immediately at a window table. Marissa didn't know it, but he had made a special request for this table. It overlooked a small field with a pond, and the clear night allowed the moon to reflect off the water. It was a bit of a cliché, but Oscar was a romantic at heart. At least he thought he was. Marissa wanted to make a joke about him not planning for any fireflies but thought better of it. She didn't want to hurt his feelings. She found his boyish romantic nature a nice change.

Oscar held the chair with its back to the door for Marissa to take a seat. He didn't like to sit with his own back to the door. Something his father taught him as a boy. Oscar couldn't remember going to a restaurant where his father wasn't seated with his back to the wall. A quirk he now carried forward. As he sat down, a waiter appeared to take drink orders. Oscar was about to order a bottle of wine when Marissa interrupted. She smiled and asked the waiter to return in a moment.

Oscar was surprised. "Is everything okay?"

"Yes, it's just that wine is what led us down a bad path last night, and I want us to be clear-headed so we can enjoy every part of tonight."

Oscar agreed but wondered what she had planned. The waiter returned, and they ordered sparkling water. Oscar could have done with at least a beer to settle his nerves. After all, the pressure was now on, he thought. She had a plan for the evening; he was excited and worried all at the same time. Oscar thought to himself that it had been a while, if that's what she meant.

21

CATHY ARRIVED AT KYLE'S office much earlier than she had anticipated. She couldn't help herself; the waiting seemed endless. She pulled out the sticky note with the passwords, made sure no one was looking through the glass in the door, and then booted up the administrator's computer. The morning shift nurses were due to arrive around 7:00. They will be busy getting their updates from the night shift nurses. The CNAs will be occupied with getting the residents ready for breakfast. Arriving early, Cathy had some quiet, uninterrupted time before she had to start her day.

She stared at both passwords and couldn't get her mind off the second one. *What are you protecting? What are you up to, Kyle?* It got the better of her. She glanced over the desktop icons, looking for anything that didn't look work related. There was nothing. She checked the documents file, still nothing out of the ordinary. She hit the icon on the bottom left of the screen again to pull up the menu. Cathy was about to press the search bar when a knock on the door startled her. She looked away from the monitor, causing her to hit the shutdown command accidentally. She panicked as the computer continued to shut down. Cathy waved the gentleman in, trying to act like nothing was going on. Cathy didn't recognize him.

"Hi. Sorry to bother you, but I'm looking for Larry the IT person."

"It's Lenny, and who are you?" Cathy asked while waiting for her heart to restart.

"I'm Ken Andrews, from your software company. I'm here to do routine maintenance on the system." He flashed his ID badge, and Cathy pretended to look at it. She was still in recovery mode.

"Have a seat in the lobby while I call Lenny and tell him to come up to meet you."

"Thanks. Sorry to startle you."

"Oh, you didn't. I just, um, didn't sleep well last night." Cathy thought to herself, *How lame.*

As the stocky middle-aged man returned to the lobby, Cathy motioned like she was about to smack herself then picked up the phone and called Lenny.

Cathy took a deep breath then restarted Kyle's computer. A request for username came up on the screen. She typed in the username she had written on the sticky note. The machine made a second demand; this time it wanted a password. Cathy paused for a moment then typed in the second password, and it worked. The computer was compartmentalized. Cathy sat there, practically holding her breath as only one icon came on the screen. Its name read "Kyle." She debated if she really wanted to know. There would be no going back. She hoped it didn't contain nude photos of women or worse, of Kyle. *Oh, come on, how dramatic*, she thought. Then the thought of a photo of Kyle in a weird sex fetish situation sent a shiver down her back. That was followed by the hope that there was something that good she could hold over Kyle. For a split second she wondered if she could actually go through with the blackmail, no matter what was there. She decided to debate that later.

She clicked on the icon. A file containing several folders with different dates appeared. Cathy opened the file with the earliest date. It was a list of every resident at Green Haven for the past ten years. Every resident was listed in chronological order according to the date of admission. Now she had to see more. The next file was the same list with red lines drawn through most of the names. As she read down the list, she began to realize that the last set of names matched her spreadsheets. The names were in the same order. The next list contained the names of current residents, but they were still alive. Her mouth went dry; she was looking at a hit list, Kyle's hit list. Long gone were the thoughts of sex photos for blackmail.

The final two files were lists of residents that Cathy didn't recognize. At the top of each were the initials, AL and EC respectively. "No! Autumn Living and Elite Care too? How?" Cathy spoke softly to herself as she stood up and paced the office.

She didn't have a jump drive, or any other way to copy the files, and printing them was too risky. What if someone else came in while they were printing? She took out her cell phone and hit the camera icon. Cathy snapped photos of each list and then one of the file screen showing the time stamp of each file's creation. The last photo she took was of a desktop image of the solitary folder named Kyle. She wanted to be able to show Kyle's methodical thinking.

As she logged out of the secret site on the computer, she wondered where Kyle actually went today. Maybe he wasn't coming back. Maybe he got what he was looking for or killing for and left so he wouldn't get caught. It wasn't like Kyle to take days off without giving a one week notice.

Cathy didn't register the first two rings of the desk phone. She picked up on the third. It was Lenny. "I need everyone to log off the system. By the way, why are you logged in on Kyle's computer?"

Cathy was silent for a long moment then responded, "Kyle is out and wants me to sit up front. You know, so it looks like someone's in charge."

"Whatever. Look, the system is going to be down for ten to fifteen minutes. Please don't sign back on until I tell you it's okay." Lenny's voice was hurried, so he dismissed the Kyle's computer thing without a second thought.

"Okay, got it." Cathy held her breath, hoping Lenny wouldn't ask any more questions. He didn't. Cathy heard the click of the phone from the other end and nearly fell over with relief.

Cathy sat back in Kyle's chair, looking at the blank screen of her smartphone. She was trying to decide whether to call the police or reach out to a board member and let them handle it. If for any reason she was wrong, she would be fired and never would work as a nurse again. Her name would be tainted forever. Still feeling the salt-covered wounds of Pharmatek, she decided instead to get all the information and be 100 percent sure before saying anything.

The cell phone in her hand buzzed, and she dropped it. The screen faced up as it hit the carpet; Cathy could see the caller ID. It was from Kyle. She let it go to voicemail. A minute later the phone pinged telling her that Kyle had left a voicemail. Her body was rigid from the fear of the discovery she had just made. Cathy could barely breathe. This was all too real. She picked up the phone and listened to the message. Kyle said that he was coming back early and would be in that afternoon. Cathy had hoped he was on the run and not returning. Now she would be face to face with a murderer. She reached for the phone on Kyle's desk to call the police. Cathy stopped herself again as she considered that she might still look involved. Everything still pointed to her. Kyle might say she planted the lists on his computer to frame him. She needed to make sure she was in the clear before she called the police.

Cathy was leaving Kyle's office when she realized she hadn't returned the computer to its original password, and then fear overcame her; the system was down. What if it didn't come back before Kyle returned? Would he know that she found his secret? Cathy felt her entire body tremble at the thought of Kyle finding out that she was tampering with his computer. He would know, without a doubt, it was her. Cathy went back to the desk and called the IT guy. "Lenny, how long before the system is back up and running?"

Lenny heard the panic in her voice, and he softened his tone. "Why, is everything okay?"

"Lenny, how long?" Cathy was almost yelling into the phone.

"Jesus. About five or six minutes more."

"Thanks." Cathy hung up without any further conservation.

Cathy again paced the floor in Kyle's office as she waited for the okay to turn on the computer. She wished the password led to a secret dating site or porn or anything but Kyle being a killer. Lenny came on the intercom and said it was okay to turn the computers back on. She ran around the desk to hit the on button. She made sure the monitor began to load the system. It prompted her for the username and then the password. Cathy put in both using the first password. When the icons returned to the screen, Cathy took a deep breath and fell into Kyle's plush, high-end office chair. Kyle could return, and he would never know she had discovered his secret.

She left the office, her mind filled with all sorts of reasons Kyle was killing residents. Cathy was brought back to the present when, for the second time this week, she walked right into Father Brendan. He smiled and told her that Sister Diane might start getting jealous if this continued. She apologized and asked them why they were at Green Haven on a Friday. Sister Diane answered that they decided to do some quick makeup time for missing the other day. Cathy moved past the holy couple and headed for her office. The holy couple didn't even register with her, not now. All Cathy could concentrate on was Kyle—the how, the when, but most of all, the why.

Sitting at her desk, she was still trying to make sense of what she just discovered. Her smartphone had Bluetooth capability, as did her printer. It was Green Haven's policy not to enable the Bluetooth on the office printers so that sensitive information could not be sent or stolen. This was definitely confidential information, Cathy joked, trying to make herself feel better. She turned on the printer's Bluetooth then paired her phone with it. Her printer at home had the same capability, and after several attempts she managed to figure out how to make it work. She printed out the photos of the lists, but they were too small to be of any real use. She put the photos back in the printer and enlarged them until they were large enough to read, but they had become somewhat blurry. Cathy turned off the Bluetooth before anyone might get a Bluetooth notification from their smartphone.

Cathy scanned her tiny office for anything that could conceal the new larger copies. She spotted an old satchel that she carried years ago hiding under a stack of old nursing books. The books had not been opened in years. Cathy had stopped noticing that the books or satchel were part of the office décor a long time ago. She moved the books to an open spot on the floor and placed the dusty satchel on her desk. The zipper of the satchel had been in its current position and fought against movement like the arthritic joints of most of Green Haven's residents. Cathy managed to get it to open and shoved in the copies. She then turned her attention to the original printouts of the lists, grabbing them and running them through the shredder next to her desk. After making sure that every page had been completely shredded, Cathy put the satchel under her arm and headed for her car. When she was certain no one was watching, she hid them under the front seat. She walked back into the building, trying to act normal. She'd have to be her usual self, especially when Kyle returned. If all went as usual, he'd cut her down for a few minutes then return to his normal activities. Her mind came up with all new ideas of what Kyle's normal was. She asked herself if it was possible to call killing residents normal.

Cathy got back to her desk and attempted to go through her regular pre-morning report routine, but she was unable to shake the thoughts of Kyle killing poor, or rather rich, elderly people. After the morning report meeting, without Kyle, she returned to her desk and managed to work right through lunch. It was 1:00 pm when Kyle knocked and opened her door. He never waited for a reply to the knock. After all, he was everyone's boss. He gave her a grim smile and commented on how at least the place was still standing. He closed the door and left. Cathy felt it hard to swallow as she thought that a killer was in the building.

She hadn't been able to eat much at lunch, and now hunger had started to overcome her. Cathy noted that this was becoming a recurring problem that she needed to address when all this was over. She headed down to the employee area to retrieve a snack from one of the vending machines. Cathy usually threw something in her purse for a mid-afternoon snack, but in the hurried excitement of the morning she forgot. While reaching for the bag of pretzels she just purchased, she heard the intercom come on and call for Dr. Passed to north wing.

Cathy felt her heart drop. She raced out of the break room and down to north wing. It was Grace Harding; this time she was dead. Father Brendan and Sister Diane had beaten Cathy to the room and were waiting outside. She asked them to wait because she forgot the form. As she headed back to her office, she asked the nurse if anyone was with Grace before her death. The nurse said she gave Grace her meds about an hour ago, the CNAs had been in and out of the room, and there was nothing abnormal. Cathy continued to her office to get the form. The whole time she was trying to figure out how Kyle could get in and out of the room without being noticed.

Cathy returned to Grace Harding's room and went through the motions like she always did. Father Brendan and Sister Diane were patiently waiting to perform their ritual. Cathy looked at them then returned to the body, checking around Grace's neck. She recalled that Grace had been saying that a large man was trying to choke her. There were no marks on her neck. Cathy knew Kyle killed her, but how and when? She turned to the priest and told him to go ahead.

Once again, a resident with a "nurse may pronounce" order died, and Cathy was no closer to figuring out how it was being done. But it was too much of a coincidence that Kyle came back this afternoon and a resident died. She wanted to go to his office and confront him. She wanted to know how and why, but she couldn't let him know she knew. He would most certainly run or kill her. Either way, she knew that all fingers still pointed toward her. Cathy returned to her office, clueless of how the murderous administrator was getting away with it and how to catch him and keep herself safe. She sat in her tiny office, leaning back with her the back of her head resting against the wall and wondered if she could catch Kyle before he finished framing her or worse, turned his sights on her.

22

Bishop Anthony and Sister Diane left the convent in the bishop's car. They drove for about half an hour before pulling into a parking lot. Sister Diane read the sign out front and turned to Bishop Anthony with a look of confusion. "Green Haven, a living well place, I thought we were meeting a priest from a small parish?"

"We are. He's working and I didn't want to take him away from his duties. So, you're meeting him here."

"May I know his name so I don't feel too awkward when I'm face to face with him?"

"My apologies, his name is Father Brendan. He has just taken over Green Haven from an older priest who retired. I think you two would make a good team, but let's not get ahead of ourselves." He gave her a boyish smile that didn't seem to fit his demeanor. This made Sister Diane more hesitant.

"No offense, Bishop Anthony, but I like being at the convent. I'm not looking to make a change."

The bishop, in an all-knowing matter-of-fact disposition, replied, "Aren't you looking to make a difference?"

"Um, yes. Sure I am," Sister Diane answered with a great deal of uncertainty.

"Good, then meet him, go around with him for the day, and we'll talk tomorrow. Father Brendan knows you're coming, and he was told to take you back to the convent at the end of the day."

"You're not coming in?"

"No. Go ahead, he's waiting at the door for you. You'll be safe with him."

Sister Diane got out of the car and headed for the door. She looked back at the bishop like a child off to her first day of school. The bishop, who was quite pleased with himself, smiled and waved for her to continue forward. From a distance, she could see that Father Brendan was quite handsome, but she was a sister and he was a priest. She looked up at the sky and mumbled, "Wrong lifetime." She reached the entrance, and Father Brendan opened the door, greeting her with a less satisfied smile followed by a cheerful hello. Sister Diane was unsure what to make of his mixed greeting. He called her by name then introduced himself. She wanted to say she already knew but decided to let it go. That would be impolite. Father Brendan extended his hand, and Sister Diane shook it, noting the size and strength it possessed.

Sister Diane looked around the lobby of Green Haven wide-eyed as she asked, "Is this a nursing home or a five-star hotel?"

"Yes, can you believe it? It's nicer than any hotel I've ever been in."

"Can I make a reservation for about thirty years from now?" Sister Diane jested.

The priest laughed. "Not unless you have a rich uncle willing to leave you lots of money or are planning to steal from the collection baskets."

The shy sister stood silent for a long moment. "Sorry."

Father Brendan realized she didn't know him or his sense of humor. "No, it's okay. I was just kidding. All the residents here come from very well-off families. Either old money or self-made."

"They really are lucky, aren't they?" There was a feeling of coming from the wrong side of the tracks in Sister Diane's question.

"Actually, no. Their families place them here and, sure, at first they visit, but as time goes on, most of the residents here are forgotten. Most of the time we might be the only outside people they see for weeks or months."

Diane stopped walking and protested, "That's horrible."

Father Brendan nodded then asked if she had worked with seniors before, and she shook her head no. Father Brendan started her off lightly, visiting several residents who were coherent and talkative. Then he took her into rooms with the less coherent and finally those who were bedridden and didn't even know they were there. This was how Father Timothy broke him in. Before entering each room, Father Brendan gave her a bit of background about his work with the person so she could engage.

Sister Diane didn't realize she was to engage with the residents. She understood that she was to meet Father Brendan and tag along silently. She had been thrown into the deep end and wasn't happy about it.

After about five or six encounters, she started to relax and things went smoothly. Father Brendan's laidback style was nice, and she could relate to it well. The residents seemed to like his family-like attitude. Most of the residents dropped the Father and just called him Brendan. He was years younger than every resident they stopped to see. To most, he was like a visiting son. Sister Diane found this warming and appealing. Even when they started entering the rooms of residents who had no idea they were there, he didn't treat them differently. His compassion made her feel better about the non-responsive condition of the resident. Sister Diane thought it was a God-like gesture to give the resident someone who talked to them and treated them with respect. She wondered, "Do you think they can hear us?"

"I like to think that we're communicating with their soul. Their body is merely the pod holding the soul to this earth, and it's our job to keep that soul going."

"Father, those in bed, what's their quality of life? Why hasn't God called them home?"

"Both excellent questions. As for the quality of life, I think it's poor at best. As for God calling them home, that one I don't really have an answer for. I'll tell you what I've been told. They must still have some purpose to serve here. Truthfully, I wonder if He's forgotten to visit them too."

"Do you believe that?" She tilted her head and looked over her eyebrows at him.

Father Brendan's voice lowered, and his good nature turned somber. "I don't really know. It just seems so pointless, and it makes me so sad for them."

Sister Diane could feel the angst in his voice; she too wanted more for these poor residents, but she said nothing. After all, this was her very first encounter with the priest and the residents.

Sister Diane found herself wanting to be that person who saw past the outer layer to reach their souls. Father Brendan gave her that chance when he asked her to speak with the residents, all the residents.

By midday they had finished with Green Haven. Sister Diane was exhausted. She was not used to that much walking and interaction. She was no match for Father Brendan's six-foot-three stride and was now lagging behind the priest. He slowed to allow her to keep pace.

The convent was quiet, and everyone went about their business each day. She also tended to shy away from a conversation. As they got into his car, Father Brendan asked if she wanted some lunch. She sat silently for a moment as she stared at the small handbag on her lap.

The embarrassed look on her face gave her secret away, and Father Brendan quickly interjected, "Oh, don't worry, it's on God. The Church gives us food money. We take an oath of poverty, not starvation."

She smiled and agreed. "Well then. I think it might be a sin to go against God."

They were both still laughing as they pulled up to a burger joint a few blocks away from the convent. Both ordered a cheeseburger and lemonade.

During lunch they chatted about their pasts and how they both came to the Church. Father Brendan told her about Fathers Matthew and Timothy. How grateful he was for both of them. Sister Diane told him about wanting to become a nun, but she found it too rigorous and so she became a sister. How she was allowed to live at the convent. She told him she loved her work at the convent and how Bishop Anthony had insisted on this meeting. Father Brendan wanted to ask if she regretted the meeting, but he kept quiet.

They spoke of Bishop Anthony for a short moment. Neither was willing to commit to a firm opinion. They didn't know each other and feared any backlash from harsh comments about their boss. Both did agree they didn't fully understand the man. Both were unaware of the similarity of their courtships by the bishop. They did acknowledge that the gray-haired, barrel-chested holy man seemed to get what he wanted when he wanted it.

Sister Diane asked, "What do you have planned for after lunch?"

"I'll visit another nursing facility for about two hours then head back to the parish. Do you want to tag along?"

Sister Diane sat for a moment, staring at the empty dishes on the table as though contemplating the idea and then she responded, "No, thanks. I've been gone longer than I thought I would be, and I don't want to leave Mother Superior hanging." She clenched her hands under the table, as she knew this was only a half-truth. Sister Diane was not accustomed to so much interaction and, while she liked it, it made her tired and in need of some quiet downtime.

Father Brendan let out an over-dramatic sigh then smiled. "Okay, I'll drop you off at the convent as soon as we're done here."

He continued to smile, but on the inside, Father Brendan wanted her to come along. He liked having the company. It reminded him of his time with Father Timothy. The thought of Father Timothy's company and then the loss of it brought a hollowness to the center of Father Brendan's chest. He fought back the urge to beg her to come along.

He dropped her off at the convent. As she was getting out of the car, Father Brendan rolled down the passenger side window, again showing his perfectly straight white teeth. "You're a natural. You did a great job today with the residents."

Sister Diane gave a thank you bow, then she turned and walked into the convent grinning uncontrollably. Even though she was tired, there was a lightness in her step. She went straight to her room. Her full belly and all the excitement of the morning made her sleepy. She lay down on her bed and fell asleep, intending just a twenty-minute catnap.

Two hours later Sister Diane awoke to a knock on her door. It was a young nun letting her know that she had a visitor. She asked who it was. The nun told her it was the bishop.

23

CATHY SAT AT HER desk, looking at the death certificate with Grace Harding's name on it. She could have prevented this if she called the police when she found Kyle's secret lists. Cathy silently contemplated: *What am I doing? I'm a nurse, not a TV detective, and certainly not one in real life.*

She stopped herself as a new thought brought more fear. *What else did Kyle do to point the police in her direction? What hasn't she found yet? What's your plan, Kyle Strong? Does he hate me that much? There has to be more.* Cathy's mind had taken over, and she was lost in a loop of conspiracy theories with hundreds of reasons for Kyle's actions. What she was most sure of was that Kyle had to be arrested and found guilty. If he weren't, she'd be next on the list. She had to be able to prove it before going to the police. This was quite clear now. Her brain hurt; she massaged her temples then opened the top drawer of her desk and removed a bottle of aspirin. She poured two into her hand and swallowed them without anything to drink.

She recalled the red marks on Kyle's list went back to about two years ago. Why did Kyle start killing residents two years ago? What happened? The conspiracy ideas were beginning again. This time Cathy quickly turned her attention to her computer. She needed the list to pull up the names of residents from two years ago, but they were in her car. Then she remembered her phone had Kyle's lists on them. She turned on the printer's Bluetooth again and printed out just one list. She grabbed the list off the printer and returned to her monitor. Cathy typed in the name of one resident; nothing came up. The resident was archived and off the central system. She didn't know how to retrieve an archived name. Cathy picked up the phone and called Lenny. She asked the IT guy to come up to her office to help with a computer problem.

As Lenny entered the room, his smartphone pinged. The phone alerted him that a Bluetooth connection was available. He looked at the Bluetooth name and didn't recognize the device. He looked around the room and noticed the printer with the same name.

"Hey, why is the Bluetooth on your printer turned on? You know that we aren't allowed to turn them on." Lenny raised an eyebrow at her.

"I have no clue. I didn't know my printer had Bluetooth. And I wouldn't know how to turn it on even if I knew it had it." Cathy realized she sounded too defensive, but she couldn't go back now.

"Okay, I'm turning it off. If it goes on again let me know immediately."

Cathy tried to think quickly. "It must have gone on when the system was reset."

"That's impossible. Don't worry, I won't say anything. Besides, no harm done, right? What did you want anyway?" Lenny winked at Cathy, letting her know she owed him one.

"I need to look up information on a resident from a few years ago."

"Why?" Lenny stood there with his arms folded across his chest, trying to look as authoritative as possible.

"Because a family member called looking for the information, and I'm trying to help them. I understand there is an archived section; I just don't know how to get there."

"If it's from two years ago, it's not in an archived section; it's in the inactive resident section. I can walk you through it in a sec."

He started to go into a long, complicated explanation about how the system was set up, then stopped himself. Lenny liked to show off his computer prowess whenever he got the chance but not around Cathy. When she was in the room, he was overwhelmingly attentive. He had a long-time secret crush on her. The problem was that it wasn't a well-kept secret. He was a boyish-looking man that might be surprisingly attractive if he had someone to dress him. Lenny wore a brown polka-dot shirt, tan corduroys, and navy-blue canvas sneakers. Rumors flew around the halls that at thirty-one years old Lenny was still a virgin and still living with his mother. Early on there was the suggestion of a pool to "devirginize" the computer wizard. Half of the pot would go to the woman brave enough to undertake the task. There were no takers.

Cathy knew he was harmless. A while back she had thought about taking him out to help him become more of a man, not in a sexual way. But she, too, was concerned about any rumors that might be spawned from the mission. She knew Lenny was attracted to her so she pretended to mistakenly touch his hand when reaching for the computer mouse on the desk. This would send Lenny into a tailspin and hopefully get him to forget about the printer's Bluetooth. Lenny retracted his hand quickly. In fact, he stepped back from the desk entirely.

Cathy asked while looking over the top of her cheaters at him, "Is everything okay?"

Lenny sensed that he may have overreacted and cleared his throat. "Yes, um, why?"

Cathy smirked on the inside. Any external positive display would send too much of the wrong message. She didn't want to use the innocent man more than she already had. She felt sorry about the several lies she had told only seconds earlier.

Lenny took her through the steps of getting into the inactive resident section, keeping a safe distance the entire time. Cathy was sure the distance wasn't just for fear of sexual harassment, but for sexual anything. As Lenny was leaving the room, he tried to puff out his concave chest and again told her that he would keep the printer just between them. Lenny's effort to be her superhero confirmed that her hand mishap had worked. He would think about that all day.

Lenny closed the door, and Cathy let out a quiet laugh, replaying Lenny's hands on his hips and flared chest. Part of her thought the rumor might be worth helping the poor man when this was all done.

She pulled up the name Renee Gold, a resident who died in June two years ago. She called the death certificate up on the screen. There it was: "nurse may pronounce." She had been filling out the forms for so long she had lost track of how many she had done. Cathy pulled five more of the red marked names; all the death certificates were the same. She then pulled up a name not marked in red; it didn't have her signature or the words on it. She was being set up. "Damn you, Kyle. You're trying to get back at me by setting me up for murder." Cathy was sure of it now. "Murder? Couldn't you just fire me?" Cathy found herself verbalizing her thoughts at a level that could be heard by a passerby.

"What an ass!" Cathy realized she was almost yelling. She could feel her shoulders drawn up toward her neck and the heat from the flush in her face.

Cathy needed space. She logged out of her computer and stepped out of her office. She was walking toward the front door when she saw Father Brendan. This time she didn't walk into him. He side-stepped her just for fun. Cathy stopped and asked, "Father, can we talk for a minute?"

Father Brendan responded with his own question. "Would you like to go to your office?"

Cathy wanted to scream no, but she kept her voice and body language in check. "Can we talk in the parking lot?" The confused priest followed her out of the building and midway through the parking lot.

Cathy turned to face Father Brendan then looked to see if anyone was within hearing distance. "Father, do you visit our other facilities?"

"Yes. Sister Diane and I are headed over to Elite as soon as she comes out of the building." There was confusion in his response.

Cathy paused for a moment, deciding if she wanted to continue the inquiry. "Were you guys at either of the other buildings in the past few days?"

"Yes. Why?"

"Did you see Kyle there?" Cathy decided she was going for it all.

"Yes, we saw him at Autumn Living yesterday afternoon. What's going on?"

"Nothing, I just wanted to make sure everything was okay with him." Cathy stayed calm and relaxed as she concluded that lying was surpassing habit and becoming an addiction. She thought, *Now I'm lying to a priest. What's next?*

"I saw him leave right before you stopped to talk with me. He looked fine."

"Thanks, Father."

"Okay. Is there something bothering you?" Father Brendan stood there perplexed but concerned. In all his time at Green Haven, the director of nursing had not once confided in him.

"No. I'm fine. Thanks again, Father. Say goodbye to Sister Diane for me." Cathy walked away from the priest and right to Kyle's office. The answers were there she could feel it. Knowing that Kyle had left for the day, Cathy entered his office. Through the windows in Kyle's office Cathy looked out onto the parking lot to make sure the holy couple left. Her heart was pumping even faster now, and the heat returned to her face, sending beads of salty warm sweat down from her forehead. Kyle's car was not in the administrator's parking spot. Looking at the sign marking the spot reminded her that Kyle had assigned himself a closer parking spot about three years ago. Maybe he was setting up a quick escape just in case someone caught on to him. Cathy grinned, thinking perhaps Kyle was just a bigger pompous ass than she initially thought. He probably wanted everyone to know he could do whatever he wanted. He answered to no one. Cathy could feel the coolness returning to her body as she realized that it was Kyle's arrogance that would get him caught. The chance that it might be her who caught him gave Cathy great satisfaction.

She refocused her attention on the computer. What else was hidden in that thing? She couldn't take the chance of snooping around it now that everyone knew Kyle was back. She decided to go through his desk. The desk drawers and the right-side filing cabinet were locked. The left side was not; Cathy began her search there. After about ten minutes of shuffling through files, she came up empty. What she was looking for must be locked away, and only Kyle had the key.

She would need a new plan to catch Kyle the murderer. She went back to her own office. Cathy sat thinking about all the crime shows she watched with a serial killer as the villain. All those killers had a pattern. It was their MO; she chuckled. Kyle must have a pattern. In the shows there was always a trail leading to the killer. Where was Kyle's trail? He's using the death certificates to set her up; she felt the tension in her shoulders start to grow. That was the only part of the trail. The answer was there, or at least it started there. She pulled up Kyle's red-marked list on her phone. She wished she had stronger cheaters as she squinted, trying to read the names of ten more residents. She wrote them down on a sticky note. Cathy then logged back into the system and printed out the necessary information for those residents. She shredded the sticky note, logged off, and headed for the parking lot.

24

OSCAR ORDERED THE *enchiladas con mole* while Marissa ordered *fajitas con carne*.

"When I go out to eat, I like my food already assembled. If I have to put it together, then I'm doing the work and still paying them." Oscar smiled.

"Do you really know where those hands assembling your food have been? The less they touch my food, the better I might be," Marissa retorted with a fiendish look.

They each laughed. Dinner was filled with small talk and constant dancing around the subject of work and the previous evening.

"I love the blue dress you're wearing. It looks new and expensive," Oscar told her.

"It's not new, and yes it was expensive." Marissa was thinking about their first meeting and the borrowed green dress.

"More expensive than the green dress you wore when we first met for lunch?" It was like Oscar was reading her mind.

"Oh yes. That green dress was practically free. But I didn't keep it long. I mean, I gave it to Goodwill." Marissa had to catch herself because on the inside she was laughing at the thought; if he only knew.

"But it looked brand new."

"No, it wasn't. As a matter of fact, I barely ever wore it." Marissa played along hoping that Oscar would never figure out her white lie. He didn't. His thoughts revolved around keeping this night going on forever.

Both enjoyed each other's company. After dinner they walked arm-in-arm back to Oscar's car. He once again opened the door for her; she again thanked him.

On the drive back to Oscar's home, Marissa commented that she was glad tonight didn't go like last night. The words leaped from her lips before she realized she had broken her own rule. Oscar pulled the car to the curb in front of his home and turned toward her. He was a romantic. He steadied his voice and with the utmost confidence, he spoke, "Last night is the distant past. I've wanted to ask you out on a real date for a while now. We're having a wonderful evening, and I don't want it to end. I want you to stay over again tonight. Except this time, I don't want us to fall asleep."

Oscar sat there for what seemed years when Marissa leaned in and kissed him. Without a word, she got out of the car and started walking up to his front door. Oscar went to get out of the car but had forgotten to place it in park; the vehicle lunged forward, catching against the curb. He quickly parked the car and headed for the front door.

No other words needed to be said. Oscar led her, or perhaps she led him to his bedroom. They undressed each other, both wanting to take it slowly. Neither had been with someone in a long time. Neither had forgotten how to perform. Their bodies fit together well, which made the long absence irrelevant. It was as though they had been lovers for some time, knowing each other's intimate wants. Afterward, they lay in bed together gently touching until they fell asleep.

At 7:00 am the next morning Oscar's alarm jolted them out of bed. It was Friday, still a workday, and both had to be on their way. Oscar wanted to join her in the shower, but she told him she couldn't be late. Oscar agreed. They showered separately; Marissa dressed quickly while Oscar took his time. She had no time for breakfast or even coffee. Marissa told

Oscar to call her later. She reminded him that he had the number from the other night. He didn't need to be reminded. In a blink, Dr. Marissa Oliver was gone.

Oscar poured himself a cup of coffee and sat down on one of the kitchen stools. He didn't really have to be at work at any time. He was the boss. He picked up the newspaper and tried to read it, but all he could think about was Dr. Oliver's perfectly shaped body lying next to him. He recounted that when he and his ex-wife had first dated it didn't feel this good. A smile ran across his face. He wondered if she had a change of clothes in the car. Then he pictured her changing into a new set of clothes. Typical guy, he thought. He knew she was more, much more than just a sex partner. At least in his mind, he hoped she was feeling the same way. She did tell him to call her later; that meant something, right?

Marissa pulled into Green Haven and parked in the furthest parking spot she could find. She opened the trunk of her SUV and pulled out a clean dress and undergarments. She hadn't planned ahead for last night. She made it a habit to have a clean dress and undergarments in the car just in case. Marissa worked with sick people who bled, threw up, or whatever. That meant having a change of clothes ready or wearing someone else's body fluids for the entire day. No, she was always prepared with a change of clothing.

She opened the front and rear passenger doors to create a sort of changing room and waited until no one was in sight. She slipped the fresh dress over her head and allowed yesterday's dress to fall to the ground. She quickly stepped over the old dress and threw it into the back seat of her SUV. She then climbed into the front seat and unclasped her bra, sliding it off under the fresh dress and put on the clean one. Marissa then slid her underwear off and stepped into the fresh pair as she exited the SUV. There, good as new, she thought to herself as she walked into the building.

Dr. Oliver tried to walk around the halls of Green Haven in the stoic persona that she had always portrayed, but a smile kept coming to her face. It didn't go unnoticed by the staff as they walked by with one finger wagging fiercely behind their backs. Marissa knew the staff was on to her, but they would never know who the gentleman was. She was reviewing charts on north wing while her mind kept replaying last night. She wanted Oscar to call; if he did, she couldn't answer sitting at the desk. It was too risky. She slipped into a nearby hallway bathroom and texted him not to call. She wouldn't be able to answer, but she wanted to know if he was thinking about her.

Oscar was delighted to get the text. He was putting on his shoes and getting ready to leave when Marissa's text landed on his phone. He texted her with a causal but coy, "Oh, hi," followed by a smiley face emoji. He knew she was at Green Haven and had already decided to drop by. This wasn't out of the ordinary since he owned it. He would walk past Marissa and give her a passing hello and keep going. It would be fun and daring. Oscar got into his car and flipped on the radio, half listening to some news show as he drove to Green Haven.

Dr. Oliver saw Oscar coming down the hallway and felt the sweat droplets begin to form all over her body. She wasn't sure if it was from fear or excitement. Her heart started to beat ten times louder. She would be furious if he did anything to harm her credibility. Marissa was about to duck into a room when she heard his voice call out to her. *Damn it. Please, Oscar, don't do this*, she screamed in her head.

He walked up to her, said good morning, and kept going. She covered her mouth with her hand to hide the large ear-to-ear grin she was unable to control. He was having fun, but he was still respecting her station at Green Haven. *He'll pay for that.* She walked into the room of an incoherent resident, pulled out her cell, and texted him, "You'll pay for that."

Oscar's phone pinged. He pulled it out of his pocket and read her text. He typed back "LOL" as he let out a boisterous laugh. Marissa had confirmed that she was on board.

25

CATHY REMOVED THE PAGES from underneath her seat and placed them on the passenger seat as she started to drive home. She kept thinking she needed more proof that Kyle was the killer and that he was setting her up. Right now, it looked like she might be the killer. Then it dawned on her, she already had proof of both. It was Kyle's computer. The dates showing when the files were created would show he was the killer. She knew where he hid the password to the secret files. She knew the password; that meant she could change the password and lock him out. This would keep the proof intact for as long as she needed it. Kyle would find out, and he may run, but she'd be in the clear. She'd take a photo of the passwords written on the backside of the blotter as proof that it was Kyle. They're in his handwriting. Finally, those detective shows came in handy.

She pulled into her garage, grabbed the papers, and went into her home to start putting all the pieces together. The thought of being able to show Kyle's plan made her more determined than ever to bury her arch-enemy for good. Her muscles twitched faster; her fingers moved more swiftly. Cathy had gone past feeling like a TV detective; she was a bonafide superhero.

As she added the new names and information to her spreadsheet, she noticed the dates the residents were dying. Cathy kept writing in the days of the week. It was odd; almost all the deaths on her spreadsheets occurred on a Tuesday or Thursday. Kyle was killing the residents on specific days of the week. She wondered what was so special about Tuesday and Thursday.

The earlier dates were also of residents who had been at Green Haven for a long time, most of them more than seven years. What did all these residents have in common? Cathy took out a separate sheet of paper and started writing down common points.

1. Long-time residents
2. Died on Tuesday or Thursday
3. Have "nurse may pronounce"
4. All were older residents
5. All were in poor health

Her superhero status dropped down a few rungs as she concluded she was missing something and that something still eluded her. Cathy felt she was making progress but it was slow and frustrating; nothing like the one-hour crime shows she watched. As the Green Haven DON, Cathy knew every resident on the list. She recalled that they were either bedridden, incoherent, both, or had some other deteriorating condition that would soon render them incapacitated. *Kyle, how could you? They were helpless. You're supposed to protect them.* Cathy could feel the anger starting to build, and she realized she had to keep calm to find the answers she was looking for. She raised her hands above her head and took several deep breaths.

Lower down on the page she started a second list of what she had on each resident.

1. Death certificate
2. Chart information
3. . . . .

Cathy stopped writing. She didn't have the contracts that each resident signed. She needed to get them, but they were in the corporate office, and there was no way she could get in there and not get fired or arrested. This would take time and some serious thought. Now she too had created lists that made her look like the killer. She thought about destroying the sheets. But she couldn't shred them. She heard on the news that the FBI has people who reassemble shredded documents. They would have to be burned before she attempted anything.

Hours had passed, and Cathy was getting tired. She put everything away. Her belly grumbled, letting her know that it also needed some attention. Cathy went to the fridge and took out a wedge of sharp cheddar. She pulled some crackers from a cabinet then sat on the couch and pressed the remote's power button. The television flickered to life. A news story was playing about a politician who had stolen campaign funds. The news reporter covering the story stated that if you want to catch a crook, follow the money.

"That's it!" Cathy screamed. The money. Each resident, actually their family, agrees to a single yearly payment that doesn't change for as long as the resident stays at Green Haven, Inc. She wondered if Green Haven, Inc. was in financial trouble. Were the long-term residents no longer profitable? But why would Kyle be killing them? That's just insane, she thought. Maybe Kyle was being blackmailed into committing the killing? Maybe they promised him something big. Whatever it was, Kyle was still killing people. Perhaps he's just a psychopath afraid of losing a job from a place that tolerates him.

The contracts, Kyle, the murders, how did it all tie together? Cathy's mind was spinning. Her stomach let out a second massive roar for food. She hadn't started eating, and her body was getting upset with her. Cathy quickly cut a portion of cheese from the wedge, placed it on the cracker, and started eating. She could do no more tonight. She would go in early tomorrow and set her plan in motion. First, she would change the secret password. No, she stopped; there's more proof in the locked drawers. He was hiding something in that cabinet, and she needed to find it. Changing the password would definitely tip him off. She had to wait on that. She wondered if he unlocked the filing cabinet while he was there. Tomorrow, during the morning meeting, Cathy would ask to be excused, rush back to Kyle's office, and see if the cabinet was unlocked. Kyle would be busy throwing his weight around. He'd be occupied for at least an hour. She needed just a few minutes to search the drawers of the cabinet. Cathy thought if she found evidence quickly, she'd have time to change the password too. If the evidence in the filing cabinet was strong enough, she wouldn't go back to the meeting. Instead, she would head to her office with the evidence and call the police. Kyle wouldn't suspect anything. She knew exactly where he'd be in the building, and the police could take him immediately.

If the cabinet was locked, his key might be in the office. The key should be easy to spot on a key ring; it would be small and different than car or house keys. She'd unlock the cabinet and proceed with her plan. Either way, it's a good plan.

Try to set me up. I'll show you. You murderous jackass! Cathy thought as she took a second bite of the cracker topped with cheese.

Too much television, Cathy told herself. *After it's over, I have to get a life outside of work. Maybe I'll write a book about this.* She laughed as she thought perhaps they'd make a movie out of it. She wondered who'd play her. Cathy sat back on the couch, tired from the day's adventures, and closed her eyes. She fell asleep trying to decide which actress would be worthy of playing such a super sleuth as herself.

26

SISTER DIANE STRAIGHTENED HER clothes and went to meet with Bishop Anthony. She worried that something had gone wrong. She wasn't scheduled to talk with him until tomorrow. Did Father Brendan say something? Sister Diane didn't want the bishop to think she was ungrateful for his faith in her.

She met him in the convent's front sitting room. Bishop Anthony smiled as she walked in. Sister Diane took this as a good sign and started to calm down, but she was still worried about what couldn't wait for less than twenty-four hours.

"Good evening, Sister." Bishop Anthony's voice was pleasant; his posture was relaxed.

"Yes, um, good evening, Bishop Anthony." A concerned look still flashed across her face.

"I know we were supposed to meet tomorrow, but I was passing by and wondered how today went? I spoke briefly with Father Brendan, who told me he was delighted to work with you. I wanted to hear your thoughts." He removed the silver spectacles from his face and placed them into the inside pocket of his traditional black suit.

"Yes, uh, he's a nice man and a wonderful priest. He cares a lot about his work. Oh, and the people too." Sister Diane was now visibly fidgeting in her chair.

"It's okay. He had only good things to say about you. I pride myself on being a good judge of people. I'm human; it's my only vice, hopefully. I'll get right to the point. I want you to move from working at this convent to working with Father Brendan. He could use the help. Before you say anything, I've already cleared it with the Mother Superior." The look on the bishop's face was one that sent a clear message that no was not a possibility.

"Bishop Anthony, I like it here. I don't mean to offend you, but I'm not sure about leaving." Even though she had read the bishop's face correctly, her fear of leaving the convent was more overpowering.

"How about a two-week trial? So I'm not offended." The bishop paused to let the reality of the request sink in. "If you don't like it, you can come back. Okay?" Again, the bishop was not going to take no for an answer as he stood up and was making his way to the front door.

Sister Diane looked down. "I guess so. Where would I live?"

Bishop Anthony turned around to look at the mousey sister. "For the two weeks you can still live here. I'll have Father Brendan pick you up in the morning and drive you back in the evening." He again turned and started walking. "Good, it's settled."

"Um, okay?" Sister Diane was still trying to make sense of what just happened.

"He'll be here at eight tomorrow. You two will make a great team. I know it." The Bishop waved goodbye as he stepped out of the convent.

Sister Diane stood there stunned by the request, which she finally grasped was not a request at all. She couldn't say no. The good bishop had his plan well under way before meeting with her tonight. She concluded that Bishop Anthony had made up his mind long before she was even asked to meet Father Brendan. She now wondered if Father Brendan knew of the plan. Was he in on it?

Sister Diane told herself that she had to let the two weeks happen. She would watch closely as she allowed Bishop Anthony's plan to unfold. Then she thought, he's a bishop, a high holy man, what she was thinking would be evil in nature and against the bishop's very core. Maybe he saw something in her that she couldn't or wouldn't see in herself. This notion comforted her. She liked the feeling that someone wanted to keep her and make her feel that she belonged. This new feeling took over and she decided she needed to trust the bishop.

Sister Diane was up and ready the next morning by 7:00 am. She found herself excited. If the bishop believed in her enough to give her a chance, she was going to make the most of it. This time she placed twenty dollars in her purse for lunch. She couldn't expect Father Brendan to buy lunch every day. She thought about making her lunch but didn't want to be caught off guard if they were going out to lunch again.

At 8:00 am sharp Father Brendan pulled up to the sidewalk in front of the convent. Sister Diane saw him approaching and came out. He got out and opened the car door. She told him that would not be necessary. He kiddingly said to her that she didn't need to get used to it. He was just trying to make a good impression on their second day. This broke the tension; Sister Diane was grateful.

"Are we going back to Green Haven today?" Sister Diane inquired with childlike glee.

"No. Today is Friday, so we're off to Elite Care, another facility owned by Green Haven, Inc."

"How many facilities does Green Haven own?"

"It's actually Green Haven, Inc. that owns the facilities," Father Brendan explained

"I don't understand." Sister Diane's brows creased together.

"Confusing, I know. So, Oscar Green created Green Haven, Inc. Then he built Green Haven Nursing Facility, then the Autumn Life and Elite

Care facilities. Green Haven, Inc. is the corporation, and Green Haven is the facility." Father Brendan pointed at three different spots along the top of the dashboard as he listed the facilities then pretended to cover all of them when he spoke about Green Haven, Inc. the corporation.

"That's very complicated. And, if you don't mind me saying so, it's silly."

"The Green Haven facility is named in honor of his father, and all the facilities have a cornerstone engraved with 'For you, Dad.' The priest turned away from the road to look at his passenger.

"His dad must have been an extraordinary man. Did you know him?"

"No, I've never met the father or son." He returned his gaze on the road.

"What are the other two facilities like?"

"Green Haven was built for the rich, and the other two surpass it." He refrained from looking at her as he slightly rolled his eyes. "I'm not sure I'm dressed well enough for whichever one we're going to." She waved her hands over the plain dress she had put on for today.

"Elite Care, and that's funny." Father Brendan laughed.

"Well, I wanted to say they were five-star hotels for rich folks, but I thought that might be too judgmental." Sister Diane now brushed the wrinkled material of her dress on her lap as if she were preparing to enter a lavish upscale gala.

"It's okay. I think it almost every time I walk in." He brushed the lapels of his black suit to keep with the charade.

Both laughed as they arrived at Elite Care. Sister Diane noted that it was more elegant than Green Haven. It was almost too stuffy to live in. Father Brendan told her that if he had the chance, he wouldn't mind retiring here. She was feeling more comfortable, and this time she made the joke that their pay wouldn't cover a day here. He nodded in agreement. They entered the north wing of Elite Care, and Sister Diane asked, "Are all three facilities set up the same way?"

Father Brendan looked over his shoulder to make sure no one could hear them. "Yes, I've heard that Oscar Green has a motto, basically 'if ain't broke don't fix it.'"

They started with the coherent residents just like the day before. Sister Diane was curious. Why he didn't just go room to room? Why all the back and forth? It was not very efficient. But again, it was just her second day, and she didn't want to ask. She followed the priest around the building for the next three hours. She only helped when she was beckoned. Father Brendan was willing to let her join in; she just didn't want to crowd his style. She wanted to watch and learn more before venturing forward.

After they were done at Elite Care, she asked Father Brendan where they were going next. Yesterday's afternoon nap and a good night's sleep prepared her well for today. The father replied that on Fridays they visited one facility and took the afternoon off.

"Even the holy like time off from work. Besides, there will be plenty of times that we'll be called in on the weekend or even on a Friday afternoon. So, I've learned to enjoy the time off."

His continued upbeat attitude made it easy for her to feel comfortable around him. She found herself thinking that in another life they could have been good friends. She giggled as she told herself that she was lying. She meant more than friends. With a smirk still on her face, she inquired, "May I ask what our normal schedule will be?"

"Mondays we'll go to Autumn in the morning and make some home visits in the afternoon. Tuesdays we'll be at Green Haven and then go where needed in the afternoon. Wednesdays we're at Autumn and then Elite. Thursday it's Green Haven then onto the hospital if we have residents there. And Fridays you already know."

Sister Diane nodded in approval. "It's good you have it all laid out."

"Actually, you have to thank Father Timothy. He created the schedule. It works well, and we can cover a lot of ground in a short time. How about some lunch?"

"Sure. I'll buy my own today," Sister Diane said with a great deal of pride. More than she had intended to display.

"That won't be necessary. I already told you. We get a food stipend. In fact, our lovely bishop increased it when you joined me." He waved his hand in the air as if to mimic the bishop himself.

Sister Diane now had confirmation that the bishop had planned her transition well ahead of the two-week trial she almost agreed to. She also understood that the bishop planned this to be a permanent move. She quickly decided she would still decline if it wasn't what she wanted. A small but unnoticeable frown passed through her lips for just a moment as the she realized her last decision wasn't an option.

They had lunch at a diner that Father Brendan learned about while working with Father Timothy. During lunch Sister Diane asked, "What happened to Father Timothy?"

The young priest truly loved his mentor and had feelings of great loss when the older priest chose to retire. Sister Diane asked why Father Timothy retired so suddenly. Father Brendan told her that he didn't know why. He went on to tell her that he gave no warnings and hadn't even discussed it with him. He was just told one day by Bishop Anthony that he would be working alone until further notice. The bishop further conveyed that Father Timothy retired without giving a reason other than he knew his people were in good hands. The young priest hadn't heard from Father Timothy since the day before learning of his retirement. Father Brendan mentioned that he made several attempts to contact Father Timothy but never got any response. He finally stopped trying.

"I'm trying to be a good priest, so I'm trying to find forgiveness for the way Father Timothy handled the whole thing. It's still hard. I'm glad

Bishop Anthony keeps in contact with him. He tells me Father Timothy is doing well. I still worry about him, but I have to respect his privacy." Father Brendan's eyes begin to redden as tears well up.

Sister Diane would never ask another question about the older priest. She could see that the pain was fresh and would be with Father Brendan for a long time. She knew the pain of abandonment very well, and she would make every attempt possible to spare him from it.

They finished lunch. Father Brendan dropped her off at the convent telling her he would be back on Monday at 8:00 am. As he drove away, Sister Diane stood in front of the convent thinking about Father Brendan's pain and the sorrow that resides deep inside of him. She whispered, "He hides it well." As she climbed the steps to the convent door, Sister Diane's thoughts shifted to Bishop Anthony. He indeed was a spiritually good man, but he had a plan. He had reached out to both of them during their time of need, saw their potential, and set a plan in motion. The bishop was right; she liked working outside the convent. Sister Diane didn't need the two weeks to decide. She didn't care what the bishop's plan was; she wanted to work with Father Brendan. Their bond was tangible, and she wanted it to continue.

27

CATHY ARRIVED AT HER office just before 7:00 am. She logged in and started gathering the rest of the expired residents' information. She filled in her spreadsheet furiously, concentrating on the date of admission and date of death, including the day of the week. Cathy created an additional column on the spreadsheet that showed how many years the resident lived at Green Haven. She would later match that to Green Haven's opening date. The director of nursing found a new fire within herself as she continued to look through the names. Over and over, she was forced to read the bold blue-lettered phrase; she knew it would be there, and yet her eyes could not stray from its call. "The bastard was consistent," Cathy repeated this with each eyeful.

The pattern was there; she had found it. Every resident had been at Green Haven for a long time; all were quite old and had a low quality of life. Every resident he murdered was failing in one way or another. Then she thought, *Did he convince himself he was doing them a favor? Is he really just a twisted psychopath?*

Around 9:00 am the start of the morning meeting was announced. Cathy logged off and headed for the front conference room. It was larger and didn't have glass windows, which made it more private. All the cast members were present. Kyle was standing at the head of the table with his hands on his hips, giving a "how dare you make me wait" glare at each of them as they walked in. Kyle made it his thing to get there first and demean everyone with his "king of the hill" look.

About ten minutes into the meeting, Cathy interrupted, asking to be excused for personal reasons. Everyone understood this was code for having to use the restroom. Grudgingly, Kyle told her to go. She headed straight for his office. Once inside, she directed her attention to the filing cabinet; it was still locked. She pulled on the desk's top drawer; it was open. Cathy rooted around inside it and found keys. She tried them in the cabinet's lock and heard the clicking of the lock's mechanism as she turned the key. Quickly Cathy pulled the upper drawer open and started flipping through the folders. This drawer contained all the files on the employees of Green Haven. She was tempted to find her file to see what the ass had written about her. That had to wait for another day. She closed the upper drawer then pulled open the bottom drawer.

The door to the office opened. It was the receptionist; she had come in to place a letter on Kyle's desk. She asked what was going on. "Why are you in Mr. Strong's personnel files?"

Cathy asked her not to say anything; she told her she needed information on a nurse she thought might be stealing medications. The receptionist seemed to buy it. Cathy was not happy about lying, but so much more was at stake than a small lie. The receptionist turned to leave when Kyle came through the door, both surprise and anger blanketed his face as he threw his hands in the air.

"What the hell is going on here?" Kyle's voice was booming and frightened both of them.

"I found her going through your desk. I had nothing to do with it," the receptionist quickly responded, trying to keep from cowering to the floor.

"Is that true?" He glared in Cathy's direction.

"Yes," Cathy told him, trying to keep her own fear in check.

"Leave!" he commanded his receptionist.

"No, stay!" Cathy said, her fear now palpable.

"Leave now, or you're fired! And don't say a word to anyone about this!"

The receptionist quickly left the office, making sure not to look back. Trembling, she closed the door on her way out.

"Start talking!" Kyle stood at the front of his office. Rage burning from his eyes at her.

"I know . . . I know what you've been up to. You're a killer." Cathy returned the hatred with her own glare.

"What? Are you out of your mind?" His hands were now in the air again. This time a look of shock overcame his face.

"I found your kill list in the secret section of your computer. Don't try anything. Everyone saw us come back to your office." Cathy, now standing, kept her eyes fixated on him. She attempted not to show the fear that filled every inch of her body. She knew that if he wanted, he could kill her before anyone could come to her rescue. He could hit the front door running and make it to his car before anyone could stop him. She would be dead, and he would be gone.

"Sit down and shut up! I'm not the killer. I thought you were. I was putting together the pieces on my own." His appearance became less threatening with each word.

"I don't believe you. I just can't figure out why you only kill the residents on Tuesdays and Thursdays."

"Wait, what?" It was evident that Kyle had yet to see this part of the puzzle.

"All the killings happen on Tuesdays and Thursdays. You came back yesterday, Thursday, and Grace Harding died. No one died when you were gone. She tried to tell us that a big man was trying to kill her. It was you."

"No, it wasn't. I took a couple of days off to go to the other facilities. I was following a hunch that it was happening there too. I just couldn't figure out how you were killing residents at the other facilities. Actually,

I couldn't figure out how you were doing it here." Kyle was now seated in one of the chairs in front of his desk.

"Me! I'm not the killer!" She refused to take her eyes off him. She was still scared that he might lunge at her without warning.

"Since you're in here searching my office that's obvious now." Kyle pointed at the filing cabinet drawer still half open and the keys dangling from the lock.

"Wait, you're really not the killer?" Cathy's shoulders relaxed as she sat in Kyle's chair.

"No, that's what I'm telling you. Can we exchange chairs for appearance's sake?"

Kyle circled around the desk to the left while Cathy made it a point to go around the right side of the desk. She was still playing it safe.

Kyle shook his head in disbelief. "I can't believe I'm saying this, but we need to work together. We need to compare our findings. What were you looking for in my files?"

"The contracts that the residents sign. You have a copy of them, right?"

"Yes, why?"

"I thought you were killing them for money."

"Wow. Okay, I'll let that go for now. Let's get back to the meeting. We'll talk later. It's too dangerous here."

"No, this can't wait." Cathy was now standing again.

Kyle slammed the filing cabinet shut then leaned on the desktop with both elbows. "Listen, if you're not the killer, and I'm not the killer, then someone else here is doing it. So, we have to keep with the normal routine, or they'll get spooked, and we'll never find them."

"Okay, that makes sense, but we're not done with this, do you understand?" Cathy was trying hard to keep a stern exterior while still fearing that a sudden move by the administrator could end her life.

"Yes, and keep in mind I'm still your boss outside of all of this. Appearances." Kyle was pointing to the door. Cathy understood the gesture.

Kyle relocked the filing cabinet and put the keys in his pocket, making sure Cathy saw where the keys were before she left his office. Before returning to the morning meeting, Kyle stopped at the receptionist desk to tell her that it was all okay. It was just a big misunderstanding. Cathy was just trying to protect Green Haven. Still, he didn't want her to say anything to anybody, as there was an inquiry in progress. The receptionist was skeptical; he was too angry for it to be "just" a misunderstanding, but she agreed.

Cathy sat in the remainder of the morning meeting trying to decide if she believed Kyle. Either he was telling the truth, or he was the best liar she had ever come across. He did give her a piece of information she didn't already have; the murders were also happening at the other facilities. If Kyle was lying and he was the killer, how could he do it at Autumn Living and Elite Care? They have their own administrators. What if he lied to throw her off? What if Kyle was playing her? Cathy's mind was in overdrive; she remembered nothing of the morning meeting.

Cathy didn't have a chance to look in the bottom drawer before she was interrupted. When the meeting was over, she would immediately demand to look in the bottom drawer. She wouldn't give Kyle the chance to remove anything. Whatever was in there would prove he was telling the truth or lying. Cathy was still afraid of being alone with Kyle, but she wasn't going to lose this opportunity. This might be the only chance she had to clear her name.

28

Around lunchtime, Dr. Oliver went out to her car and pulled out her phone. She called Oscar, who had left the building hours ago. He picked up on the second ring.

"Were you waiting with the phone in your hand?" She was testing him.

Oscar thought about lying, but with a childish grin he replied, "Yes."

Trying to sound angry, Marissa continued by starting a discussion regarding his little game earlier that morning, but she couldn't hold the lie. She found it as fun and tantalizing as he did. She wanted to meet up this afternoon at his place. He didn't say no.

After a quick return into the building to finish signing charts, none of which she could really concentrate on, Dr. Oliver hopped back into her car and headed for Oscar's place. Oscar met her at the door, his shirt half undone. She stepped in and kicked off her shoes while asking him to pour her a glass of bourbon. Oscar wasn't in the mood for drinks but didn't want to seem like a schoolboy about to have sex for the first time, even though he was feeling every bit of that excitement. Marissa sat down on the couch, slowly sipping her drink, making sure Oscar could see every embrace her lips made with the glass and even the movements of her slender neck muscles as the bourbon made its way down her body. She was making him pay for this morning.

"How did the, uh, morning go at Green . . ." Oscar was bidding his time the best he could.

Marissa waggled a finger at him. "No shop talk, rules."

She had made it clear on several occasions; she didn't want their relationship to affect her work or her reputation. Oscar understood. She called him to the couch and placed the empty bourbon glass down on the coffee table. Oscar sat close to her. Marissa slid her hand inside his shirt and stroked his chest. They kissed and found a way to make the afternoon pass.

"How about a reservation?" Oscar asked as he rose from the couch without clothing or modesty.

"Oscar, I've already told you that it's not good to be seen in public together a lot. Let's stay in. I promise you'll be happy with the choice." Marissa made sure Oscar saw her eyes map his naked frame.

Oscar understood. He wanted more, but great sex wasn't a bad second choice. She agreed that someday they might make it more. Oscar wanted some planning in their relationship. He didn't want it to become "call you on a whim" or "if I just happen to be extra horny this week." He wanted to see her every day, but for now, he would settle for set days of the week. They agreed on Tuesday nights and Friday afternoons, and if that led into the weekend, that would be fine too. There would be no funny looks at work or long conversations in the hallway. Both agreed that while at work it was Dr. Oliver and Mr. Green.

The no-shop talk meant neither knew if there was a problem brewing unless it was brought up at the board meetings. It was better this way. With no previous knowledge, they would be hearing everything for the first time and wouldn't give away any accidental bedroom chatter. Even though there wasn't any, about work that is.

These rules carried on. Both had become very comfortable with what they had. Oscar already had children and wasn't looking for more. Marissa seemed to have misplaced her nurturing mother instincts. The occasional breaking of the rules concerning extra afternoons, or nights or days, was an option that both would exercise from time to time. Their libidos were well-matched, and saying no happened very rarely.

As much as they kept their relationship a secret, they did go out to dinner and occasionally someone from one of the facilities would see them. Rumors that flew around the facilities would die quickly because there was no proof and because they were the medical director and the owner. Neither Dr. Oliver nor Mr. Green ever addressed any of the rumors. This would only give more credence to them. No one wanted to get fired from a place that paid exceptionally well and was built to look like a five-star hotel. Besides, working somewhere else would definitely be a step or two down.

Most of the time they met at Oscar's place since it was larger and better kept. Marissa wasn't much of a cook and less of a housekeeper. She had a cleaning lady who came in twice a month. It was on those occasions that she might even consider inviting Oscar over. This was fine with Oscar. He too preferred to stay at his place. He was comfortable there. He secretly hoped that Marissa would become so comfortable there she might want to move in someday.

Their relationship grew quickly to its peak and reached a comfortable plateau, at least for Marissa. Oscar had tried to push the issue a few times throughout the years, but he was only met with resistance and backing away. At times he wondered why she was so afraid to commit. Oscar thought, with the years moving forward and her reputation well established, what would be the harm? He rarely asked her. It was better to keep what he had than risk losing it all. He had lost it all once before, and he didn't want to go back down that road. Oscar convinced himself, eventually, that she was right. This was better for both of them. If it didn't work out, he wouldn't lose half of everything, or like before, almost everything except for what Lacey didn't want.

Dr. Oliver and Mr. Green would arrive and leave Green Haven, Inc. separately. They would attend social and business gatherings alone. They would show no signs of any other type of relationship other than professional. Marissa was clear and stern about this. Oscar agreed. He had her on Tuesdays and Fridays and most weekends.

In Oscar's world of deal making, compromise was the key. He unknowingly extrapolated it to his personal life. Marissa demanded secrecy for her own needs. The sting of a failed previous marriage kept Oscar in check, and Marissa knew this. She counted on Oscar's fear of losing her and controlled him with it when necessary. Oscar's challenges became less and less with time.

29

CATHY FOLLOWED KYLE BACK to his office immediately after the morning meeting. She was following too closely; he could almost feel her breath on the back of his neck. Just before entering the office, Kyle spun around and whispered, "Give me some room." The determined director of nursing backed off a few steps.

They entered the office; Kyle closed and locked the door. This made Cathy a little nervous, but she was fully committed. Kyle sat down behind his desk and motioned for her to sit. She had her reservations but sat anyway. Kyle reached under his desk. Startled, Cathy stood up and moved to the door. Her mind raced back to detective shows where the villain had a gun taped to the underside of their desk. Her hands reached for the lock as she kept both eyes fixed on Kyle's hands. Kyle looked at her puzzled. He pulled his hands from the desk and placed them in the air as though surrendering.

"Oh Jesus, you still think I'm the killer. I'm not. And I'm not going to hurt you. I thought you were the killer, remember?" Kyle showed her the keys in his hands. He had been reaching into his pocket to retrieve them.

"You could be just saying that." Cathy was still standing at the door. Her eyes were glued on his hands.

"Please sit down." Kyle pointed to the chair with his free hand.

Cathy sat back down. Kyle kept his hands in plain sight, only moving them involuntarily as he spoke.

"John Perkins, do you know who he is?"

"Yes. He's the dead board treasurer."

"Unfortunately, that's right. Anyway, he contacted me just before his death. He wanted to ask me about some financial numbers regarding this facility. He said there was something odd about the books and he needed to take a closer look."

Now feeling more courageous, Cathy decided to apply a full-court press. "How do I know you weren't embezzling money and you killed Mr. Perkins because he found out?" Cathy was leaning forward with both elbows on the chair's armrests, her tone daring him to lie.

Kyle, agitated, stood from behind his desk. Cathy almost fell over backward from her chair trying to back away.

"No, I'm sorry. I'm not a killer, nor am I a thief. I didn't know what John was talking about. Besides, I already believed you were the murderer."

For the first time since she had known Kyle, Cathy could see he was afraid. "Okay. What did Mr. Perkins tell you?"

"That's just it. We never met. He died two days before our meeting." Kyle sat back down in his chair and placed his hands on the back of his neck.

"That does seem pretty convenient." Cathy was trying to sound convincing, but she no longer believed he was the killer.

"A, I'm not the killer and stop thinking that. B, I can see how it looks. I thought you were the killer and a ruthless one at that."

"So, you want me to work with you?" Cathy had now relaxed and sat comfortably in the chair. Her fear had faded.

Kyle had come to the conclusion that if Cathy was not the killer, then his whole theory was wrong and the killer was still out there and could be hunting for him next. He kept this to himself. "Yes. If you were looking around my office for evidence, you must have information pointing to me as the killer. I don't want to go to jail, and I'm pretty sure you don't either.

Let's pool our information and figure this out." Kyle seemed to be almost pleading with her. His voice wavered as he spoke.

"Um, okay." Cathy remained guarded.

"Good. First, let's agree that neither of us is the killer and we might be getting set up. No, I don't know by whom. I was hoping you might have information that might lead to that."

"First, what do you have in the locked filing cabinet?" She was pointing to the keys.

"What? It's just the hard copies of what you already saw on my computer. I needed to have it in case something happened to my computer."

"You kept them here?" A look of amazement came over Cathy as she thought, detective shows' rule number one—don't keep incriminating evidence around where people can find it.

"Yes. Why not?" Worry flashed across Kyle's face. He began to think he might have made a grave mistake that could land him in prison.

"Because if someone finds them, you go to jail for murder. They read like a hit man's grocery list." She thought to herself, *What an idiot! He couldn't pull off these murders, at least not alone.*

"Fair enough. What were you looking for?" Kyle, trying to give the appearance that all was good, asked as he unlocked the file cabinets.

"The resident contracts. And evidence on you." Cathy shook her head as she considered that she may have to start from the beginning.

Kyle told her that the contract copies were stored in another locked filing cabinet and asked her why she wanted them. Cathy tried to be patient as she started to explain that the killer was murdering residents who had been at Green Haven for a long time. He asked what the reason was. Cathy told him she suspected it had something to do with financial reasons, especially after hearing of Mr. Perkins' death and now his planned meeting with the board treasurer. She stressed that the contracts might be the key to helping them find the killer.

Kyle expressed that there would be too many to just walk out of the building with them. She asked if they could both sneak them out, go over them and then return them in the morning. Kyle thought silently for a moment then agreed. He suggested they should meet somewhere away from Green Haven later that day.

Cathy said they could meet at the town library. She still was not willing to fully trust Kyle. She added that he was to bring whatever information he had collected and she would do the same. This made Kyle nervous. He wondered if she was playing him. He, too, didn't completely trust her. He okayed the library meeting for 4:30. They would meet in the library lobby. Cathy left his office and returned to hers.

It was almost lunchtime. Cathy decided to go home and get her papers. She wanted to make copies of everything. When she returned to her office, she made another set of copies then she wrote notes detailing everything she and Kyle had discussed. She chronicled her concerns of Kyle being the killer and how he tried to make it sound like she was the killer. She explained about the "nurse may pronounce" notation on the death certificates. How both she and Kyle had noticed independently that there had been an increase in deaths at Green Haven, and finally that if she died or went missing after her meeting at the library, he was responsible. She then placed everything in a large yellow envelope and sealed it. On the outside of the envelope, she wrote that day's date and the words "for police only." Cathy placed the envelope in the top drawer of her desk. She didn't lock it. If tonight was going to be her last night, her killer would be found. She was going to make sure of it.

Cathy put the first set of copies in the revitalized satchel, turned off the lights, and headed for Kyle's office. He was sitting at his desk. She could see this through the window in the door. Kyle waved her in. Dr. Oliver was seated in a chair in front of Kyle's desk. Cathy apologized for the intrusion and asked Kyle if the files were ready for her to review. Kyle reached for a thick stack of files on the corner of his desk, picked them up, and handed them to her. She was about to leave when Dr. Oliver asked if she could offer some help. She went on to say that she knew how tedious chart reviews could be.

Cathy was frozen in place, unable to reply. Kyle interjected that those are not chart reviews; they were old resident contracts that needed some final assessments before they could be sent to storage. Cathy gave him a glare. Kyle quickly added that it was customary to review the contracts to see if anything was overlooked after the resident had died or moved out. Cathy added that it was just another part of the small print in her own contract. Dr. Oliver jokingly said she was happy that her own contract didn't have any fine print; at least she hoped it didn't. Both Kyle and Cathy laughed. The visibly nervous DON quickly left the room, preventing any further discussion on the matter.

Once she closed the door behind her, she mumbled the word "idiot." Apparently loud enough to draw the attention of the receptionist, who then asked if everything was okay. Cathy nodded and kept going.

Cathy placed the files in the satchel on her arm then threw her jacket over the top for good measure. She planned to put the satchel in her car after leaving Kyle's office, but with Dr. Oliver sitting in his office, she would have an unhindered view of the parking lot, and that meant seeing Cathy place the contract filled satchel in her car. Cathy returned to her office and placed the satchel, with jacket atop, on the worn armless chair that Green Haven had so graciously given her for guests who might need a place to sit. Cathy spotted the letter opener sitting on her desk and slipped it into the satchel. After all, how much could she trust the man who had made work a living hell for years? Cathy left her office to make a routine visit of the wings. The dealings with Kyle had built up tension that she was now feeling in her neck and shoulders. Her attempts to stroll the hallways normally failed, as a few nurses asked if she was tired or feeling sick. After numerous check-ins, reviews, and a final return to her office, Cathy headed out the door with all the necessary papers, files, and spreadsheets she had safely tucked away in the satchel. She had a certain amount of comfort knowing that she had laid out everything in great detail for the police. She got into her car and headed for the library. Her only thought was, *Kyle, don't you screw me over.*

30

SISTER DIANE CALLED BISHOP Anthony to request he move forward with the transfer and make it permanent. She didn't want to offend the nuns; they'd been so good to her, but she needed to find purpose in her life. Bishop Anthony was right; that wasn't happening living in the convent. Now she wanted to be part of the real world. Sister Diane was willing to fully commit for the first time in her life.

Bishop Anthony found her a small apartment quickly. Sister Diane's days were filled with Father Brendan and her nights with learning how to be in a space that was all her own. In the convent, she had a small room with minimal décor. Bishop Anthony had placed her in a small, one-bedroom apartment. She had her own refrigerator and her own private bathroom. She received a slightly larger salary working with Father Brendan. Money was never a concern of Sister Diane's, but now she found she liked looking at the beautiful things she might buy to hang on her very own walls. Even though the apartment was tiny compared to others, to Sister Diane it felt like a palace, her palace. She had lived poor, and now she thought she might give modest a try.

As the weeks turned into months, she and Father Brendan became used to having each other around. They had nothing more than the utmost respect for each other, but their closeness did raise some concerns among the other priests in the parish. Bishop Anthony quickly ended those concerns and any others. Any priest wanting to advance in the Church would need the bishop's blessing, so it was not a good idea to speak out against those he took a particular interest in.

The holy couple was well received by the residents of all three facilities. Apparently having a man and a woman together made it more family-like. The residents enjoyed the feeling of family visits. The father and sister were doing well, and the bishop heard the praises.

At the request, or rather gentle demand, of Bishop Anthony, Father Brendan met with him once a month on a Friday afternoon, without Sister Diane. The bishop insisted they meet alone to discuss her progression and other matters at hand. He explained to Father Brendan that these were matters only concerning for the clergy. Bishop Anthony told him Sister Diane needed to become a nun to be considered for their private conversations. Father Brendan was uncomfortable with deceiving Sister Diane, but like the other priests, he understood the power the bishop had. He would tell Father Brendan the issues they discussed were coming from higher up on the chain of command. He did wonder if the bishop was having the same conversations about him with the sister. Father Brendan would never ask either of them; he figured she too was afraid to make any mention of it.

Their conversations ranged from the day-to-day life of a priest, to the most critical difficulties facing the spirituality of man and how the Church was or wasn't meeting man's needs. The bishop always returned to saying that spiritual leaders must take actions to ease the struggles of man. During many of the visits, Father Brendan thought it might be faster to start at this point then call it a good conversation. He enjoyed his meetings with the bishop, but he also enjoyed his Friday afternoons free. He often wondered if the bishop called these meetings to make sure to keep him from mischief. This would make Father Brendan laugh as he wondered what mischief can a priest get into.

Sister Diane met with the bishop on occasion, but not regularly. The bishop didn't ask her about the father. Instead, they would talk about how she was and what concerns she might have. Bishop Anthony liked her but didn't feel the inclination to share such deep concepts with her. Church matters were for the men of the Church. Probably one of the only archaic thoughts the bishop still clutched. He would ask her how she liked working with the residents at the facilities and how she might change things. They discussed her feelings about belonging to a greater cause. Sister Diane's most significant concern was the lives that had no real joy left in them. Those who lay in bed with no idea they were even alive. She told him that she could relate to those residents who felt helpless and alone. She would continue saying that, for much of her life, she had the same feelings. Bishop Anthony would always assure her that the Lord must have a plan for them. Sister Diane would always agree, but she secretly wished that she would be let in on the plan.

"Bishop Anthony, do you think that God has allowed us to create medications to extend our lives?"

"I believe that God allowed man to discover many things to bring ease to his life, but it's man that pursues immortality in God's likeness. It's a modern-day Adam and Eve story on a much grander scale." The bishop sat there cleaning his glasses, speaking as though he had been pondering this for years.

"Does that mean that Christ will have to die on the cross again?" Sister Diane sat on the edge of the chair as she nervously asked the question.

"I don't know. Perhaps it's us who are dying on the cross now. Just much slower. Science and medicine create the cross and then nail us to it with the drugs. Maybe, the Lord calls us home and the medication prevents us from going."

Sister Diane would remember this conversation over all the rest as she saw the consequences of it every day.

During lunch on Wednesday afternoon, between Autumn Life and Elite Care, Father Brendan's curiosity or maybe his guilt overpowered him, and he asked Sister Diane if she still spoke with the bishop. The sister shifted uncomfortably in her chair.

"On rare occasions. Why are you asking? Did he say something to you? Did something happen?" Her full attention was now focused on the priest.

"No, no. I was just wondering, that's all." Now the young priest was shifting in his chair, creating loud creaking sounds with every move and causing more discomfort to Sister Diane. He could no longer hold back the deception and blurted out, "I've been meeting with Bishop Anthony regularly, and I was just curious if you were."

The sister's fury was flaming up, burning away her discomforted fear. She frowned and clenched her fists but made no sound. She just waited.

"Say something, please." Father Brendan reached out with both hands.

She moved back from the table. "Why didn't you say something earlier? Did you talk about me?"

Sister Diane didn't wait for an answer. She rose from her chair, pushed it in with a loud crash against the table, spilling the water, and walked out of the diner. Father Brendan looked around at the other patrons embarrassed. He gave a sheepish grin as he placed two twenty-dollar bills on the table, an amount much higher than the check would be, but he wasn't waiting. He rushed out after Sister Diane, who was now leaning against the car with her arms tightly folded.

"Should I be worried about my job?" Tears streamed down both cheeks as the fear returned. She was now pacing the sidewalk in front of the car. The fear of being tossed from yet another family was too much to bear. The thought of having to return to the convent, to a small room in the back. The unwanted orphan child swooped in with a vengeance.

"Why?" Father Brendan asked.

Her pacing stopped inches from his face. "I don't know what you and the bishop were talking about."

Father Brendan stepped back, feeling uncomfortable with the intrusion to his personal space. "I was asking you if you talked with the bishop because I'm worried about my job."

"Why would you be worried? That makes no sense." Her tears had stopped.

"Really, do you recall how I got this job? First, I worked with Father Timothy, then I replaced him with no warning. So, I was wondering if that was going on again. Only this time I'm Father Timothy." Father Brendan was now staring at the ground. He was ashamed about not coming forward sooner. He knew what it was to be betrayed by those close to you.

"You're a priest, and I'm a sister. And I don't want your job."

"I didn't want Father Timothy's job. I was told to take it." Tears now welled in the priest's eyes.

There was a long pause as Father Brendan was replaying his history with Father Timothy. How the kind old priest had taught him everything. How he held nothing back and then he was gone without even a goodbye. He was feeling the pain all over again.

"Father Brendan, Brendan!" She was now yelling his name, trying to bring him back from whatever painful memory he was reliving.

"Sorry. I was just, uh, thinking. Listen, your job is safe." The priest was still shying away from her as he tried to hide his tears and his shame.

"So is yours. We're a good team." Sister Diane placed a hand his shoulder then removed it with an abrupt jerking motion. She realized that it might send the wrong message to onlookers; after all, they were standing on a sidewalk.

They got into the car. He still thought, *I taught her everything, just like Father Timothy taught me. If Bishop Anthony removes me where will I go? What will I be forced to do next?*

She yelled out his name again. This shocked him back into the present, again.

"Why all the secrecy? What's going on?" A sense of fear was returning to her.

"First, it wasn't a secret, and second, I don't know if anything is going on."

She hoped he wasn't lying, but her fear was telling her not to trust him. He also hoped he wasn't lying. There was little dialog as each was deep in thought about how to handle the information they just learned.

Halfway to the Elite Care, Father Brendan broke the silence. "Do you want to continue on, or should I take you home?"

"Why would I want to stop? Please just keep driving to Elite Care." She looked at him, utterly amazed by the question.

If her job was on the line, the last thing she was going to do was quit early and have the bishop find out. He would think she couldn't do her job. She turned to Father Brendan and inquired why he asked if she wanted to end early. She almost demanded to know if he was going to end early if she did, or if he would go on without her. He hadn't thought it through. He just knew she was upset and was trying to help. Father Brendan pulled the car to the side of the road and shut off the engine.

"I wasn't hiding anything from you until about five minutes ago. I'm not worried about your job. I'm still worried about mine. Unfortunately, it's not up to us." Father Brendan sat looking straight ahead. He could not make eye contact with her at this moment.

"What? Why?" Sister Diane looked straight ahead. She also didn't want to make eye contact.

"I already told you. This is exactly the way I replaced Father Timothy. Bishop Anthony assigned me to Father Timothy, who taught me all he knew and then he suddenly retired. I don't think he retired. Maybe he was fired or forced to retire. All because of me!" Tears began to flow from his eyes again; still, he couldn't face her. The shame he felt for what happened to Father Timothy was all pouring out.

She knew that he needed her help. With the utmost compassion, she asked, "Didn't you ask?"

"I did, and I was told he just decided to retire." Father Brendan removed a white handkerchief from his inside breast pocket and wiped his eyes. There was no denying the free flow of tears.

"But you don't believe that. Do you?" This time she placed her hand on his shoulder and left it there.

Father Brendan finally looked at the sister. "I guess I don't."

"Then we can find out together. It might well get us fired." She gave a tiny chuckle.

"Just leave it alone. We both like our jobs. I'll continue to meet with the bishop and make sure I . . . we stay in his good graces." Father Brendan feinted a smile that Sister Diane didn't accept.

"Are we not in his good graces right now?" She now sensed her own fear returning.

"No, no. You know what I mean. Look, let's not start this all over again." He now grabbed her hand.

He restarted the car and headed for Elite Care. They continued the conversation agreeing to discuss any matter that might put either of them at risk. While they understood they had to trust one another, both had pasts that made them unwilling to fully commit.

31

THE LIBRARY WAS BUSY at this time of day. Cathy waited for Kyle in the lobby. After he arrived, they found an isolated table near the back.

"I created these spreadsheets to better track what was going on. Actually, I made them to see if anything was going on."

"You did this in a matter of days?" Kyle looked at her as he held the stack of papers in his hand.

"Yes, why?" She shot him a look as if to say, *Yes, I'm that good. If only you could get past that one damn mistake, you would know it.*

"I've been putting stuff together for about three months, and I don't have as much as you do." Kyle reached for the flimsy folder holding the copies of his lists.

"I know, I've seen the hidden section on your computer." Cathy waited for the backlash.

"Wait! You what?" Kyle was speaking loudly now and standing over her.

"We're in a library, and yes, a while back I overheard you talking to Lenny about setting it up, and I knew that you kept your passwords on the backside of your blotter."

"I should fire you right now! When this is all over, I'm beefing up our computer security." Kyle attempted to slam the folder on the table for a dramatic effect, but he only managed a meek whoosh from the air that leaked out from between the folder and the table. Both looked at each other.

"Hold those thoughts for later. Right now, we have to clear our names." Cathy was trying hard to fight back the laugh that Kyle would most certainly be offended by.

Kyle understood. He apologized and told her it was just a joke. She ignored the old Kyle that was trying to creep back into the conversation.

She explained how the deaths at Green Haven seemed to take place on Tuesdays and Thursdays, how the residents had all been there for a long time, and finally how all the deaths occurred with residents who had "nurse may pronounce" on their charts. Kyle already knew most of this but let her go on. When she was done, Kyle stated that he hadn't discovered that most of the deaths fell on two specific days.

"I'm guessing we don't need to go over my stuff. Since you already broke into my computer and read everything." Kyle waived the folder in the air then tossed onto the floor next to the table.

"Well, since we're on the same team now. Yes, I can't believe I'm saying that too. I didn't just read it, I, uh copied it too." Cathy pulled away as she waited for the blowback from Kyle. There was none.

"You know that I suspected you at a point, right? Well, you know that day you left an hour early?" Kyle was now smirking as he placed his hands behind his head and leaned back in the library chair.

"No. You didn't." Cathy was impressed and slapped him on the arm.

The smirk left Kyle's face as he confessed. "I tried, but I didn't know your password, and I couldn't ask Lenny."

"You wouldn't have found anything. I was already paranoid because I'm being framed. By leaving all those lists on your computer, you framed yourself."

"How do you know all this?"

Cathy shrugged her shoulders. "Too much alone time at home with a television."

Cathy smiled. She was gaining a new perspective and respect for him. Kyle stood, placing his hands on his hips and trying to fight back a grin as he told her that they'd still have to discuss boundaries. For now, the Pharmatek wound and the years of pouring salt into it had faded.

Kyle started with the first contract on the top of his pile. Anna Sparks came to Green Haven just over six years ago and she, or rather her family, was paying $6,500 a month for her to be there. Kyle flipped to the back of the contract containing a section that gave an estimated cost of a ten-year stay at Green Haven. They were both shocked when Kyle read aloud the figure of $41,300 per year. They both knew that this number was grossly underestimated. Cathy did the math on her phone's calculator. She told Kyle that the estimate, when broken down into a monthly number was only about $3,400 per month. Both realized the numbers were off.

Kyle told her that was just over a fourth of the real cost of staying at Green Haven. Cathy asked who would be so stupid to create such low figures. Kyle added that the person should have known that it would put the company in the red and eventually out of business.

Cathy thought out loud, "What if the person didn't know how to figure the numbers correctly? What if his motive was just to get the place filled up as quickly as possible? What if it was more about looking good?"

"Oscar Green? You think Oscar is behind all of this?" Kyle was shaking his head.

"What if he just wanted his father's name to live on? We've all seen that damn testimonial to his father on the corner of the building. And what nursing facility doesn't take any insurance at all? It makes your client base very narrow." Cathy's eyes were wide, and she spoke faster as her brain played out the scenario.

"Oscar? I don't see it." Kyle placed one hand on the contract and the other almost in Cathy's face as if to ask her to stop.

"Maybe murder wasn't his original plan, but he has to get rid of all the financially bad contracts to bring in more sustainable ones." Her fast cadence was now accompanied by quick, jerky hand movements.

"Oscar, a killer? Nope, I don't think he has it in him. I agree about the money part. He may have had no clue of what he was doing, but wouldn't the board correct it immediately?" Kyle spoke softly, almost at a whisper as he looked around to see if anyone was listening.

"John Perkins! Didn't you say he wanted to look at the financials when he contacted you? Think hard, try to remember everything you can." Cathy had removed the cheaters from her face and was now flaying them in the air around Kyle.

"Shhh. He said he wanted to go over financials of the dead residents. Oh crap! He was coming to look at the contracts, wasn't he? He must've figured it out." He grabbed the glasses from her hands for fear of catching an arm in the eye.

"Let's check more of the contracts to see if there's a pattern. Sorry, too many detective shows." Cathy's speech was returning to a more normal pace, and her hands were now reaching for the next contract and her eyewear.

As they went through the smuggled resident contracts, the same pattern continued to appear. Green Haven was slowly being bled dry by honoring contracts of the long-standing residents. Someone was making room for new residents whose deals would be profitable. After about three hours of searching contracts, collecting the data, and transferring it to Cathy's spreadsheets, both were weary and needed to stop.

It had been a long day and even longer afternoon. Kyle asked if she wanted to get a quick bite before going home. Until now, the thought of having a meal with Kyle Strong would have made her go on a lifelong hunger strike, but now it seemed like the right thing to do. Now they were a team, and he wasn't acting like the vengeful prick of a boss she knew. They decided to go around the corner to a diner that Father Brendan told

Kyle about. They agreed it must be okay to eat there if it had the blessings of a priest.

They sat down in a booth away from the crowd. It would make it easier to discuss anything that might come up. The waitress came over to take their drink orders. She then turned to Cathy and asked if she knew Father Brendan. Cathy thought this was an odd question but answered that she knew him in passing only. The waitress said that he and Sister Diane came into the diner a lot. She followed up with how they were good people. Cathy smiled, and the waitress left. She looked at Kyle and put her hands in the air. Kyle pointed to her shirt. In all the excitement she had forgotten to remove her Green Haven badge. She rolled her eyes and unclipped the badge, shoving it into her purse.

They ate dinner and recapped the afternoon's work, occasionally looking at a spreadsheet to verify some question either might have had. The aftermath of such intense research had drained them. Kyle yawned and motioned for the waitress to bring the check. Cathy was not going to let him pay for her dinner; they hadn't come that far yet. The waitress placed the check on the table. Cathy reached for the check; Kyle took it from her hand. He told her that the least Green Haven could do before it went under was buy them a crappy meal. She looked at him, confused. He smiled and said to her that as the administrator he gets a small expense allowance as long as he submits the receipts. She let go of the check.

Kyle placed cash in the check holder and took the customer copy to submit to Green Haven. He took out a pen and wrote on the copy, "Dinner meeting with DON to discuss her performance."

Cathy could see the letters DON that Kyle had written on the receipt. "What did you write on the receipt?"

Kyle replied, "I have to record what the receipt is for, so I put down it was for your performance evaluation."

Cathy jokingly asked how bad her performance evaluation was.

Kyle answered, "Oh the worst yet." He smiled. "We have to keep up appearances."

Cathy didn't comment, nor did she smile. She knew they were entering a new era in their work relationship. Cathy thought how strange that it took a murder spree to get a better work environment.

They agreed at the library that Kyle would get in early Monday to remove some more contracts so they could compare them to the information they already had. He opened the door of the diner to allow Cathy to leave first. They both found this odd. What was happening to their relationship? She thanked him for opening the door. She found the whole series of events strange and unnerving. Cathy made a joke about thanking Green Haven for dinner. She moved toward Kyle and gave him a hug, accidentally placing her hands over his chest.

Kyle didn't expect this display of emotion and stepped back. Cathy was just as shocked by it. She quickly held out her hand, and he shook it. Cathy was trying to make sense of why she just hugged the man who tormented her for so many years. She made a mental note not to touch Kyle ever again. She now wondered what Kyle was thinking but didn't dare ask. They each walked their cars, making sure not to look back at the other.

Cathy didn't go directly home. Her spreadsheets were now filled with new information. She needed to make copies, so she drove to a nearby convenience store she knew had an old copy machine for public use. She made copies of everything. The store clerk became annoyed with having to make changes several times before she finished. She also bought a large padded envelope and stamps. She placed the copies inside with a note to her sister, Lisa. The note requested that Lisa not read any of the contents or tell anyone about receiving it. She asked Lisa to place the envelope in a safe place. She signed and dated the note as well as each page of the copies. Cathy addressed the envelope to her sister, drove to the post office, and put the envelope in the mailbox. Exhausted, she headed for home, already dreaming of sleep.

32

MONDAY MORNING, 6:00 AM, Cathy turned on the television as she made breakfast. She switched the channel to the local news and couldn't believe what she was hearing. The news anchor was talking about breaking news of a local man who was found dead in his apartment this morning.

"Kyle Strong, administrator of Green Haven nursing facility, was found dead by his landlord, who heard a loud noise and knocked on the door. There was evidence of a struggle." Cathy dropped the glass bowl she was holding. It crashed to the floor, shattering, creating shards of blue glass that swam in a scrambled egg sea. She let them sit on the floor.

She knew she was next. They had gotten too close to figuring out the truth. But how, who? There was no time to waste. She had to go to the police before the killer got to her. Scared, Cathy first made sure her door was locked, and then she started picking up the pieces of broken glass. Her hands were shaking so much it became difficult to pick up the glass. The palm of her right hand began to bleed as the jagged edge of glass protruded from it. The blood immediately dripped onto the floor. Cathy ran to the sink, removed the small shard, and began to wash the wound. She used a towel to dry it and could see she was going to need stitches. The police were going to have to wait. Her nursing skills instinctively kicked in. She applied a pressure dressing, got dressed, and headed for the walk-in clinic four blocks away. It would be faster than the hospital emergency department. Cathy thought there would be less of a trail going to a random walk-in clinic than the regional hospital. She needed to stay hidden until she could get into the hands of the police.

After filling out all the paperwork, Cathy saw the physician assistant and was told she'd need a few stitches. Something she already knew. Even though the clinic was nearly empty, Cathy couldn't shake the feeling of being watched. More specifically, being watched by the killer. She realized that her mind was again adrift in an ocean of extrapolation of detective show reruns. Cathy was now actively talking to herself.

"Stop it! You have to stay in control. Your life depends on it."

"Are you okay? Maybe we should get you to the hospital. How exactly did you cut your hand again?" the PA asked, now more skeptical of the whole situation.

"No. I'm fine. I just don't do well with seeing my own blood."

Cathy became acutely aware that she was very close to winning a ride to the psych ward for a three-day vacation. Cathy smiled, telling the PA she would just look away and everything would be fine. The PA bought it. Cathy understood that being locked in a psych ward might be safe, but it would start a flurry of questions that would eventually implicate her to far worse deeds.

The local anesthetic took hold quickly, and Cathy's right hand was sutured and dressed. She squirmed now and then and gave the occasional whimper for good measure. She was told to see her regular doctor, have the hand looked at further, and in time, have the stitches removed. Again, something she already knew. A prescription for an antibiotic was called in to her pharmacy. She'd get it later.

During the clinic performance, Cathy concluded that she couldn't go to the police just yet. She needed to secure Kyle's computer and make a final sweep to see if she had left any evidence tracing back to her. She couldn't have anything pointing to her. The police would eventually get around to searching Green Haven, and they'd find the envelope in her desk suspecting Kyle. They might think that she killed him before he could kill her. She had to get to her desk.

Cathy pulled into the parking lot where five or six police cars were parked. She could see through the large front windows of Kyle's office that the police were already going through Kyle's belongings. She decided to go in and tell the police all she knew about what was going on at Green Haven. Hell, after she told the police, there would be no job anyway. Cathy got out of her car and walked into the building. She was met by a police officer, who asked her name. She told the officer and was immediately escorted inside. The officer told her to sit in the lobby and a detective would come to speak with her. The officer stood between her and the front door. Something Cathy noted immediately. Cathy told the officer she had information they needed to know. The officer again asked her to sit, and he would get a detective. A few minutes later, a Detective Oaks came over and asked her to follow him. They walked into the front conference room; a room Cathy had been in many times since coming to Green Haven. Now it felt entirely different. It seemed much smaller and closing in on her. Something was not right.

"For your protection we're going to tape our conversation. You should also know that we've been trying to reach you for a few hours now. Why haven't you been answering your phone?" Detective Oaks maintained eye contact with Cathy during his entire statement.

Cathy's eyes were fixed on the mini video camera whose tiny red light shined at her like a lighthouse beacon in some parallel universe.

"Nurse Arden. Are you paying attention?"

"I'm sorry. Yes. I left my cell phone at home." Cathy tried to focus, but the red light called her like a siren's song.

"Where were you?" The detective's eyes were still fixed on her. He was watching every twitch, every breath she took.

Cathy held up her right hand, bringing Detective Oaks, full attention to the new bright white bandage wrapped around her it.

"What happened to your hand?"

"I was making scrambled eggs when I saw the news about Kyle. I dropped the bowl, then when I started cleaning it up, I cut my hand on a sharp piece."

"Where were you for the past hour?"

"At the walk-in not too far from my home."

"Tell me again how you cut your hand."

"I . . . wait, what are you thinking?"

Cathy looked directly at the detective, trying hard to not show the fear of her realization. She started playing back yesterday's events with Kyle in her mind. She had been with him in the library. At one point his voice was almost a shout. After dinner, on the street, she had tried to hug him, and he pulled away. Anyone watching would surely think they were arguing.

"What was your relationship with Mr. Strong, uh Kyle?" Detective Oaks showed no emotion and no body language. He was stone cold.

"He was my boss." Cathy remembered the detective shows and tried not to show any emotion or body language of her own.

"Is that all he was to you?" The detective was tapping a pen on the table while looking at papers that rested on top of it. Other than looking at her bandaged hand, this was the only time he took his eyes off of her.

"Yes!" The thought of anyone thinking that she and Kyle were anything but coworkers made Cathy's mind want to scream in revolt. She wanted to say she hated the man but thought better of it. The truth was that after yesterday, she didn't hate him. She didn't say that either.

"A waitress at a diner not too far from here says you had dinner together last night. She remembers because she saw your badge." He was now staring directly at her with the pen clenched tightly in his right hand.

"Yes, that's true. But it was a work-related dinner." Cathy was now unable to keep her uneasiness hidden as her feet began to shuffle under the table.

"The receptionist says you both left here around 4:00 pm yesterday. Dinner was around 7:00 pm, according to the waitress. Did you go anywhere with Mr. Strong before dinner? Maybe back to his place?"

"Yes, I mean no. We met at the library. Do I need a lawyer?" Cathy was now in panic mode, but she recalled that the people being interviewed always asked for a lawyer.

"That's up to you. You said you have information to share with us."

"Yes, yes. Someone is murdering residents at Green Haven," she almost screamed.

The detective flipped through his notes. "Do you know who Martin is?"

"No. Yes, he's the head of facility operations here." Cathy's eyes darted away from the detective.

"I think you might what to consider an attorney before you go any further." Detective Oaks placed the pen on the table then stood up.

"I didn't kill Kyle! That's crazy. We were working together to . . ."

"Miss Arden, I'm going to take you in for further questioning at this time. You should know that a search warrant is being used to go through your apartment as we speak."

"I'd like a lawyer." Cathy saw that her worst nightmare was unfolding before her.

Oscar Green sat in a back office with a younger detective who explained to him what was going to happen next. The authorities were going to do a full investigation into Cathy Arden and the death of Kyle Strong. They already had a statement from the receptionist that there was a large and rather loud argument earlier yesterday between Mr. Strong and Miss Arden. Oscar was stunned. He was finding it hard to believe that his dream was the setting for a murder.

Dr. Oliver was walking in as Cathy was being escorted out of Green Haven in handcuffs. Dr. Oliver identified herself to the officer at the door, who then verified her credentials. She knew Oscar was here. His car was in the parking lot amidst the police cars and who knows how many unmarked vehicles. She asked to speak with Mr. Green. After a short conversation with a younger detective, Dr. Oliver was taken back to the same room Oscar had been sitting in patiently. They were both told this could be an active crime scene and not to touch anything. They were not to leave the room without an officer. Oscar and Marissa looked at each other, both thinking the same thing. Would their personal relationship be revealed?

"Oscar, don't say anything about us that isn't work related. We came in separately and for now, there is no us outside of Green Haven. Can you do this?"

"Yes. Does that mean that we're still good after this?" He reached for her hand.

"Oscar! Focus. Right now, we have to be professional only," she demanded as she pulled away from him.

"Okay, okay. I got it." Oscar sat back down.

Marissa had seen the news about Kyle and came in to see if there was anything she could do. Oscar filled her in on the rest. She told Oscar she had spoken with the receptionist shortly after the fight between Cathy and Kyle must have occurred. She explained that the woman was visibly shaken. Oscar told her she needed to tell the police this. Marissa clarified she came in to help the residents and she didn't want to be involved. She admitted to Oscar she didn't see or hear any of the fight. She told him it wouldn't make a difference. Oscar went along with this, too.

Marissa could see Oscar practically dancing in his chair like a small child waiting for the church sermon to end. "Oscar, look at me. You have to keep it together. We didn't do anything."

"Then why are we hiding things from the police?" His hands grasped tightly onto the armrest of the chair.

"You know our relationship is inappropriate. If it gets out, I'll be fired, and you'll be kicked off the board. This has nothing to do with the murder. Relax and sit still."

"So, they won't care." His hands let go of the chair's arms.

"Oscar, if they know, it could slip out in a press conference, and then what?" Her voice was now softer as she tried to reason with him.

"Fine." Oscar had now regained a comfortable appearance.

In Kyle's office, a team of officers looked for any clues to Kyle's murder. They came across the locked filing cabinet and no keys. They picked open the lock and found nothing but an empty space. They searched the computer and found nothing out of the ordinary. They looked at every item in the office and finally found the passwords written on the underside of the blotter. One of the junior detectives asked the receptionist if she could recognize Mr. Strong's handwriting. She identified the writing on the back of the blotter as Kyle's.

A second team was rummaging through the director of nursing's office looking for evidence. Her computer was turned off. They fired it up, and a request for a password came up. Lenny, the IT guy, was already called to come into Green Haven to assist with any computer issues. He was asked if there was any other way into the computer.

"I always build a back way into the computers I set up, just in case of situations like this." Lenny's sunken chest was once again making an attempt to peacock into glory.

"You mean, like a murder?" The uniformed office at the door sneered, letting Lenny know his place.

Lenny's shoulders sunk forward, causing his chest to return to its normal divot shaped position. "Gosh, no! I mean, uh, when someone can't remember their password or, uh, they get locked out for any reason."

The officer got up from the chair and gave a hand motion for Lenny to sit. He sat at the keyboard and typed in some words, and the computer responded. Lenny rose from the chair to allow the officer back into the system. He stood there as the officer went through Cathy's computer. She

system. He stood there as the officer went through Cathy's computer. She found nothing. She asked Lenny if he had noticed anything out of the ordinary about Nurse Arden. At first Lenny said no, but then he recalled that the Bluetooth on her printer had been turned on one day last week. The officer looked confused.

"HIPPA regulations are very strict and very clear on access to people's information, so Green Haven's policy prohibits connecting to any Bluetooth devices." Lenny's nervousness caused his pitch to rise as he spewed word after word without thinking.

"How does that apply here?"

"The other day Cathy called me into her office to help her find records on residents that were no longer here. When I walked in, my phone pinged, telling me that a Bluetooth device was active near me. Cathy's printer Bluetooth had been turned on. She said she didn't know how it got on. She said she didn't even know how to turn it on." Lenny began to sway back and forth.

"Do you think she was lying?" the officer asked while quickly scribbling notes into a small notebook.

"I don't know. She said that it must have gone on when we rebooted the system, but that's not possible."

"What's your opinion, Lenny? You have to tell us the truth, or else we could get suspicious." The officer could see Lenny was spinning out of control and wanted to nudge him over the edge.

Lenny raised his hands. He didn't want to be the one to get Cathy in trouble, but he was more afraid of lying to the police. "She could have been in on it. But she didn't even know how to search the system for dead residents. So, I'm not sure." Lenny had moved to a corner in the room and literally had his back against the wall. An irony that was not lost on the officer standing at the door, who smiled at the other officer sitting at the desk.

The officer made some notations in the small pad sitting next to her on the desk. Lenny tried to see what she was writing, but she glared him away.

The officer opened the top drawer of Cathy's desk, and there was a large envelope marked "for police only." She radioed Detective Oaks to ask him to come to the DON's office so she could show him what she had found. Detective Oaks and two other detectives appeared seconds later. He asked Lenny to leave the office. He looked at the others and said it just can't be this easy. Detective Oaks put on a new pair of gloves, placed the envelope on the desk and began to open it. He started to read the letter to himself, but then thought it better to read it aloud so everyone in the room could hear the same evidence if they needed to testify.

The dated letter in the envelope detailed how Cathy was afraid of Kyle, her confrontation with him earlier in the morning, and that he now knew that she was onto his plan. It also described how Cathy believed that Kyle was killing residents at Green Haven and framing her for the murders. The last section of the letter detailed that she was meeting him at the town library later that day and if she had gone missing or turned up dead, the police were to blame Kyle Strong.

A call came over the radio for the detective in Cathy's office requesting that he and the IT guy return to the administrator's office immediately.

"Put everything back into the envelope and bag it all. Do it by the book. No mistakes." Detective Oaks let out a breath of frustration and left the tiny office. As he headed down the hallway, he grabbed Lenny by the arm, pulling him along.

An officer sitting at the computer asked Lenny if he knew why there was a second password. Lenny told them that a short time ago Mr. Strong asked him to set up a second user on his computer that would require a different password. The officer asked him if he found this strange. Lenny replied that he worked in a place with so many rules and regulations regarding computers and information that nothing was strange. He told them he was the IT guy and not the regulations person. If the boss wanted a second username or password on his computer, then he got it. No questions asked.

One of the officers restarted the computer and typed in the password when requested. A single folder was now on the desktop; she opened it. The officer took a screenshot of the page. She had a second officer with a camera take a photo of the page. She opened the folder then the first file. A list of Green Haven residents appeared on the screen. It meant nothing to the officers. They opened each file in the folder and copied the secret files just in case. The officer then disconnected the computer and had it taken to the lab for further investigation.

Oscar called one of the officers and told him that he and Dr. Oliver were ready to leave the building. Detective Oaks saw them in the lobby and asked for their phone numbers in case he had questions. Both of them gave the detective their numbers along with a business card. Oscar and Marissa left the building and headed in opposite directions without any indication of a personal relationship.

Father Brendan pulled into the parking lot with Sister Diane in the passenger seat. Both looked at each other with amazement and fear. They had heard about Kyle on the radio and changed their plans to make sure the residents at Green Haven were okay. Marissa recognized Sister Diane and stopped them. She explained the situation to them. Father Brendan stated that the residents needed them even more today. Dr. Oliver countered that there were already too many people in the building, and it would be better if they came back tomorrow when they were scheduled. She went on to say that it might be too much change for the residents at this time. She insisted that showing up on a different day in the middle of all this commotion might send the wrong message. Sister Diane agreed. Father Brendan didn't say a word, turned the car around, and left Green Haven. Not a word was spoken between them.

33

THE OFFICERS OPENED THE door to Cathy's apartment and saw the television still on and the appearance of a rushed exit. They carefully moved into the apartment, finding a large pool of dried blood and shards of broken blue glass on the kitchen floor. As they traveled deeper into Cathy's home, they found spots of blood on the carpet leading to the bedroom. A towel lay on the bed fixed in a contoured shape from the crusted blood.

The officers looked at one another and in an almost instinctive manner began to open closet doors and drawers around the apartment searching for more clues. An officer pulled out a large folder marked G. H. on it. In the folder were spreadsheets, lists, and contracts. He looked at the other officers and told them to be extra careful. Everything by the books; this one could be a serial killer. He called Detective Oaks to fill him in.

A second officer opened up the trashcan that was standing in the corner of the kitchen and found broken glass covered in blood. He called over the senior officer and showed him the contents. "Don't touch it. Leave it for forensics." The senior officer stepped into the hallway to make a second phone call to the detective. He returned shortly and told the team to bag the bloody towel and papers and lock the door; they had enough.

Cathy had been placed in an interrogation room and asked if she had an attorney to call. She did not. She didn't know any attorneys. She didn't even know anyone who knew an attorney. She asked them to assign one to her. In the crime shows, they always said that an attorney can be provided for the suspect. She figured having any attorney for the moment was better than going it alone.

A few hours later, an older, overweight gentleman, Brian Landers, walked into the interrogation room and introduced himself as her attorney. Cathy thought she might wake up from this dream to find she was an actress in a detective show, because her attorney was just too much of a cliché for all of this to be real.

Without saying hello, he abruptly said she had already told them too much and they were thinking she killed Kyle and possibly others. Cathy told him over and over she didn't kill Kyle. She was about to start from the beginning with the whole story when he stopped her.

"Don't say anything right now."

Cathy's eyes widened; her attorney didn't want to hear her side. The attorney caught the look of confusion on her face. She was about to overrule him but stopped when he raised his hands to indicate a rather forceful "shut up, now."

"You can tell me when we get out of here. For now, shut up. Please! Do you understand?" His jolly smile turned into pursed lips, and his eyes opened to almost insane.

"Yes." Cathy thought about asking for another attorney, but he did say he was getting her out of here, or something to that effect.

Detective Oaks returned to the room and asked if they had enough time to get acquainted. Cathy gave a worried looked at her lawyer as he told the detective they were good for now. Detective Oaks started with questions, and Attorney Landers responded that his client would not be answering any more questions.

"Are you charging my client with anything at this time?" He was staring directly at the detective.

Cathy almost smiled at hearing the detective show line but snapped back to reality as she imagined how much worse a yes from the detective would be.

"We're working on it." Detective Oaks understood the rules of the game and knew that Attorney Landers was just playing his part. He took no real offense to it.

"Then let us know when you're done working on it, and we'll come back. If you still need us." The attorney placed his hand on the back of Cathy's chair, signaling her to stand and walk out of the room.

Cathy froze for a moment as the power of her attorney's action overtook the room. He had put the mighty detective in his place, just like on television, only much more dramatic. All she needed now was a "Don't leave town" comment. She looked back at the detective as they walked down the hallway. He didn't give her the satisfaction, just a cold stare that kept her in the seriousness of the moment.

For the first time since cutting her hand this morning, she noticed the pain. She needed something for the pain. She asked her attorney if they could swing past her place for a change of clothes and some pain medication for her hand.

"Unfortunately, that is not in the cards, as they say." Attorney Landers informed Cathy that her apartment was considered a secondary crime scene. "I'll make sure we get you something for the pain. Don't worry."

"What do you mean my apartment is a crime scene?" Cathy felt the cold shiver of daunting gloom run down her spine.

"Apparently the place is covered in blood." There was an unspoken "did you do it?" behind the statement. Cathy understood the tone and held up her hand.

Attorney Landers had defended many guilty clients. He never asked if they actually did it. His job was to defend them. He knew he couldn't sleep at night if he knew the answer to that question. He decided long ago not to even consider it. Secretly, he wondered if she injured her hand struggling with Kyle before killing him.

Once inside the car, Cathy couldn't hold it in anymore. She started from the beginning and didn't take a breath until she reached the point where she had met her attorney. When she was done, Attorney Landers took a deep breath and asked her where all the proof of this was. She recounted she had two sets, one in her office and the other at her home. Attorney Landers surmised that the police now had both sets and were planning to use them against her. He didn't share this information with her just yet. Cathy didn't share the set sent to her sister.

"But why and who murdered Kyle?" Landers asked, trying to make sense of everything he just heard.

"I don't know. We must have gotten too close to what was going on. Just like John Perkins."

"Who is John Perkins?"

"Green Haven, Inc.'s treasurer. He was killed too, for the same reason."

"We'll keep that to ourselves for now. Okay?" The attorney knew that any related murders would just be considered the continuation of her alleged killing spree.

"Okay." Cathy still didn't know what to make of her attorney.

"Let's get you to a place I know where you can spend the night."

"I have money if we stop at an ATM."

Attorney Landers shook his head. "No, I don't think that will work either. They're probably already looking into your bank accounts."

"I didn't do anything wrong." Her voice was now pleading for a teammate.

"Actually, you did. You should have gone to the police right away. Now all the evidence points to you."

"I didn't think they'd believe me. Do you believe me?" Cathy felt the moment of weakness come over her, but it was too late, she already spoke the words of a guilty and desperate client.

Landers realized he had overstepped and offered a kind, "Of course I believe you. I'm your lawyer."

Cathy sat quietly, thinking that they distrusted each other. She knew that if she could get the paperwork, she could prove to him and the police that she was innocent and that Kyle was killed for what they knew. Suddenly a deep fear set in. Cathy just remembered that she was now on the hit list. She looked at Attorney Landers, wondering if he was actually an assassin hired to finish the job. Cathy took a deep, clearing breath. "Were you paid?"

"It's too early for that."

"No. Were you paid to kill me?" Cathy had her right hand on the door handle readying herself to bail from the car and roll on to the pavement just like in the movies. It was the only thing she could think of to get away.

"Do you understand the concept of a public defender? Especially the defender part?" Landers saw her hand on the door handle. "Don't do it. I'm not in the mood for an ER visit."

"Kyle was killed, and I'm pretty sure I'm next on the list. Just tell me if you were hired to kill me. She stared at the attorney with the same defiant look she had used in Kyle's office only days earlier.

"I was hired to defend you; that's it. Look, you don't have much choice at this point." He pulled the car to the side of the road and unlocked the doors. "You have to trust me."

"I could say the same to you." Cathy fought hard to make sure her voice didn't shake.

"Fair enough. Okay, I wasn't paid to kill you. I'm not going to kill you, and I don't know if you're on a hit list, but I'm going to do my best to keep you from being crossed off it. We good?" Attorney Landers restarted the car. Cathy gave a smile at the hit list line and started to relax.

Landers drove to a motel on the opposite side of town. It was a rundown structure with two floors and endless exterior doors, most of which had various degrees of damage. Cathy wanted to protest as she sat there with her arms crossed. Her hand was now throbbing.

"It looks like crap, I know, but it's clean. No bedbugs or roaches, and the sheets are fresh every day. I use this place quite a bit for clients. Come on, room 105. It's around the back."

Cathy didn't say a word. She followed him to the front door of 105. It seemed not to have any damage. That's a good start, she thought. He opened the door; the interior was circa 1970, wood paneling, light brown shag carpeting—at least it was brown now—and a floral bedspread.

"All the comforts of home." He gave her a fake smile, trying to lighten the mood.

"What about the pain medication for my hand?" She held her right hand in the air and made a painful gasp as she moved her fingers.

"Had my assistant pick up some extra strength something or another. It should be on the sink. Lock the door and don't open it until I come back in the morning. No one knows you're here." He handed her the key and started out the door.

Cathy wasn't sure if that was a good or bad thing. She closed the door, making sure that every possible lock was locked.

34

OSCAR CALLED MARISSA AS soon as he got into his car. He asked if she wanted to come over. She looked out her car window at him with amazement. He told her it wasn't for sex; it was to discuss what just happened. He added that they could get a bite instead. He just needed someone to talk to. She agreed. They both drove back to his place. Inside, Oscar went over to the bar and poured himself Scotch and Marissa bourbon. She pointed to her watch.

"First of all, it's never too early, and second, after what just happened, I don't care. You know, I remember my first sip of Scotch. My uncle always drinks Scotch. When I was thirteen, he and my dad were sitting in our living room; he asked me to pour him a Scotch. I went over to the bar and opened the bottle. I took a sniff from the bottle; I must have made an awful face. When I handed him the Scotch, he looked at my father and then told me to take a sip. It was the worst thing I'd ever tasted. I almost puked right there. He and my dad laughed. My uncle told my father that at least I wouldn't ever steal from the liquor cabinet. Look at me today. Now it's my drink of choice." Oscar held the faux-crystal glass in the air as he admired the bronze-colored liquid.

"Did you?" Marissa was trying to look interested, but her mind was a million miles away.

"Did I what?"

"Steal from the liquor cabinet."

"No. There were only a couple things you didn't do to my father. One was lie, and the other was steal."

"You momma's boy." She gave a faint and very fake smile then realized she had been harsh.

Marissa knew he needed to calm down, so she let him finish, and then she came up with a story about why she drinks bourbon. The truth was she just preferred it. The lie worked; Oscar was relaxed.

"How are you so calm?" Oscar paced behind the bar taking sips of the Scotch.

Dr. Oliver remained seated on the couch. "In my line of work, death is common. You get hardened to it. Not because you want to, but because you have to."

"This isn't a death! It's a murder, and the killer was my employee." Oscar was almost yelling, and now he was pacing well beyond the bar.

He was on edge again. Marissa assured him it would all blow over as soon as the next politician or celebrity caused a scandal. She called him over to the couch and put her arm around him as she continued to explain that the only thing people like more than a murder is a scandal.

He laughed because he knew it was true. If he could weather a week or two, surely something new and more eye-catching would put Green Haven on the has-been list fast.

Oscar picked up the remote to turn on the news. Marissa took it from his hand and kissed him hard. Oscar forgot about Green Haven for the next hour. Dr. Oliver always knew which medicine was right. Marissa got up from the bed and dressed. He asked if she was leaving. She sat on the edge of a chair to put her shoes on and smiled. She was good for just leaving without much being said. A trait that Oscar found incredibly annoying yet oddly sexy. He heard the door close, and he reached for the remote. The television came on, and a commercial was playing. Oscar flipped through the channels; there was no mention of Green Haven. Kyle's death didn't even get a sound bite. He was amazed. He sat up in bed and looked at himself in the mirror.

Oscar's cell phone rang; it was Marissa. "Miss me already?" He hoped that she had changed her mind and was coming back.

"Turn off the television. It's only going to upset you."

Oscar looked at the phone as if it were spying on him. "Actually, there's no mention of any of it."

"Really, how odd."

"That's what I thought. But I'm not unhappy about it. Maybe the police are keeping a lid on it, or maybe I'm not as important as I think I am. Thank God." Oscar lay back down on the bed.

Marissa drove home. She called Green Haven to tell them she was taking the day off. Then she headed for the shower and a change of clothes. She flipped on the television as she got dressed. She too was amazed. How does he do it? How does he keep out of trouble? Not a single word about any of it. Marissa thought that soon she would be looking for a new job. Not an experience she would enjoy. Marissa had become very comfortable in her position as medical director, a seat on the board, and decent sex. She smiled as she thought about how good life was turning out. After a bite to eat, something Oscar failed to deliver, although, that might have been more her fault, she hopped into her car to start her errands for the day.

Oscar lay in his bed thinking it was one of the strangest days of his life. A murder, an arrest, and sex all in the same day; he was content to just lie there for a few more hours. He was hungry. Pizza, that's what this day needed. Oscar picked up his phone and ordered a cheese pizza. He chuckled; just cheese was good. He'd already had enough excitement for the day. As he waited for his pizza, he began to wonder why no one from the board had called him. They'd need to have an emergency meeting to discuss a plan. They'd need to find a new administrator and a new director of nursing in addition to a new treasurer. Then it hit him. Did she kill both Kyle and John? Why? How did she even know John Perkins? Something was going on. Cathy Arden had never shown any signs of being a killer. So why did she snap now?

The doorbell rang. As Oscar put on his robe and walked to the door, he decided that the police should handle Nurse Arden. He signed for the pizza, giving the deliveryman a ten-dollar tip. Oscar's father always said to keep the delivery guy happy; he's handling your food with no one else around to witness it. Oscar poured another Scotch and sat on the couch with his pizza. He was about to turn on the TV when thoughts of the board returned to his mind. He picked up his phone and dialed Elliot Jenson, a board member. He left Elliot a message about having an emergency board meeting and asked him to call back ASAP. Oscar dove into his pizza. Four slices and two Scotches later, he was sprawled out on the couch in a full-belly coma. He didn't hear his phone vibrating. It was Elliot returning his call. The board was meeting in an hour to figure out what to do. Elliot apologized for the short notice, but everything was last minute.

Five hours later Marissa returned to check on Oscar. She had been at the emergency board meeting. She was unable to call him from the meeting, as that would have drawn suspicion. She used the key that Oscar had given her. A key that she reluctantly took; it was too much of a commitment for her. She never offered Oscar a key to her place, and he never asked for one. As she opened the door, there was Oscar laid out on the couch, robe undone exposing more than she was expecting to see. She couldn't help but let out a loud laugh that startled Oscar awake. Out of instinct, he almost threw the empty Scotch glass that was still in his hand. This made her laugh even harder.

"What have you been up to?" She was standing in front of him with one hand holding her stomach and the other wiping the tears of laughter from her eyes.

"I wasn't expecting any company, and I got hungry."

"Close your robe, please. Why didn't you answer your cell phone?"

"I didn't hear it." He was now standing and adjusting the robe that had betrayed him.

"Elliot said he tried to reach you about an hour before the meeting. He said he left you a message."

"Damn! I must have slept through it. Tell me what happened. I'll call the board later and make my apologies."

Marissa recapped the meeting, telling him the board would naturally look to fill the necessary positions immediately. As far as the reputation of Green Haven, Inc., they had decided to wait it out. Since there hadn't been any mention of Green Haven on the midday or evening news, waiting seemed to be the best road to take. She continued that the board was curious as to the lack of media coverage, but they were not going to look for trouble.

Oscar looked at her and asked what time it was. She looked at her watch and told him it was 6:30 pm. Oscar had slept for the better part of five hours. Marissa wanted to make a joke about the sex wearing him out, but she figured he had been humiliated enough for one day.

35

CATHY DIDN'T SLEEP AT all last night, again. Her life was currently on display, she was a suspect in a murder, and all she wanted to do was go home. The attorney knocked on her door at 9:00 am. For the last several hours she had been working hard to wear down the already threadbare carpet. Tears had been cascading from her checks the entire time as she attempted to figure out how she got caught up in all of this. She opened the door, and Brian Landers Esq. was standing there looking fresh as could be imagined.

"Good morning. Today is a new day. My office has done a little digging into what you told me last night. I believe you. So now we have to move forward." He handed her a pair of blue jeans, a white top, and a rather old-maidish sweater. Cathy looked at him, amazed and confused.

"I think they'll fit. After all these years, I'm a pretty good judge." Landers placed both hands on the lapels of his jacket and grinned.

"Why would I lie to you? And thanks for the clothes. Well, maybe not the sweater. Do you mind if I skip it?" She flung the sweater on the bed as she headed for the bathroom to change.

"Be my guest. I found all this at a secondhand store not too far from here. Don't worry; it's clean. I checked. Sorry, I didn't want to purchase any undergarments for you. We're not there yet. That was a joke." Landers closed the outside door and sat on the only chair in the room. He quietly waited for her to come out of the bathroom.

Cathy found his overly cheery outlook unsettling. She knew nothing of the man other than he sprang her out of jail. She was grateful for that.

"Mr. Landers, I didn't thank you for getting me out of jail last night. Thank you."

"That's my job, and call me Brian. I think we're going to be spending a lot of time together in the weeks to come. We have to go back down to the police station today and talk with Detective Oaks again, but this time I'll be sitting there with you. I won't let you answer or say anything that will harm you."

Cathy's tears began to flow again. She was afraid. The interrogation room had served its purpose, and Cathy thought for a moment that she would suffer some form of PTSD for a long time as a result.

"If it becomes anything less than civil, I'll stop the interview and we'll leave." Brian was now standing with his hands tucked under his middle-aged love handles, desperately looking to make contact with his hips.

Cathy was finding more comfort in his words, and his cliché persona added much-needed levity into the air. She grabbed her purse, thanking Brian again for remembering to pick it up while they were in the station. They headed down to the car and started for the police station. On the drive, Brian explained that the police might be fishing for information and she should only answer the question that was asked with as few words as possible. He told her not to look evasive but don't offer information they weren't asking for. Cathy could hear her heartbeat get faster. She was scared. Brian could see it and told her she'd do just fine.

Truth is Brian had no idea. He knew as much about Cathy as she knew about him. What Cathy didn't know was that she had been released to Brian with the understanding that he would bring her back to the station for further questioning today. This made him think they had a lot more information on her, and none of it was going to be good. Attorney Landers had been practicing law for twenty-two years and took his fair share of charity cases, but this was going to be a high profile one when it hit the news. He had to bring his A game. He hoped he remembered what that was after all these years.

Once inside the police station, they were escorted to a larger, cleaner conference room where the same video camera had been set up. Cathy looked at Brian, who assured her it was standard procedure. Detective Oaks entered the room and sat down at the head of the table. He immediately began tapping the pen. Brian looked at Cathy as if to tell her this was just his way of unsettling her. She understood the look.

Cathy again was hypnotized by the red light from the camera. She couldn't stop staring at it. Brian called her name twice before she returned to the room.

Detective Oaks asked if they needed anything before they started. He asked Cathy to recount Friday's events from the minute she got to work to the minute she went to bed. Cathy again looked at her attorney, who nodded for her to start. He knew the police must have most of the details already and he would stop her if she was about to say anything incriminating.

Cathy told the detective how she thought Kyle was a serial killer and the plan she had to steal his keys and unlock the filing cabinet. How she was going to change the password to the secret section in his computer and then use the files to prove he was the killer. She added that Kyle came back to his office unexpectedly from the morning meeting and caught her in the filing cabinet. She again looked at Brian, who again gave her a reassuring nod to continue. She explained how she hadn't been able to change the password because Kyle came in. Cathy then backtracked, remembering that the receptionist came in first to place a letter on the desk and she had to lie about why she was in the office. When Kyle came in, they started to argue and he asked the receptionist to leave the room. Cathy stated that she was afraid and wanted the receptionist to stay, but

Kyle made her leave. She was staring at the red light again, but this time she was able to pull herself back.

"Why didn't you call the police?" Detective Oaks asked, again without looking up from his papers.

"I regret that now. I didn't call because I thought Kyle was setting me up out of revenge."

"You thought he was killing people to set you up for his own revenge?" A non-believing frown came over the detective's face as he finally looked at Cathy.

"No, I didn't know why he was killing people. I just thought he was framing me out of revenge." They were now looking eye to eye. Cathy was refusing to let her fear of the detective win.

He asked her to continue. She explained how Kyle started to fill her in on his own investigation and how he thought she was the murderer. Then she shared that Kyle asked her to agree that neither of them was the killer. They both thought it was too dangerous to discuss their findings at work and decided to meet at the town library at 4:30 pm. Cathy asked for some water. Detective Oaks reached for the camera, and the red light disappeared.

When he left the room, she asked Brian if it was okay to lay this all out. He told her to tell the truth and not to worry about it.

Detective Oaks returned with two glasses of water. He sat down and turned the camera back on. He asked Cathy to please continue.

Cathy told him that after a few hours of comparing their information and searching through resident contracts together, they were tired and called it quits. They went to dinner, at Kyle's request, and afterward went their separate ways. Then yesterday morning when she was making breakfast, she turned on the news and heard Kyle was dead. She dropped the bowl she was using and cut herself trying to clean it up. She went to the walk-in for stitches and then drove to Green Haven.

Detective Oaks asked if that was her entire statement. Cathy stood up and said that there was no more to tell except that she didn't kill Kyle; they were working together.

Attorney Landers placed his hand on Cathy's forearm signaling her to stop talking, then he interjected, "What Ms. Arden means is that she and Mr. Strong were working together to solve the killings, not to commit them." He made sure the Detective understood the difference.

The Detective reached over and turned off the camera. He opened the door and allowed them to pass out of the conference room. As they were headed down the hallway, he called out to Cathy and reminded her not to leave town. Cathy let out a small smile, making sure the detective didn't see it.

They walked out of the building and headed for Brian's car. Cathy asked how he thought it went. He replied that the police didn't ask her any questions, which meant they knew what she was going to say and had already checked the facts. He muttered just a little too loud that they must have more.

Cathy felt her skin turn cold. "What does that mean? And don't hold back."

Brian turned and looked at Cathy. Again, he placed his hand on her forearm, this time for comfort. "The police are not telling us everything. I can sense this."

"Sense it? Let's go back and ask them." Cathy made a turning motion like she was heading back into the police station.

Brian was now holding onto her arm more tightly. "That's not how it works."

"How bad is it really? Don't lie!" Cathy was standing only inches from the attorney

Brian took a step back. "I'm not lying. I think it's bad, but I don't really know."

Brian had managed to walk them over and into the car as their conversation continued. He didn't want to keep talking in front of the police station. The video cameras would watch every interaction, and since they were in public, the footage could be used against his client.

"What's next?" Cathy said as she entered the passenger seat.

He started to drive and ignored the question, following up with one of his own. "Where are all the papers you were talking about?"

"The originals are at my home and copies are in my desk at work."

A cold stare came over Cathy's face as she remembered the envelope to the police in her desk. It informed the police about Kyle and her fears of how he might kill her. She told Brian about the envelope in her desk. Brian sighed heavily and turned the car around. Cathy asked where they were going. Brian answered they were headed back to the police station to explain the envelope. Cathy still didn't mention the envelope mailed to her sister. This was her insurance policy. They walked up to the front desk and asked for Detective Oaks, who appeared almost immediately.

Brian informed him of the envelope and the need for Cathy to explain its contents. The Detective told him they already had, it and it was in the hands of the state attorney as evidence. Brian turned to Cathy and calmly walked her out of the building. She asked him what that meant. He looked at her and replied that things just got much worse. Cathy wanted to return to her apartment. They drove there and went to the apartment door. Brian made a call to the detective to ask if it was okay to return to the apartment. He told Brian they were finished there. Cathy unlocked the door, and they went inside.

The entire apartment had been turned upside down. The police had inspected every inch of the place and left it a disaster. Cathy sat at the kitchen table and cried. The blood was still on the floor, all the cabinets and drawers were emptied everywhere. Cathy then looked at a kitchen drawer. "They found it."

"Found what?" Brian already knew the answer by the look on Cathy's face.

"The envelope. Now what?" Cathy sat back down on the kitchen chair. "I'd like to be alone."

"I can stay and help you clean up." Brian had been doing this long enough to know that leaving a client alone in this state was not a good thing.

Cathy asked again if she could be alone. Brian told her he would call her tomorrow so they could plan a strategy. Cathy could only think of the mess her home and life had become. She heard the closing of the door behind Brian but was unsure of anything he might have said as he was leaving. In the silence, Cathy wanted to cry, but no tears would come.

36

FATHER BRENDAN PICKED UP Sister Diane at 8:00 am as he did every weekday. Over the past two years, they had become very used to each other's habits. Both enjoyed one another's company and ignored the minor annoyances that come with working so closely together. They shared their personal opinions only with each other and were a good balance. The holy couple understood that the work they did was necessary and essential. Father Brendan called their work "peaceful mercy." He would sometimes go on at length, explaining how he came up with the terminology. He told her they offered peace to those who wanted it and mercy to those who needed it. Sister Diane found it better to just let him finish than to rudely tell him that he had already sung his own praises on this subject. Internally, she would laugh at the of thought how she was giving him the peace by letting him go on, and she was taking the mercy by just allowing him to finish. Any interruption would make the conversation drag on or start over

It was Tuesday, and Green Haven still had a police car parked in the lot. They looked at one another and continued into the building. A policeman had been posted at the entrance of each wing. No doubt they were taking the serial killer theory quite seriously. Father Brendan stopped in the restroom while Sister Diane headed for north wing. The residents were being confined to their rooms, so there was no need to go searching for them. This would save a great deal of time.

Father Brendan caught up with the sister three rooms into their visiting rounds. The general attitude of the residents was fear and confusion. The residents they visited were comforted by the familiar faces and appeared more relaxed after their visit.

After a quick check of the residents, Father Brendan made a motion that it was time to leave the facility. Sister Diane moved toward the door in agreement. As they walked into the lobby, Detective Oaks was standing there and asked if he could speak with them. Father Brendan agreed as long as it might be swift because they were behind schedule. Sister Diane, staring at the ground, told him this was not a typical day at the facility.

"We normally come on Tuesdays and Thursdays, but given the circumstances, we spent extra time with the residents today, so we're behind. God's work doesn't punch a time card." Sister Diane had become fond of this phrase and used it when she could. Father Brendan rolled his eyes at her.

"Sister, I'm sure your work is greatly appreciated, so I'll only take a minute or two." Detective Oaks looked at her with as much kindness as his grumpy demeanor allowed.

"It's okay, Diane, we have a few minutes." Father Brendan placed his hand on her back as he stared at the detective. There was an immediate competitive nature between the two men that both engaged in willingly.

Detective Oaks' phone rang. He looked at the caller ID and asked if their conversation could happen another time, soon. Father Brendan waved as the detective trailed away before finishing his sentence.

Dr. Oliver was entering the building as Father Brendan reached for the automatic door button. After a subdued "good morning," she asked what the climate was in the building.

Sister Diane whispered as she leaned in close to Marissa, "It's spooky. Everyone's quiet, and no one wants to make eye contact."

Father Brendan repeated the word in the form of a question, "Spooky?" They all laughed quietly. He added, "It's tense, and having the police roaming around isn't helping anyone. Especially us."

Dr. Oliver was about to say something when Oscar came through the door. He was cheerful and smiling. Apparently, the day off yesterday did wonders for him. They all greeted him, and then Father Brendan excused the sister and himself.

"Marissa, I mean, Dr. Oliver, have you had any time to assess the condition of the residents?" His face was still sporting an "all is well" colossal grin.

"I'm just getting here like you are, Mr. Green." She gave a look of "stop overacting."

"I'm trying to sound official." The grin now left his face.

"Stop right there." Dr. Oliver got in close enough to give him a poke in the chest without being noticed.

"Please give me an update when you can, Dr. Oliver." Oscar walked away, rubbing his chest.

"Idiot! It's a good thing the sex is great." Marissa walked in behind him, just close enough for Oscar to hear her. He smiled but didn't turn around.

Dr. Oliver wondered if the police had charged Cathy yet. They must have enough evidence to prove she killed Kyle. She sat down at the north wing nurses' station and started reviewing the charts tagged for her. She whispered quietly, "At least there shouldn't be any deaths today." Marissa looked around to make sure that no one heard her off-color joke. The rest of the morning went smoothly, if you didn't count the police watching every move she made and an intrusive detective intent on letting everyone know he was in charge.

Detective Oaks asked Dr. Oliver for a minute to go over some questions. She didn't have a chance to reply. "How long have you been the medical director? Have you noticed any changes around here lately?"

"Since the place opened and no. I like to . . ."

"How well did you know Kyle Strong, how about Cathy Arden? Oh, how about that priest and nun?"

"She's a sister, not a nun, and his name is Father Brendan." There was a tone of annoyance in Dr. Oliver's reply. She wasn't accustomed to being spoken to in this manner, not at Green Haven.

"Sure. How well do you know them?" Noting her flippant nature, he returned the irritation.

"I didn't know any of them well. I'm the medical director. I keep my distance to maintain an aura of authority with the staff. You get that, being the detective in charge. Don't you?" Dr. Oliver was aware of his frustration, but they were both gladiators, and she was determined to let him know this point.

He smiled but didn't say a word. He understood her perfectly. He even agreed with it, but he wasn't going to give her the satisfaction of acknowledging it.

Marissa thought she was successful in reaching common ground with the detective, maybe even eked out a victory, so she leaned in to ask her own questions. "Why are there still police on the scene? Don't you have Kyle's killer in custody? The residents are spooked."

Detective Oaks didn't answer. She also wanted to ask why he was looking at Father Brendan; he's a priest. But she figured the detective wasn't in the mood to answer questions, just ask them. He thanked for her time and walked away before actually finishing the sentence. It was a thing with him.

Oscar sat in the back office as he always did and started making calls to the board members, apologizing for missing the meeting. He claimed he had come in early and had become overwhelmed with the whole matter. He said he went home and laid down to rest, accidentally leaving his phone in the car. This worked on everyone but Elliot, whom Oscar had called. He furthered his lie by telling him that he was in his car when he called Elliot. Elliot didn't really care either way. The truth of the matter was that the board was much happier when Oscar didn't show. The only reason he was still on the board was because Oscar was the sole owner of the properties. It was a fact the board had discussed many times, but no one was willing to sign on the dotted line for the loans.

By noon Oscar had enough of groveling and left for lunch. Marissa's car wasn't in the parking lot, so he called her. She went right into their agreement and that toying with it would not end well for him. She knew that wasn't entirely true, but when it came to both their personal and professional relationship, she demanded the upper hand. It was almost time for her next raise. Dr. Oliver thought asking for a raise was beneath her. She saw it as a yearly obligation that Green Haven, Inc. had to honor without being told. She dove into a second round of rule-breaking consequences just for good measure. Oscar sat in his car, contemplating his decision to call her. He wasn't going to ask if she wanted to get lunch. He merely said he was checking to see how she was after dealing with the situation inside Green Haven. Dr. Oliver replied she was fine and she had to run. That was good with Oscar, who now thought it was a full morning of groveling.

37

HE WAS STARTLED BY the buzzing of the phone in his pocket. He reached inside and pulled out the phone. She only called him in an emergency. He answered without saying hello.

"Are you there?" He could feel the uneasiness in her voice.

"Yes. What's the problem?" His tone was one of being unnecessarily bothered.

"Everything is as we thought it would go. All is in place, perfectly."

"Okay. Then why are you calling?" His annoyance increased.

"They're being looked at too."

"I'll handle it. I always handle it." He sighed as he removed his glasses and rubbed his temples to soothe his irritation at the call.

"I don't want to . . ."

The phone went dead. He had hung up on her. She hated the way he treated her. This would have to change.

Detective Oaks finished his phone call and stood in the Green Haven hallway shaking his head. He texted his team, which he usually resisted at all costs, and asked them to meet him in the lobby. Once everyone arrived, he started to inform them of the phone call he'd just received from the forensic team. He told them it might be true that they have a serial killer on their hands. He explained that the number of deaths at Green Haven had dramatically increased in the past two years, and over 90 percent of them pointed to the director of nursing. He then ordered them to find everything they could to tie it all together. He wanted to know the how and the why immediately. Detective Oaks informed them that Cathy Arden was no longer just a person of interest; she was now considered the number one suspect. Finally, he told the team that if anyone found anything new, he wanted to know right away.

Cathy sat in her apartment trying to start the cleanup, but she was frozen in her chair. Her home phone rang. It was Brian. He had gotten a tip from the station that the police now thought she was the murderer and most likely would be coming to pick her up. He wanted her to be prepared for it. "I'm trying to reach Detective Oaks to arrange for you to surrender. It'll look better that way."

Cathy hung up the phone. She walked to the bedroom and pulled a suitcase from the closet. She had watched enough detective shows to know she could never prove she was innocent if she was in jail. She packed quickly and then headed for the door, grabbing her keys and purse from the counter on the way out. The quick motion sent a painful remembrance through her right hand.

Cathy drove to the bank and withdrew all the money from her savings and checking accounts. She was thankful that she had beaten the police to the accounts. She then drove to a supermarket parking lot and left her car there. Cathy took a local bus to the bus station and bought a ticket in cash. She would get a motel room and call her sister to retrieve the envelope. She might have to wait a day or two for it to arrive. On the bus, Cathy tried to calm down. She realized soon she would be a fugitive. Cathy removed a pen, some old receipts, and torn pieces of paper that had once served as list holders. She now needed to use them to formulate her plan. She started making a more detailed plan trying not to draw attention to herself. She knew she was shaking and had to stop. She fought back the tears with the waves of anger that silently grew inside her. She would have to gain control if she wanted to be on the run. Her hand ached as she wrote on scraps of paper.

Detective Oaks sat in the conference room looking at copies of the evidence he had sent over from the station. He was trying to figure out how she killed the residents. The staff gave statements that Cathy was in her office when most residents passed away. He concluded she must have been working with someone. What if he had it all wrong? What if Kyle Strong was working with her and then he had a change of heart? She killed him to keep him quiet. It was a possibility, but it didn't sit right with the detective. He stood up and walked around the room. If he figured out the why, maybe the how would reveal itself. He knew he was missing a lot of pieces and picking up Nurse Arden now would be a mistake. His phone vibrated for the third time; it was Attorney Landers. He ignored it again.

Oscar finished lunch and drove to his construction office. He thought about calling Marissa again, but that didn't go too well last time, so he decided against it. In his office, he turned on the small television to see if there was any mention of Green Haven. There was not. He thought the police must still be keeping it quiet. He was thankful for that. He called Elliot to ask if the board was making any progress on filling the positions and if he could help. Elliot wanted to call him an idiot but told him that the board couldn't do anything with the police still in place at Green Haven. He explained that the board would wait a few more days then place a temporary person there, and when the police were done, they'd hire the necessary personnel. Oscar thought this was a good plan.

Bishop Anthony called Father Brendan to request he and Sister Diane meet him later that day to go over the situation at Green Haven. He said he wanted to see how they were doing. He asked if they could please grab dinner before coming over, as he had to leave directly after the meeting. They would meet at his office around 6:00 pm. Father Brendan thought this was odd, but the whole situation was odd. He told Sister Diane they were being summoned to Bishop Anthony's office at 6:00, so they'd better get a bite to eat before heading over there. It was nearly 4:00 now. They decided to stop at 5:00, get a quick bite, then head over to the bishop. Father Brendan was unable to shake the eerie feeling he had about tonight's meeting. The bishop had never requested a meeting with both of them at the same time. *Why now?* he wondered.

The bus pulled into the station, and Cathy took a cab to a motel about twenty minutes away. She didn't use a credit card because that's how the cops knew where you were on television shows. The motel was an hourly dive that smelled like pot and who knows what else. It was on a slightly lower rung from Attorney Landers' place, but it would have to do. She put her suitcase on the dresser then checked the room for bedbugs and other disgusting items she could think of. She decided that she would sleep in her clothes, if she slept. The motel was located near a low-end shopping mall that had various stores and restaurants. She walked into one of the small shops and asked to borrow the phone, claiming she left her phone at home. Trying to stand so no one could hear her talk, Cathy called her sister. Lisa hadn't heard anything about Green Haven, nor had she received the envelope.

"It's Cathy. I'm in trouble. Big trouble." She kept her hand over her mouth to shield her conversation from others. Cathy looked around again to make sure no one was eavesdropping then she continued. "I'm being framed for murder; actually, lots of murders."

"What? That's insane!" Lisa voice was now two octaves higher and screeching.

"Just listen, please. I sent you an envelope. When you get it, don't open it, just hide it. Don't tell Bill! I'll call you again tomorrow to see if it came. I'm okay for now."

Cathy hung up the phone before Lisa could say a word. Lisa wanted to call her husband, but Cathy had asked her to say nothing, just to wait. Cathy knew the call had sent her sister into a world of chaos with a million questions. She just hoped Lisa could hold it together long enough to get the envelope. She hoped the police wouldn't find her sister and interrogate her too.

Father Brendan drove to the diner they ate at almost every day. Sister Diane looked at him as if to say, "really?" He told her they didn't want to keep the Bishop waiting. As they ate dinner, they discussed multiple possible conversations they were about to have with the bishop. He'd never called them over together, so why now? What changed? This time the priest verbally spoke his questions. They decided to stop speculating and finish their dinners so they could actually find out. The holy couple was experiencing the tension they recalled when they first met. They sat in the car for a long moment and then decided that whatever the bishop demanded they would stand united. They would give no response until they had time to confer with each other. They were a team. Father Brendan started the car, there was a loud explosion, and the car was engulfed in flames immediately.

38

MARISSA DROVE TO OSCAR'S home to surprise him. She let herself in hoping not to find him sprawled out naked on the couch again. He had not gotten home yet. She was hungry, and they both knew she couldn't cook, so she opened the kitchen drawer that held the menus; the pizza menu was on top. She placed it on the bottom of the pile without a second thought.

"Tonight, it's Indian." She loved Indian food. Oscar tolerated it for her. She knew she was selfish, but why change now? She told herself it was what Oscar loved about her. She ordered saag paneer, chicken tikka masala, and a double order of naan. Oscar liked the naan. It was like eating Indian pizza crust. Marissa called Oscar and told him to pick up the food on his way home. She told him she was already there waiting.

Oscar practically leaped out of his chair and headed for the car. After picking up the food, he arrived home to find Marissa in his bathrobe lying on the couch, pretending to be passed out. The robe was open. He wanted to laugh, but she was beautiful. She opened one eye as he came over to her. He gently climbed on top of her, and she kissed him. She pushed him to one side and got up. She was hungry; sex could wait.

"You know I have a housekeeper. It could have been her opening the door." Oscar wasn't happy Marissa had chosen food over sex but tried to make light of it.

"It would have been a bonus for the housekeeper." Marissa winked at him as she pulled the lid off her tikka masala.

They laughed as they sat in the kitchen to eat dinner. Neither had heard about the explosion. Both were full after dinner, and the thought of sex on a full stomach didn't sit well with either of them. They sat on the living room couch. Marissa turned on the television to find a movie while Oscar surfed the web on his phone.

"Oh my God!" Oscar's eyes nearly leaped out of his head. He sat up in a quick jerking motion.

"What?" Marissa was now sitting upright and staring at him, waiting for a reply.

"Look at this. Father Brendan and Sister Diane are dead." He turned the phone to show her a photo of the car fire.

"What? How?" She was unable to ask much more.

"It says here that his car exploded with them inside." Oscar looked up. "Poor bastards, they didn't even know what hit them."

"That's terrible. Does it say what the cause was?" Marissa was regrouping.

"It says it may have been caused by an unknown fuel leak from an accident the father had—crap!—while in the Green Haven parking lot not too long ago. What the hell is going on? It's like someone's out to get Green Haven or maybe just destroy me. Why even mention the name?" Oscar went right past standing and was pacing in front of the coffee table. It was more of a slow sprint back and forth across the living room.

"That's crazy. It's just a coincidence." Marissa got up and grabbed him to stop his panic.

"I don't think so." Oscar tried to break free from her grasp.

"Why would someone want to get Green Haven or you? Everyone loves both." She was trying hard to calm him and herself. She sensed there was more to this than the reporter mentioned.

Oscar sat down, silently trying to think what enemies he might have. He finally spoke, sharing with Marissa that he didn't have any real enemies. He didn't know anyone who could do things like this. She said maybe it was Cathy. She asked Oscar if he thought she just snapped and now she's on an all-out killing spree. Oscar didn't reach that conclusion, but now that he had heard the possibility, it could be true. He told Marissa they needed to call the detective and ask for protection. She told him not to go overboard.

"You're not leaving tonight. I want you here so I know you're safe," Oscar told her.

"Okay, okay, I'll stay, but in the morning, I'm leaving for work. You know I really need to bring one set of clothes here for these sudden overnighters."

Oscar gave a broad smile as he thought that one set could lead to two and three and eventually everything. Marissa realized much too late the consequences for both her and Oscar of what she had just said. She chose to let it go. Besides, it kept Oscar busy and seemed to lessen his fear.

Oscar walked over to the front door and made sure it was locked. For good measure, he then checked all the windows and even the back door. Marissa watched him then headed for the bedroom. She was now ready for some good sex and sleep. She needed to take her mind off her own fear.

Oscar was in no mood for sex. When they got into bed, Oscar pulled her close as if to protect her all night long. She wanted to ask what happens when you fall asleep, but that would just make him try to stay awake all night.

Cathy returned to the motel. She again checked for bedbugs and other creepy crawlies. There were none. She turned on the television, wanting to find something to fall asleep to. The television was tuned to an adult movie. Cathy changed the channel, thinking that it must be appropriate for a place like this to start on that channel. She stopped on a sitcom. She removed the comforter from the bed and lay down over the sheets. She had decided earlier that she was not getting into the bed. She tried to watch the sitcom but could only concentrate on what the rest of her life might be if she couldn't prove she was innocent. She thought about calling Brian.

He would tell her to come back, that she was making a mistake. He would then have to call the detective and tell him she left. She decided not to call him. She flipped to the news to see if they were looking for her. She sat up when she saw the story of the car death of Father Brendan and Sister Diane. She knew it was all tied together somehow. There was no mention of her anywhere on the news. No one was looking for her. She was sure they would be soon. Cathy became more worried as she wondered if they were going to try to pin the holy couple's death on her too. Then it hit her. They were always there. Always. They were near each time. But now they're dead. Her mind was now moving so fast; a thought was only half coherent before the next one took its place. The one thing she was most certain of was that this was no coincidence. *I have to be careful. I have to tell Oaks . . . I have to call him.* Cathy's mind stopped. *I'm next.*

Detective Oaks was reading the initial report on the car fire. The fire department had determined the explosion was caused by a gasoline leak in the engine. The report concluded that it was merely an unfortunate accident. He didn't believe it. This was too much of a coincidence. Too many people associated with Green Haven, Inc. were dying. He called in a junior team member and asked him to do a search, in the morning, for anyone associated with Green Haven, Inc. that died in the last six months. He told him to exclude residents for now. It was late, so he decided to call Attorney Landers back in the morning. It was time to go home and get some rest. He put on his jacket and left the office.

He had long ago made peace with the fact that he'd never see heaven, but the actions he had taken to honor his brother's wishes were far worse than anything they did while he was alive. He did have some resolve in knowing that he'd be in hell with his brother. He smiled as he took another sip of Scotch and reread the letter.

Dearest brother,

Soon you will be all that is left of our generation. I know that my time is coming to a close. We have done as much good as bad, and I can live, or die, with that. Together we have done well, but now I must ask you to do one last good deed alone. My son, your nephew, is all that is left in this world of our name. I ask you to see that he never knows of our deeds and that you watch over him until your last breath. His heart is in the right place, but, as you well know, his intellect is not that of ours. I have shielded him from our doings and only allowed him to prosper from our abilities. I need you to continue this until the day you reach your end. I know this is an enormous burden I ask of you. To help you, I have ensured that you have the necessary funds hidden at our usual location. I believe you are up to it. Thank you for honoring my last wish.

Your loving brother, Oscar

He reread the letter, taking his last sip of Scotch. It was a request he couldn't say no to. His brother knew this. "Damn him."

39

CATHY WOKE UP THE next morning later than she intended. She checked the shower for bugs, mold, or anything else she might see then slipped in and out of her shoes only long enough to take a shower. She decided she would buy shower sandals today for tomorrow's shower. She opened the suitcase, took out underclothes, a pair of jeans, and a shirt, then put them on without letting them touch the floor or anything else. She closed the suitcase, leaving yesterday's clothes, now also her last night's sleepwear, on top of her luggage. On her way out of the door, she hung the "do not disturb" sign on the outside handle. She noticed a small coffee shop adjacent to the mall yesterday and went there for breakfast. As she ordered, she could hear the news being played over the speaker system. There was no mention of her or Green Haven. The broadcaster gave a short recap of the fiery death of clergy members. He continued to say the car fire had been ruled an accident for now. She didn't believe it. She, like the detective, knew much more than the public.

Cathy finished her breakfast then walked to the pharmacy a few doors down. She purchased a pair of scissors, gloves, a plastic tablecloth, hair dye, a large bottle of hydrogen peroxide, and some generic aspirin. She was going to have to change her look if she wanted to stay free. She went back to her room, leaving the "do not disturb" sign on the outer handle.

Cathy headed for the sink area, opened the plastic tablecloth, and placed it on the floor. She was thinking that her crime show watching days were finally paying off. She removed all of her clothing, including her shoes. She stood on the plastic tablecloth.

She took out the scissors and cut her jet-black hair back to shoulder length. Next, she read the instructions on the hair dye. She dowsed her hair with the hydrogen peroxide and applied the dye accordingly. Soon she'd become a sandy blonde. She let the dye set for the instructed time frame then turned on the water for the shower. She cursed. "Crap!" Cathy had forgotten to purchase the sandals. She got into the shower and rinsed off. After the shower, she wrapped everything in the plastic tablecloth, placed it in the plastic bag from the pharmacy, dressed, and headed out of the room. She disposed of the bag in a garbage can at the mall. The can would be emptied sometime today, she thought. There was nothing to do until her sister received the envelope, so Cathy decided the best place to hide was at a movie. There was a movie theater not too far from the mall. She could walk there. She didn't really care what was playing; she'd pick the first one starting and maybe even go to a second one.

Oscar opened his eyes to find that Marissa was already gone. He sighed; he had just been dreaming of having sex with her, followed by a large breakfast. She wouldn't skip work anyway. He got out of bed, showered, and drove to the office. He didn't bother calling her; she wouldn't pick up.

Marissa was already at work, checking on the residents and hoping to overhear something more about the investigation. There were more police today than yesterday. She had expected that. She half wondered why they just didn't close the place down. She told herself to shut up. She had a contract, but there wasn't mention of coverage if the company went under. After all this was done, she'd make sure Oscar fixed the problem. Would she still get paid? She smiled; she would one way or another. Dr. Oliver knew she had set herself up to live a good life, no matter what happened to Green Haven, Inc.

Oscar detoured from his construction office to Green Haven. He had to know what was going on. Detective Oaks met him in the lobby. They stepped into Kyle's office, which was now Detective Oaks' onsite office. The detective sat down behind the desk; Oscar smiled; this was still his facility, so he chose to stand. Detective Oaks understood the objection; he got up and walked to the front of the desk alongside Oscar.

"Let me start by saying we don't think you're a suspect. I pulled you in here to ask you some questions that are better done in private." Oaks was again looking in his notepad and purposely avoiding eye contact with Oscar.

Oscar was startled, and his body language gave away his utter surprise. He had never thought of being a suspect. Another gesture the detective didn't miss. Detective Oaks had been working the case for days now, and like the Green Haven board, he didn't think much of Oscar's intellect. The detective knew Oscar had been willed his fortune. He checked Oscar's background before the inheritance and found him to be an honest, run-of-the-mill builder with an okay reputation. The Green Haven building was his crowning achievement and also a monument to his daddy. Detective Oaks knew Oscar would do anything not to lose it, but he just didn't see the killer in Oscar.

"I know you have a board. Do you know if the facility is in financial trouble?"

"I don't really think so. The board is always worried about money. That's part of their job." Oscar truly believed what he was saying. In his mind, the financial concerns the board was having were everyday normal occurrences.

The detective wondered how or why he didn't really know the financials of his own company. Then he thought the board probably lets him stay on the board, but without much power. He saw Oscar as a rich kid in a man's body. He knew Oscar was well off but not really rich. He figured the board humored him to a point. He also knew that Oscar owned just about everything the board was in charge of.

"Did you hire Kyle Strong or Cathy Arden, and how well did you know them?" Still, the detective refused to look at the man he was conversing with.

"I didn't really know Mr. Strong well, and I didn't know the nurse at all except by face. I didn't hire either of them. I left that stuff up to the board. I'm kinda the visionary builder guy. I don't want to know about the day-to-day stuff. You could say I'm a big-picture person." Oscar was now flaring his chest in a moment of pride for his view of himself.

He asked Oscar a few more questions. None of which were of any real value and Oscar answered without any real value. Detective Oaks thanked him and walked out of the office. Oscar noticed he didn't get a goodbye; it must be a detective thing.

Marissa saw Oscar in Kyle's office with the detective as she was leaving the building. She waited in the parking lot to see if he came out. He did not. She climbed into her SUV. She was tapping her fingernails on the steering wheel, trying to decide if she should call Oscar. She called to tell him she was waiting. He hung up and exited the building. He was about to get into her car when she raised her hand, telling him to stop. He nodded and got into his vehicle. She called him using the car's Bluetooth.

"Have you lost your mind?" Dr. Oliver had both her hands raised in the air, and her voice was loud enough to hear without the use of the phone.

"Sorry, I was just speaking with the detective . . . what's his name?" His face had lost the glimmer that it carried from, what he believed, was a great interview only minutes ago.

"Oaks." She was still shooting barbs at him with her eyes.

"Yes, Oaks. He asked me all kinds of questions. Most of which I didn't know the answers to. I have to start paying more attention at the board meetings. The meeting went very well, all things considered."

"What did he ask you?"

"He asked about the financials, about Kyle, about that nurse ..." Oscar was rambling quickly.

"Calm down. What did you say?" Her voice was low and stern.

"Not much. I don't know much. I barely knew Kyle. I didn't know the nurse ..."

"Cathy."

"What?"

"Cathy, her name is Cathy." Marissa told herself it was all worth it as she placed her hands over her face.

"Whatever. He said I wasn't a suspect. That's good, right?" Oscar was now looking directly at her as he asked for approval.

"Yes, did he ask you about me?"

"No. Why?"

"I'd like to know if he thinks I'm a suspect." Once again she sounded dominating.

"Why would he think that? You had no reason to kill Kyle."

"That's true. I have to go. I'll call you later." She hit the cancel button on the steering wheel, never looking in his direction again.

Marissa started the car and left Green Haven. She wasn't satisfied with Oscar's answer. Oscar was just enough of an idiot to inadvertently say something to give the wrong impression. He said the detective didn't ask about her, so she took a deep breath to calm down. She reasoned that if there were no questions about her, Oscar couldn't say anything about her because she didn't come up. Marissa turned the rearview mirror so she could see her reflection and sternly told herself, "Dr. Marissa Oliver, get a hold of yourself. Don't create a problem where there isn't one."

40

AFTER THE MOVIE ENDED, Cathy looked around for an innocent, non-threatening person. She settled on a young, skinny girl about eighteen or nineteen years old. She figured the girl was at the movies in the middle of a workday using a credit card that Mommy or Daddy funded. She asked the young girl if she could borrow her cell phone to call her sister, who was supposed to pick her up and hadn't shown. Lisa answered the phone telling her the mailman had just delivered the envelope. Cathy asked to be picked up at the movie theater and reminded her to bring the envelope. She whispered, "Don't open it, and make sure you're not followed."

"Who would be following me, and how would I even know? And even if I did, how would I lose them?" Cathy could hear the panic taking hold of Lisa.

"Never mind. I live alone and watch too many cop shows." Cathy tried to put Lisa at ease.

Thirty minutes later Lisa pulled up, and Cathy got into the car. Lisa didn't recognize her at first and reached for the mace she had placed in her purse after their phone conversation.

"Wait! Wait! It's me, Cathy." Both her hands were up to defend against a blast of the toxic spray.

"You have me paranoid. A lot has changed since I saw you last month." Lisa managed a forced giggle.

"Yes, and that's not funny. Drive over to that mall." Cathy pointed to the car-filled parking lot of the mall only yards away from the theater.

Lisa pulled into a parking space away from other cars. She kept staring at Cathy, waiting for her to speak. Cathy's blank look told Lisa she was deep in thought. They had been very close as young sisters and could almost read each other's minds.

"It's okay to tell me. You know I can keep a secret." Lisa turned toward her.

"It's not that. The less you know, the less you'll have to lie about when the police come to question you."

"Tell me." Lisa's back was now leaning on the driver's side door so she could view her sister fully.

"In the next few days you're going to hear a lot of horrible things about me. None of them are true. When the police come, don't lie. Tell them everything. Say I called you, we met, you handed me an envelope. Tell them I cut my hair and changed the color. You can't lie! Do you understand?" Cathy was holding onto Lisa's hand tightly, causing her own hand to ache from the pressure.

"Yes, but . . . wait, what happened to your hand?"

"I cut it on a piece of broken glass. It's not important now. Do you understand?"

Lisa nodded as she sat there, unable to speak. As Lisa was trying hard to absorb the situation, Cathy took the envelope and got out of the car. Lisa lowered the window and yelled to her. Cathy didn't turn around. She walked across the parking lot and into the mall, disappearing into the crowd.

Detective Oaks called Attorney Landers demanding that he bring his client in immediately, or he would go to her place and personally arrest her. Brian explained that he had been trying to reach him for the exact same reason. Brian Landers left several messages on Cathy's phone this morning and had not heard back from her. He knew better than to share this with the detective. Detective Oaks calmed down and told Brian he had two hours to bring his client in.

After he was finished with the detective, Brian dialed Cathy's number. It went straight to voicemail. He knew this wasn't good. He tried the home phone; no answer. Brian drove to Cathy's apartment and knocked on the door. There was no answer. He had no choice; he called the detective back and delivered the bad news. Detective Oaks told him to stay there; he was on his way.

Fifteen minutes later Detective Oaks arrived with four uniformed officers. He gave Brian a despising stare-down then knocked on the door.

"Either way, if she's not there or dead, I'm going to be pissed."

"I know. Sorry." Brian half hoped she was dead for his sake.

He looked to the largest of the uniforms and told him to kick it in. Brian thought about saying that he really didn't have probable cause, but the detective just glared at him. Brian stepped out of the way. The uniform kicked the door in with one strike; the doorjamb splintered into multiple fragments. Even Detective Oaks was impressed. The officers entered the apartment first, guns raised; they cleared the place without finding Cathy alive or dead. The place was in the exact condition it was the day before. Nothing had been cleaned or even moved for that matter.

"When did you last see her?" Detective Oaks was holding his handcuffs in one hand and slapping them against his other. He was in no mood for smartass attorney crap.

"Yesterday, when I dropped her off. She was sitting on a kitchen chair. I asked if she wanted help cleaning the place. She said no and asked me to leave." Brian's ears were fixated on the slapping sound the handcuffs made as they hit the detective's large hands.

"Did you talk to her after that?" He now returned the handcuffs to their resting spot somewhere behind his waist.

"Yes, I called later in the day to advise her that she should surrender." The color now returned to Brian's face. Jail was not a good place for a public defender. Inevitably, he would run into a disgruntled criminal he failed to set free.

Detective Oaks started barking orders toward the uniformed officers. He wanted three of them to speak to neighbors. The fourth, he told to call it in. He didn't want her getting out of town. They all knew it was probably too late for that. Brian knew what was coming next. Someone at the station would leak that a murder suspect was on the run. The media would have a field day with it, and Detective Oaks would lose his mind. None of this would be good. Cathy would be guilty and sentenced before ever getting near a courtroom. He asked Detective Oaks if they could keep it quiet for a few more hours so he could have a chance to find her. Detective Oaks just walked out of the apartment.

Oscar was listening to news radio while driving home. He really didn't like listening to the news, but he thought it made him seem more sophisticated. The truth was it made him feel more grown-up. The news reporter was interrupted with the breaking news sound the station used constantly. A new reporter came on and started relaying the hot new story.

"A female serial murder suspect is on the run. Green Haven Director of Nursing Cathy Arden was missing when police showed up at her apartment to arrest her."

The reporter went on, *"Green Haven, Inc. officials could not be reached for comment."* She described Cathy's appearance then added that she could be dangerous.

Oscar yelled out in his car. "Ex, ex!" He was correct; she was an ex-employee, and he was an ex-employer. He was picking up the phone to call Marissa when it rang. It was a news reporter trying to get a scoop on the story. Oscar told the reporter he had just heard about it and hung the phone up. No sooner did he put it down, it rang again. Another reporter looking to get a jump on the story. This time Oscar said no comment. He hung the phone up only long enough to call Marissa. Her phone was going to voicemail. Oscar deduced that she must have been receiving multiple calls from reporters and turned it off. He did the same. He decided to drive to her place so they could speak in person. As he rounded the corner of her street, he could see the band of reporters waiting to pounce. Apparently, Marissa hadn't been home, or she saw what was waiting for her and made a dash for it. Oscar slowly turned the car in the other direction, hoping not to draw any attention. He didn't. He chose to drive past his home next to see if the same fate was awaiting him. It was. He backed away from the hounds and drove to a hotel. He wanted to get a hold of Marissa to order her to join him, but he had no way to contact her. He also thought that ordering her might be a bit too strong. Besides, she probably wouldn't come for fear of being found out. Then he smiled; if Green Haven were done, then she would have nothing to hide from.

Marissa had also seen the reporters waiting outside her door, but she hadn't heard the news yet. All she knew was this couldn't be a good thing. She flipped the radio on. Every station was reporting on the fugitive Cathy Arden. She had stolen the limelight from all the usual scandals making news stations rich nowadays. She went to call Oscar, but her phone was dead. She had stayed at Oscar's last night, so she didn't charge it, and she had forgotten to plug it in when she got into the car. She did so now. Marissa waited, watching the phone as it took its time gathering enough charge to come back to life. The screen finally lit up; she had twenty-six missed calls. Three calls from Oscar and twenty-three from unknown numbers. Marissa tried Oscar, but it went to voicemail. If he was getting as many calls as she was, he probably turned his phone off. She wondered where he was. She knew if he couldn't go home he would go to some swanky high-priced hotel to hide out. He was always trying to get her to go just so he could impress her. There are only three around town. She would drive by each of them looking for his car.

41

CATHY RETURNED TO THE motel after buying a new bottle of hair dye. She knew that Detective Oaks would eventually speak with Lisa. Her sister promised to tell the truth and that would include the hair color change. This time she'd be a subtle redhead. She entered her motel room and went through the process of dying her hair again. She had once again forgotten the shower sandals. Cathy grabbed her bag and left the motel without stopping at the front desk. She left the "do not disturb" sign on the door just in case she was forced to make a hasty retreat. She had the room for the week anyway.

After clearing out her bank accounts, Cathy figured she had enough money to live on for four months. She assumed that the police must have noticed by now she was on the run and frozen her CDs and retirement accounts. Soon they'd contact Lisa. She flagged a taxi and took it to the next town over, making sure to pay with cash. Cathy recalled that Brian had bought clothes for her from a secondhand store. She found a thrift shop to buy some new clothes. She purchased a pair of jeans, a bland T-shirt, and a shirt to go over it. She was walking out of the store when she realized that she was wearing shoes that were too out of character for the outfit she just purchased. Cathy remembered how her dad would tell her to look at the shoes of the beggars asking for money at traffic lights. If their shoes were expensive and in decent shape chances were good, it was a scam. Cathy never put too much faith in this until now. She didn't head back into the store for the shoes. She feared this would attract unwanted attention. Instead, she walked down to the end of the block where a large box store was located. She headed to the shoe department and picked out a pair of comfortable sneakers that were as understated as possible. Cathy looked for shoes that could handle a fair amount of walking. She might be doing a lot of it for quite a while. After purchasing the sneaker, she headed for the gas station across the street. She changed into her new look in the restroom. Cathy Arden, nurse on the run, was pleasantly surprised by how comfortable she felt in the clothes. They were not her style, but they might be after this was over.

There was a bus stop not too far from the gas station. Cathy walked to it and waited for the next bus. Any bus would do. She was thinking about the detective shows she watched and decided that she needed to get off the street. If her face was on the television, someone might see her. She told herself she needed to get a life when this was over. An older woman was standing at the bus stop also waiting for the next the bus; Cathy kept her distance while trying to hide her face. She needed to buy a book or something to prevent people from wanting to engage with her. Cathy wished she had thought to buy a baseball cap like the fugitives do on the detective shows to hide their face. She boarded the next bus that arrived at the stop and asked the driver how to get to the station.

After changing two buses, Cathy arrived at the station. She exited the bus and found a trashcan, placing the thrift shop bag filled with her old clothes into it. She sat in the terminal. Now she needed to really come up with a plan. Blindly running was not the answer. A flurry of questions ran through her mind. Where would Detective Oaks not find her? How was she going to prove she was innocent? Lastly, who did all of this and why?

She pulled out the large envelope to start making notes on the back of it. Writing things down was risky, but her mind was going in too many directions to focus.

1. Where to go
2. Who to trust
3. How to prove it all
4. Who the killer is
5. Call Oaks

Cathy looked at the list. It was a start. She tried to focus on the first item. She drew on the multitude of detective shows she'd watched. She decided that going to the nearby city would allow her to hide in the crowds while still being close enough to Green Haven to do what she needed. She could sneak in and out of town. She would figure out the actual details later. The bus terminal had a coffee shop advertising free Wi-Fi and the use of a handful of computers. She planned to use the computer to find a cheap place to stay that offered month-to-month rent. She would pay cash.

She knew she couldn't work, as that would require her to give her social security number. That would notify the authorities where she was. She would have to rely on the money she already had or find a cash-paying job. Suddenly, Cathy realized how out of her element she was. Tears began to form in her eyes; she fought them off. She had to hold it together if she didn't want to spend the rest of her life in prison. Cathy convinced herself she was doing great and she had the smarts to figure this out. Oddly, she did feel more alive at this moment than she had for the last ten years. Cathy wondered how she allowed Green Haven, Kyle, or Pharmatek to suck the life out of her.

Cathy's brain was hurting; she needed to eat. She ordered a muffin from the counter and a cup of coffee in a to-go container. She returned to the computer to find a place. It looked like motels would be her best bet. They would ask the least amount of questions and would be most happy to accept cash. She found a moderately priced motel on the edge of the city, headed back to the bus station, and bought a bus ticket. She spotted a small bookstand and bought a book to hide her face. Cathy realized she had to separate the large amount of money she was carrying into several wads so she only removed what was necessary to make her purchases. Cathy knew she'd have to spend more money, in the beginning, to get established, but she was still as frugal as possible. She entered the restroom, and once in the stall, she took out the giant fold of money from her pocket and started hiding smaller bundles in different places on her body. She placed two in the front of her underwear, one in each sock, and split the last stack into her front pockets. She couldn't take the chance of being robbed.

Cathy hopped on the bus. It had been a long day, and she was tired. She found a seat in the middle of the bus, opened the book, and pretended to read. Cathy held the book up as long as she could before falling asleep.

42

DETECTIVE OAKS WAS STANDING at his desk in the station reading the report from a junior member of his team. He started to read the names of people that had died in the last six months who were in any way associated with Green Haven, Inc.

John Perkins, Board Treasurer. Kyle Strong, Administrator. Father Brendan Pierce. Sister Diane Loretto.

The detective stopped there. He pulled out his notes. First, he found the notes he took from talking with the priest and the sister. Sister Diane told him they visited Green Haven on Tuesdays and Thursdays. He flipped back and forth through the old school notepad and found the place where Nurse Arden explained that she and Kyle had separately uncovered a plot to kill residents. He pulled out the spreadsheets recovered from Cathy's apartment and started scanning them for evidence of either a conspiracy or a conviction. Detective Oaks thought the nurse would have made a good investigator. "Not bad for a first-timer."

As he continued to analyze the data on the spreadsheets, he started drawing some of the same conclusions. The residents of Green Haven all died on a Tuesday or a Thursday. He sat there mesmerized. "Really, could a priest and sister be capable of committing murder?" He heard himself say it out loud and looked around to see if anyone else had heard it. The detective may not have been a church-going man, but he just couldn't believe it was possible. He shook his head; Cathy Arden had to be behind the murders. What if she was smart enough or, rather, sick enough to frame a priest and sister? He needed the why. The how would eventually show itself if he knew the why.

Detective Oaks called in his team. "All of you know that I'm one of the most skeptical detectives ever made, so what I'm about to tell you may make you think it's time for me to quit. I think there's a possibility that the father and sister that just died may have had a part in this mess." He held his hands up, stopping any questions asking if he really wanted to go down this road.

No one said it. They stood there looking at each other. They knew what it would be like to accuse a religious member, of any religion, of murder. They could face persecution both from without and within. Family members would come down hard, citizens would cry hate crimes, and fellow officers would shame them behind the blue walls.

"I get it. So instead of thinking I'm crazy, prove me right or wrong. Go get proof one way or another. And be very discreet. We're dealing with people's faith here. We need to be 100 percent sure if we're going to say or do anything. Especially before I go to the captain. Don't screw this up." Detective Oaks may have been speaking softly, but the words were heard very clearly and very loudly.

He split the team into two and sent half to Elite Care and the other to Autumn Life. Both teams were instructed to look up all the residents who had died in the last year. He wanted the death certificates, he wanted the day of the week they died, and he wanted all of it now.

Detective Oaks turned his attention back to the fugitive, Cathy Arden. He thought she must have something to hide; why else run? He opened the file his team had compiled on her and started to read. Her savings and checking accounts had been cleared out. Her retirement and CDs were still untouched. He figured that she must have assumed they were already frozen. None of her credit cards were used recently. She had a sister. That's where he would start. There was a phone number in the file. He called it, half expecting to get the runaround. After all, they were sisters. Even if she didn't know anything, she would be inclined to cover for her sister. Detective Oaks thought what he might do for his brother. Just about anything.

"Hello."

"Hello. This is Detective Oaks. Is Lisa Rhodes there?"

"Hello, Detective Oaks. I've been expecting your call." Her voice was calm.

"I'm not surprised. What did your sister tell you to tell me? If you're going to lie, please just tell me you have no comment. Let's save you having to get in trouble for being the sister of a fugitive." This time he was tapping his pen on the desk out of habit.

"That's just it. Cathy told me to tell you everything truthfully."

The detective dropped the pen and shook his head. "I must admit, I don't know whether to be impressed by your sister or think she's psycho."

"Go with impressed. What would you like to know?"

Detective Oaks thought it must be a genetic something or other. Both sisters were cool under pressure. He laughed; good quality for a killer. Then he wondered if they looked alike, maybe identical twins pulling off the murders together. *Oaks, you're getting old.*

"Detective, are you still there?"

"Why don't you just tell me what happened?"

He listened intently as Lisa informed him of every detail of their brief meeting, including handing over the envelope. He never had to ask a question. After Lisa described Cathy leaving her car and disappearing into the mall, he thanked her and hung up the phone. He had to admit that he was taken by the boldness of this nurse. Detective Oaks had little respect for criminals or most people in general, but Cathy Arden was growing on him.

He needed to start looking at other options. After all, that's what he told his team to do. Detective Oaks leaned back in his chair and stared at the ceiling. He took the gold shield from his hip and held it tightly in his hands. He didn't get to be the lead detective by not solving cases. He rubbed the surfaces with both hands recalling something his mentor told him: "You're a good cop if you can sort out the bull and find the truth hiding outside the obvious." Detective Oaks made a career out of this motto, and he wasn't about to abandon it now. He placed the shield back on his hip, patted it for good luck, then poured himself a cup of office gold, which was closer to tar. He returned to his desk and started taking apart the file in front of him.

43

MARISSA FOUND OSCAR'S CAR parked outside the second of three hotels she planned to visit. She walked inside and introduced herself as Dr. Marissa Oliver. She told the desk clerk she had received a call from her patient Oscar Green and was concerned for his health. "I understand that you can't tell me what room he's in, but you can call him and let him know I'm here."

The desk clerk thought that was reasonable. "Hello, it's Jessie at the front desk. There is a Dr. Oliver . . ."

Oscar caught on quickly. "Oh good! Please, send her up immediately." Oscar hung up the phone before the desk clerk could say anything else. Oscar wasn't good at lying.

Marissa went up to room 309. "Why is your phone turned off?" Marissa had a familiar look of disgust on her face as she pushed her way past Oscar and headed for the living room.

"Why is your phone turned off?" Oscar chased behind her like a young boy trying to keep up with his mother.

"My phone wasn't turned off. I stayed with you last night, at your insistence, and didn't get to charge it. Then I forgot to plug it in when I got into my car. I was a little busy. Mine is working again. Turn yours on, please." She pointed to Oscar's pocket where his cell sat in waiting.

"Thirty-one missed calls, the last from Detective Oaks." Oscar placed the phone down on the counter and was starting to walk away from it.

Marissa picked up the cell and handed it back to Oscar. "Call him back, put it on speaker, and don't tell him we're together."

Oscar didn't like the police. He remembered as a child, his father continually dealing with the police, and after every encounter, his father was in a bad mood. Oscar grew up believing the cops picked on his father because they were jealous of his success. Oscar claimed he was street smart just like his father. Oscar Green Sr. shielded his son from the particulars of his business. He wanted to spare his son a world of having to always look over his shoulder. Junior never caught on to his father's dealings. His father made sure of it.

Oscar called the detective back. Detective Oaks picked up on the first ring. "Mr. Green. I assume you're not at home. I passed by your home and saw a large number of reporters waiting for you."

"That's right. I'm in a hotel, but I don't want to tell you just in case the reporters are following you." Oscar was kind of proud about this comment and smiled at Marissa. She shook her head.

"No offense, Mr. Green, but I don't care where you are. I just have a few questions about Father Brendan."

"Father who?" Oscar was smiling again. Marissa held up a hand as if she was going to slap him if he continued to play around. This time he got the message loud and clear.

"Father Brendan, the priest at Green Haven."

"Yes. I'm sorry. It's been a long few days. What do you want to know?" Oscar didn't look in Marissa's direction this time.

"When did Green Haven start having him and Sister Diane come into the facility?" Detective Oaks now had his notebook open on his desk, and the pen was tap dancing again.

"They went to all three facilities. I don't really know the date or any of the details. Bishop Anthony handles those matters."

"Do you have his number?" The detective's pen was now standing at the ready. The tapping had stopped.

"Yes, I can text it to you."

"That would be great." Detective Oaks let go of the pen.

He hung up. Oscar turned to Marissa, telling her the detective had a habit of getting in the last word. Marissa walked over to the bar and poured herself a shot of bourbon, drank it, and then poured a second. She handed Oscar a Scotch. He asked if he had told the detective something he shouldn't have. Marissa replied that he did everything right. She was about to tell him something when her phone rang. It was the detective; he seemed to be making the rounds. Marissa was deciding whether to answer it or not. She had made Oscar take the detective's call and thought it would make her look like a hypocrite if she didn't follow her own advice. Dr. Oliver answered the phone holding a finger in the air telling Oscar to wait, then she put the finger to her lips, ordering him to stay quiet.

"Hello, Detective ... Oaks. It's Oaks, correct?" Now she smiled at Oscar. He frowned as if to say, "Why is it okay for you to do it?" Marissa shot him a "stop being a child" look.

"How many detectives do you know, Doctor?" Detective Oaks was also frowning, but he would never let the doctor put him in his place again.

"Not many. Sorry about that. How can I help you?" Oscar was again smiling as he figured out that the detective had admonished her. Marissa turned her back to him.

"Just a few questions if you have a moment."

"Sure. What's on your mind?"

"How long have you known Nurse Arden?"

"Cathy? Ever since she came to Green Haven six-plus years ago. I can't believe she murdered Kyle." Marissa took a sip of bourbon and let out a sigh.

"Can you tell me more about her relationship with Kyle?" The pen was standing tall again on the page of the notebook

"I didn't know they had a relationship. I knew he disliked her for a computer company situation that went south about five or six years back. I think he blamed her for making him recommend the company to the board. It was a real black mark on his record." Marissa turned back to Oscar, who had lost interest and was looking at his own phone.

"That was a long time ago; anything more recent?"

"Yes, now that you mention it. I heard them arguing loudly just a few days ago inside Kyle's office. The receptionist seemed very traumatized by it."

Oscar was now paying attention again. He was confused. Marissa told him earlier that she didn't want to say this to the police because she didn't want to get involved. She saw his concern and mouthed, "It's okay," to him.

"What about Kyle?"

"Kyle Strong may have been a power-hungry idiot, but he was harmless."

"Did you have any run-ins with him where you felt scared?" The pen was now marching across the pages.

"None."

"Thank you for your time."

Marissa turned to Oscar, telling him he was right; the detective did have a knack for getting in the last word. She noticed the blood had drained from his face as he stood there listening to the phone conversation. She assured him that the detective was just doing his job. He was checking all the angles. Marissa lied to Oscar, telling him that during her residency the attending doctors would speak with the police all the time if they treated a patient who was a criminal or suspected of being involved in a crime. She assured him again that this was just routine police procedure. The color started to return to Oscar's face.

Marissa sat down on a living room chair looking at her phone as if it had vibrated. She told Oscar she just received a notification that the hospital was waiting on her for a patient she sent there. She explained that in all the excitement today she'd forgotten about it. Marissa kissed Oscar on the cheek and headed for the door. She assured him she would be back in a few hours. Oscar sat there, Scotch in hand; he knew she'd lied. He remembered at one of their first encounters she wouldn't have a drink if she had to see patients in her office afterward. Now she had two drinks and was going off to the hospital. Something was wrong. Her demeanor was off. She was distant and suddenly preoccupied. He would bring up the lie when she returned.

Bishop Anthony picked up his phone and listened to the voice on the other end. "Bishop Anthony, this is Detective Oaks. I'm the lead investigator on several murders that seem to be tied together. May I ask you a few questions?"

"Of course, but I'm not sure how I can be of help to you." Bishop Anthony was wondering how the detective had managed to get his cell phone number but thought it'd be too suspicious to ask.

"Do you know a nurse named Cathy Arden, or an administrator named Kyle Strong?"

"I know of Kyle Strong; he was at Green Haven, and Cathy Arden is the nurse on the run from the same place. You have quite a mess on your hands over there. But I don't really have time for this. I lost two outstanding people of my own recently." The bishop sounded remorseful and righteous at the same time.

"I'm really sorry to bother you at this time, but I need to ask about the 'holy couple' as they were called." He suspected that this term would not sit well with the bishop. He also knew that catching people off guard caused them to say useful things.

"Fine, but please don't use that disrespectful term again. They were two people I placed together who truly helped the people they touched. You know I have a knack for finding the right person for the right job, and in this case, it was a twofer." The bishop wanted to continue with his own praises, as he had so many times before, but thought better of it.

"How long ago where they ... did you place them at Green Haven?" The detective decided to switch tactics and use the holy man's pride against him.

"Just over two and a half years ago."

"Can you tell me who was there before them?"

"A Father Timothy had been there since Green Haven opened. He was getting on in years, and after training Father Brendan, he suddenly retired. Father Brendan asked me to find someone to help work with him at the three facilities. He stated that it was a two-person job."

"That was Sister Diane, correct?" Detective Oaks was writing furiously. He would read it back later and make sense of it then. For now, he needed the new information.

"Yes, I found Sister Diane drowning in a convent. She was shy and a loner, but she had a hidden light within her. As I said before, I have a knack for that sort of thing."

"How were they working out?" He already knew the holy couple had a stellar reputation.

"I thought Brendan's outgoing personality would pull Diane from her shell, and it did. Knack, remember?" The bishop was now well past simple pride; he had reached God-like status.

"Thank you for your time and the information." This time the detective finished his sentence. He didn't want to offend his holiness, at least not yet. If it turned out that the holy couple was involved, he was certain the bishop would be a little more than offended.

Bishop Anthony was pleased with himself and reached into the drawer behind his desk to remove a bottle of Scotch he savored only on special occasions.

Detective Oaks was still finding it hard to believe a priest had anything to do with it. Equally as troublesome was the idea that Cathy Arden was capable of killing a board member, her boss, a priest, a sister, and multiple residents. It just didn't add up unless she snapped for some unknown reason. His years of experience were screaming; he was missing something. This made him more determined and outwardly more intense than usual. He grumbled in a low voice to himself, "Why did you go into the file room after all these years? Nurse Arden, tell me what I need to know."

44

THE BUS PULLED INTO the terminal, and Cathy felt her mouth go dry. She hadn't thought about the possibility of the police waiting inside the terminal looking for her. Then she remembered she had changed her appearance twice. The police wouldn't be looking for a redhead wearing used street clothes. She got off the bus, keeping her head down for good measure. Once outside the terminal, she took a deep breath and headed for the motel she found online.

Cathy's eyes darted around the street as she walked to the motel. She was scared. She reached the motel and paid for a room for the week. On the bus, just before falling asleep, she decided to move weekly to keep from being noticed. The clerk at the motel didn't even look up. He collected the money and handed her the key. Once inside the room, she did her bedbug and other disgusting items room check. She sat down in a chair to think about her next move and how to make it happen. Cathy needed a friend she could trust. What she really needed was someone inside Green Haven. She wrote Lenny's name down on the back of the envelope. Lenny's boy-like crush could be useful. She hated the idea of using Lenny yet another time, but the rest of her life may depend on it. She decided she would make it up to him in the end. She also decided that sex would not be part of the making up. Cathy was surprised to find the room had a working safe.

She removed the cash from all the hiding places on her body and locked most of it in the safe. Cathy picked up the keys from the top of the dresser and made sure she locked the door on the way out. There was no "Do not disturb" sign to hang on the door.

She couldn't keep borrowing phones. First stop was a small no-name electronics store to buy a burner phone. Cathy had heard the term many times on her detective shows but had no real idea what it was. She would sort it out with the sales kid when she got to the store. The next stop would be another thrift shop to pick up two or three changes of clothes. She couldn't wear the same clothes every day. She also needed to stop at another big box store to buy underwear. Cathy had been in such a rush when she left her apartment, she only packed two pairs of underwear, and she accidentally threw out one pair with the bag she discarded in the bus terminal earlier.

Cathy entered the small electronics store and found a clerk who looked young and uninterested. She explained she needed a phone, but she had bad credit and had no credit cards. Cathy continued, trying to bore the kid until he stopped listening. This took a matter of seconds. She thought to herself as she breathed a sigh of relief, *Thank God for the attention span of a teenager.*

The salesboy explained how burner phones are like temporary phone numbers that you buy minutes on ahead of time. Cathy grabbed the cheapest burner phone on the shelf. She didn't care anything about the phone except that it worked to call people without being traced. At the counter, she paid for the phone and one hundred minutes, all in cash. The teenager didn't make a fuss. As she was walking out, the sales boy yelled that the minutes didn't roll over, so she needed to use them within thirty days. He followed that up saying she should come back to buy more minutes if she ran out. She didn't hear the last part; she was already on the street in search of the next store.

Cathy found a thrift shop nearby and bought three more sets of what she called "don't notice me" clothes. The total was an astonishing twenty-nine dollars. She sat on a bus bench for a moment to think about all the money she wasted over the years buying clothes. Two of the items she purchased still had the original store tags on them. She had found a whole new world in thrift shops. Cathy promised to consider this new world when her new mess was ended. She told herself it would be part of her promise to get a life

Cathy walked into a sandwich shop on her way to the department store. Eating was more of a necessity than a desire these days. She ordered a large turkey sandwich, planning to eat half now and the rest for dinner back at the motel. Sitting in the corner of the somewhat vacant shop, she pulled out her list. One bite of the sandwich, and it now made sense why the place wasn't mobbed. She forced herself to eat the entire half while drinking as much of the bottled ice tea with each bite as she could. The dry, rubbery turkey covered by what she assumed might be three-week-old bread was still overpriced at five dollars and twenty-five cents. She checked off the items completed for today's outing, knowing that the underwear purchase was yet to happen. This seemed such a little thing compared to recent events, but it was the small steps that kept her sane.

Cathy debated a long time about taking the other half of the sandwich with her, but she knew she would regret throwing it out later tonight. She closed the plastic container and nearly had to force herself to put the food into the clothing bag. She left the sandwich shop vowing never to return. The thought of having the killer have his last meal from this place seemed like a good idea. Cathy decided she'd recommend this place to the killer and laughed as she walked along the sidewalk. It was good to laugh again. The recent past had been filled with such darkness that Cathy felt a part of her soul had died. Another murder credited to the killer. This time she didn't laugh.

The department store was more crowded than Cathy was hoping, but when you need underwear, you need underwear. This brought back memories of Green Haven. She frequently heard Robin, the social worker, calling family members to delicately tell them that their parent was down to their last underwear or bra. She would explain that they were either too worn, too soiled, or just missing. The last one was always met with great difficulty. Robin likened the missing clothing to a lost sock in a load of laundry. She would try to make light of it by calling it the great dryer robbery. It never went well. Cathy always felt sorry for her.

She found the underwear department and picked out three modest and inexpensive pairs of underwear and bras. She didn't care if they matched. There would be no reason to show them to anyone. Then Cathy thought about being in prison. Probably the last place she would want sexy underwear. She quickly put that thought out of her mind. She picked up a few more incidentals on the way to the registers. She paid cash. Even the young cashier was surprised by being handed money. She looked at Cathy, commenting that most people use a card for purchases that cost over twenty dollars. Cathy didn't look at her, nor did she say a word. She took her change, lifted the bag from the rack, and started for the exit.

Cathy headed back to the motel. A day of sneaking around, continually looking to see if she was being followed by the police, or worse, some hit man hired by an unknown murderous psychopath, had exhausted her. What she really wanted was her own bed. She reached the motel, walked entirely around the bottom floor once, then headed up the back stairs to her second-floor room. She sat in the wooden chair and placed her feet up on the bed. Cathy recalled how good the sheets of her own bed had felt only a few nights ago, and her eyes began to well. She rose to her feet. *No! Cathy Arden, you stop this. You'll be back at home in your own bed soon enough.* She had to believe this was a temporary state of being. The pain of being on the run for the rest of her life was too much to handle.

She calmed down and sat back in the chair when she noticed the book she had bought to hide behind. The title, which she hadn't noticed before, made her laugh. *Hiding in Plain Sight.* She started to read the description.

The story was about a boy who defended himself against a gang and was in hiding right under their noses. Close enough, Cathy thought. She might get some ideas to help with her own situation. She started to read the book. As she read, she found herself identifying with the main character. After about an hour, Cathy began to feel the day's adventure. She put the book down and thought about showering. "Still no damn shower sandals, really." Cathy silently chastised herself and then sat back down in the chair, exhausted.

45

DETECTIVE OAKS WAS CALLED into the Captain's office only to find they were being joined by an FBI agent. He was a young, just out of FBI U, rookie, probably on his first case alone.

"Apparently the powers above received a phone call and have decided that this is now a federal case. The FBI will be taking over." There was doubt within the captain. "I was not asking."

"I understand. I'd like to be kept in the loop." The detective spoke only to the Captain; no acknowledgment of the young agent was made.

"Detective Oaks, while the FBI is now in charge, of course, we'll need your input in continuing to work this case. I will personally call you with anything that comes up." The young agent might actually believe the statement and might actually call if he was ever able to get any new information.

Detective Oaks had been doing this job long enough to know that was standard FBI code for if you need to know, we'll tell you. He smiled, thinking that was most likely the first lecture taught at FBI U. Detective Oaks gave an "are you kidding me?" look at his captain.

The captain ordered him to turn over everything he had to the agent. This was not the first time Detective Marshall Oaks was forced to give a hot case to the FBI, so he had already made copies of everything, including his notebook, which by the way, he would not be turning over. He would be forced to obey his superior in turning over the information, but he would not stop working the case. A fact his captain was very aware of when he ordered him to turn over the files. The captain never mentioned anything about not working the case.

Every cop carried a second gun, and every good detective had a second set of files. One of the many pearls of wisdom Detective Oaks had handed down to him from his mentor. The FBI rookie waited for the detective to return with the box of files. The first of many rookie mistakes he would make according to Detective Oaks. The box was packed and ready to be handed over in less than five minutes. He made the agent wait a good fifteen minutes then came through the door apologizing for how long it took to box up the files. The agent appeared to accept the apology. The detective wondered if the agent could catch the killer if they were living in the same house. He furthered the thought by imagining the killer wearing a sign with "the killer" written on it.

Detective Oaks returned to his captain's office for more details. They had been working together long enough to earn each other's respect. Behind closed doors, rank was not an issue, and both spoke freely and frankly with one another.

"Before you start, I don't know." The captain's left hand was raised in the air as his right reached for the door handle closing the door.

"Okay, then why?" Detective Oaks was leaning on the back of a chair in the office.

"I don't know who or why someone pulled strings, but they wanted the case out of your hands." The captain now returned to his chair behind the desk and motioned for the detective to have a seat.

"But that kid? He couldn't find himself." His voice was louder, and the disgust was palpable in the room.

"Here's what makes it even stranger: the agent told me he was hand-picked for the case. He looked as surprised as you do now."

"Something's not right. This whole case smells bad." Detective Oaks placed his hands on his head. "I'm shaking my head a lot on this case."

"What do you have?"

"I have a nurse who I don't think did it. I have a doctor and owner who think their relationship is a secret. I have a dead priest and sister I think are somehow wrapped in it, and none of it makes sense. So basically, I have jack."

"Well, now you've gotta work it from behind the scenes." The captain gave him a smile that said "just like old times."

"Thanks, I know. I still need some behind the scene stuff to happen. Might have to work some magic. If you . . ."

"Stop! Don't tell me anything else. Get what you need quietly, and you can't tell me about it. You've been around long enough. Just make sure it doesn't mess up the whole damn case." The captain was now facing the wall pretending to look out of a window that didn't exist.

"Talk later." The detective looked back at his captain one last time, who was still pretending to look at the view from his window. Detective Oaks shook his head, and left the room.

Oaks' teams now returned from the nursing facilities, and it was as he had suspected. All three facilities had seen an increase in residents' deaths in the past year. He suspected it had been going on longer than that. Before they continued, he informed them that the case had been taken over by FBI and they were no longer officially working it.

One of the team members whispered loudly, "That never stopped us before."

Detective Oaks smiled then quietly asked his team to bury their findings for now. In a louder voice, he told his team to meet in the parking lot in ten minutes to grab a bite to eat, on him.

On the way over to the diner that Detective Oaks had picked, he started to think about a deadly duo being a priest and sister. He couldn't question them. They were dead, killed in a car accident. Again, too convenient. His detective instincts were insulted by all that he had been ignoring. He had to see how this would play out.

The four members of his team were seated in a large half-moon booth when he arrived. He pulled up a chair at the front end of the booth. It gave him a sense of authority and some separation from his underlings. This reminded him of his earlier conversation with the medical director. He told them they did good work, then he jumped right into the holy couple theory. The team mumbled but put up little resistance. They knew when he had a hunch, it was usually right or at least close. One twosome was to dig deeper into Father Brendan Pierce and the other into Sister Diane Loretto. He insisted that nothing was off limits, but they should continue to be extremely discreet. They were dealing with the Church and at the same time trying not to deal with the FBI. They all understood. He told them he would follow up with Bishop Anthony since he had placed them in the facilities.

The waitress came by for drink orders. Detective Oaks didn't see her standing by him. She asked if they were talking about the Green Haven people. Before he could tell her it was police business, she blurted out that most of them had been in the diner at one time or another. Detective Oaks gave a smile to his team. He asked if she could take a break to speak with them and flashed his shield. She looked over her shoulder at her boss and shook her head. Detective Oaks turned to the younger detective sitting to his right, motioning for him to speak with the owner. A few seconds later, he returned with confirmation that it was okay for her to go on break for as long as she needed.

The waitress sat down, still worried about the repercussions she might face later. Detective Oaks asked her to tell them as much as she could remember about each person from Green Haven. She started with Father Brendan. He had been the friendliest and the best tipper. She recounted how at first he would come in with an older priest, then alone for a short while, and then with a pretty young sister called Diane. The waitress went on about how well they got along and if she didn't know better, they could have been married. One of the team members asked if she noticed anything odd about them. She added there was nothing other than how well suited they were for each other.

Detective Oaks asked about the nurse Cathy Arden. The waitress asked if he meant the woman on TV. He nodded. She told them she had only been in the diner once and it was with a gentleman. They were going over papers. They were looking for something. She remembered going over to the table to take their order and both tried to cover up the papers so she couldn't read them. A female member of the detective team pulled up a photo of Kyle on her phone. The waitress identified him as the man with Cathy Arden. The waitress was then asked if they were arguing. She repeated that they were working together, trying to figure something out. Detective Oaks thanked her for her time then said they were ready to order. She got up looking at her boss and loudly stated that she really needed to get back to work. They all gave her a knowing smile.

During dinner they gave their opinions. They agreed that whatever the argument between Strong and Arden was at Green Haven, it had been resolved and they had combined forces to solve something. Detective Oaks placed his fork down and leaned back on his chair, his hands interlocked behind his head. He gave a dramatic pause then leaned in on the table.

"I think they stumbled onto the murders at Green Haven. I think Arden might be telling the truth. They were working together in the end. If the waitress is right about what she saw, then the killer or killers are still unknown."

"Unless they were the, what did you call them?" the youngest detective suggested.

"The holy couple. No, who would kill them if they were the killers?" Detective Oaks was irritated by the suggestion at first, but then saw the merit of the possibility.

"It's like you said, boss, there might be another killer involved," another of the underlings blurted out, trying to win favor with his boss.

"Okay, let's stop looking at Strong and Arden. We'll let the FBI rookie chase them for a while. Concentrate on the holy couple, and I'll follow up with a few other things."

He asked for the check, and the waitress brought it over. She still had a worried look on her face. As the detective reached the counter to pay the bill, he leaned in close to the owner.

"You have a terrific waitress here. One I think highly of. I suggest you keep her at any cost." He was now almost nose to nose with the owner. "I would be terribly upset if the next time I came in she wasn't here because she got fired. The change is for her, all of it." Detective Oaks turned back to look at the waitress and gave her a wink, then he walked out.

46

SHE DROVE OUT OF town heading for a bar they had met at many times before. He was sitting in a dimly lit booth in the back. She joined him. The waiter came over; she ordered a bourbon, and he ordered a Scotch. Most of their meetings lasted only minutes. This time they sat as he took his time. He wasn't concerned about being seen.

"Things are getting out of hand. How you're handling matters is drawing too much attention." She had never spoken to him like this before, and he would make sure she never did again.

She was about to tell him that she was out when she looked up to see the sternness in his stare. He had raised his hand, commanding her to stop. She had seen this before, and it frightened her each time. His hand may be older, but it seemed to have a power all on its own.

"You've become accustomed to a certain way of life. You might be about to make a dangerous mistake. One that could end the comfort you currently enjoy." His tone was as deliberate as the words he chose.

She understood them clearly. She knew he was capable of having just about anything done that he wanted. She took another sip of her bourbon and ventured the question of how he would handle all the new and unwanted popularity with the press and the police. She really didn't want to know. Her part was delivering the necessary information and keeping her head down. This had worked well for her since accepting his offer. But now she was scared, and she wanted out. Things had changed. He was going too far.

She was now sipping the bourbon at a steady pace. She told him that she had been questioned twice by a detective regarding Green Haven. She politely reminded him that he agreed to protect her in addition to paying her well. The bourbon had loosened her tongue a bit and created a dangerous spike in her courage. She caught it and sat there, hoping that he would let it slide.

He assured that he had taken care of the detective. A look of fear came over her face. He reassured her that he didn't mean in that way. He told her he called in some favors, and now the case was given to a very young FBI agent who was sure to close the case and place the fugitive nurse behind bars quickly. He added, in an almost boasting manner, that Nurse Arden was the only suspect in the murder case of Kyle Strong, administrator and her boss.

She sat there amazed and disgusted at the willingness of the man to play with peoples' lives with such disregard. It was pure evil.

He closed his grand declaration by telling her that as far as the FBI was concerned, there was nothing else going on at the Green Haven, Inc. facilities. It was merely one disgruntled employee who decided to kill her boss. For good measure, he added that if for some odd reason, the youngster became over-zealous in his work, they had already done an excellent job of pointing the finger at the nurse. This was a fact she couldn't dispute.

He ordered another round of drinks. She wanted to refuse but again was afraid, and yet she was feeling safer now than when she walked in. He had a way of making people feel safe. He knew this and used it to his advantage over and over.

He realized the alcohol was having its influence on her, so they sat there for the next hour chatting about insignificant subjects. He had ordered some bar-type appetizers to help move things along. He needed her alive and functional. Besides, another car death with someone tied to Green

Haven, Inc. would make it impossible to hide, no matter how many favors he could call in.

When he thought it was okay for her to drive, he called the waiter over, paid the tab in cash, and just left the table. It was evident to her that she was only a tool to him. But she was a tool that was paid damn well. She stood and walked through the bar, making sure to remain as invisible as possible.

She got into her car, the terror of such an evil person still clinging to her. She clearly had made a deal with the devil, and there was no way to get out. She headed back into town, her hands trembling as they grasped the steering wheel. She needed to regain her composure before returning. Pulling over to the side of the road, she exited the car, stood beside it, and vomited. She was unsure if it was the alcohol or the evil. The cool wind from passing traffic brushed against her and allowed her to regain control. She got into her car and continued her drive.

47

OSCAR WOULD BE ENJOYING hiding out in luxury if it weren't for the circumstances that forced him to be there. Now he had the added complication that Marissa lied to him in order to leave. He poured himself another Scotch and sat down on the couch. His curiosity got to him; he turned on the television. The news reporter was giving a recap of the fugitive nurse who the FBI suspected killed her boss. Oscar prayed she wouldn't mention Green Haven; she didn't. He turned off the television and closed his eyes. He lay flat on his back, holding a pillow on his chest with crossed arms. He was playing back the start of it all in his mind. His father's death, meeting Marissa in the hospital, the safety deposit box filled with money, buying the land for Green Haven, building the two other facilities, the secret affair with Marissa, and now the possibility of it all falling apart.

Oscar started to wonder about the money from his father. The man was smart, but Oscar never really knew what his father did. How did he make his money? His father told him he was an executive for some company. Why were the police always showing up? Oscar recalled his father saying that the company did a fair amount of business with law enforcement. Was the money dirty? Was all of this karmic payback for using his father's dirty money? After all, it was hidden. Oscar told himself he was getting paranoid.

He decided there was nothing to do anyway. His father was dead, and the money was spent. There was no reason to drag his father through the mud.

He brought his attention back to Marissa. Why lie now? Where did she go? Was she jumping ship? Oscar was getting angrier by the minute. His thoughts of betrayal grew almost as fast as the anger. This would be the second time in his life he was blindsided by someone he thought loved him. This time he would fight if necessary. Contract or not, if she left him and Green Haven, she would get nothing! He would enjoy every moment of the fight. Oscar now had the pillow in a chokehold.

It was another hour before Marissa returned. Oscar had managed to regain control of his emotions. She bypassed the front desk, entering the elevator for the third floor. When she reached Oscar's room, she realized she didn't have a room key. She knocked on the door while calling out to Oscar. Oscar made her wait just long enough to show his displeasure. He turned the lock and she practically burst through the door, kissing him on the lips. His anger passed for a moment, but he had to address the situation. Sex was not going to wash away the distrust that was growing in him. He placed his hands on the outside of her shoulders and held her at arm's length.

"Where did you really go?" Anger bellowed from his words.

"The hospital. Why?" She continued past him into the spacious living room.

"You wouldn't drink then go to the hospital." He held up an empty glass for dramatic effect. It happened to be his.

"I had the drink before I got the text. I had to go. I didn't have a choice," Marissa fired back with her own heat. "Besides, I was a child back then."

"You smell like alcohol now." He pointed at her in great disdain. The anger of being lied to had taken a full grip on Oscar at this point.

"You mean still, right? You're out of control! Get hold of yourself, now!" Marissa had always been the one with the upper hand in the relationship, and she felt it slipping away, but not without a fight.

"Look, I think you lied to me, and with everything else that's going on, I need to know we're a team." Oscar softened. He wasn't really looking for an all-out war. He needed her; he wanted her on his side. He sat down on the couch then placed the empty glass on the coffee table in front of him.

"Of course we're a team. I ate a breath mint in my car before I went into the hospital, but it must have worn off by now. What do you think I was doing?" Marissa knew she was back in charge as she placed an arm around his waist.

"I don't know. Maybe you're right; I am going crazy here." Oscar placed his hand on her free hand and held on tightly.

"Let's order room service, find a movie, and spend the night here." She had subdued the raging beast. Honestly, she was a bit impressed. She didn't think he had it in him.

Oscar liked the idea of food and spending the night with her. Marissa knew how to handle him. She picked up the room service menu and sat on the couch close to Oscar. She made sure they were touching. He was already looking for a movie. He took notice of the warmth of her leg against his. He had planned to hold out at least until after food and the movie. Oscar was saddened as he thought they were back to playing games. His next thought brought back the anger: *What if she never stopped playing games?* He tried to stop himself. He tried to convince himself that the stress of possibly losing the Green Haven empire was taking its toll on him and he didn't need to cause more chaos by losing Marissa.

They chose a movie and started to watch it. Oscar's eyes were looking at the screen, but his mind was in charge. He was playing back all the events of his relationship with Dr. Marissa Oliver. He recalled their first business meeting and then the meeting at her office. Now that he thought about it, the office didn't have any patients in it and none showed up the entire time he was there. *My God,* he thought to himself, *she must have been struggling, and I was her ticket to a better life.* The anger was intense once more. Oscar continued his own movie, recounting her tough negotiations with high demands. She played him from the beginning.

The doorbell buzzed; room service had arrived. Oscar looked at her as he got up to answer the door. She paused the movie, not that he knew what was going on anyway. He opened the door. It was Detective Oaks. Oscar physically jumped backward, causing the detective to let out a laugh, which he unsuccessfully tried to muffle with his hands. The detective politely insisted that he come in. Oscar escorted him into the living room area. Marissa fought every urge to scream. Instead, she greeted the detective. He smiled and told them he wasn't surprised. He tracked both their phones here. He knew this was only partially true. Detective Oaks had pinged Oscar's phone, illegally, but he didn't think Oscar was involved, so it really wouldn't affect the case. And his captain would never know about it. Marissa's presence was just an added bonus that verified his hunch about their relationship.

He sat in a chair across from the couch without waiting to be asked. Oscar remained standing until Marissa gave him a look to sit. He sat on the edge of the couch apart from her.

"Don't worry, your secret is safe with me. I don't really care who's sleeping with who as long as it doesn't mess with my case."

"Whom. It's whom."

"Really, Doc? Why do people do that? Whom really cares. And I know that was wrong! Can, no may I, continue? Good. Officially the FBI is handling the case, but I still have questions I need answered. My team already found out there has been an increase in resident deaths at all three facilities."

Oscar's face gave the expression of utter confusion and shock. The detective could see this really was new information for the owner. He knew he was witnessing Oscar's dream unravel before the man's own eyes. Detective Oaks scanned Marissa with his peripheral vision, noticing she had no response. Not a twitch, no change in her breathing, not even a look at poor Oscar, who was visibly coming undone. Oscar pushed back onto the couch and started to shake his head as he whispered to himself.

"Am I missing something? Did you remember something you want to tell me, Oscar?" Detective Oaks knew that unhinging Oscar could cause him to voice something he didn't intend to say.

"No. I'm wondering the same thing. What did I miss? I just wanted to do right by my father. I just wanted to create a place to make older people happy. I just wanted to give them what I couldn't give my father, and now it's all going to hell. And I don't know why." Oscar fell silent; his shoulders had caved in, as had his world.

The detective could see that Oscar was broken, but he still wondered why the doctor wasn't making a sound or any movement at all to console her lover. He gave Oscar a few moments to regain control, and then he continued, "I'm sorry, but I do have some more questions." He handed Oscar a napkin he retrieved from the bar.

"Thanks. It's okay, go ahead."

"I know you had a phone conversation and met with Mr. Perkins before his car accident. What did you discuss?" The notebook scribbling was running on full tilt at this moment.

"He was complaining about the long-term finances of my company, and he was calling a board meeting to give details and to ask for my removal from the board."

"Oscar, don't . . ." Marissa grabbed Oscar's arm. He yanked it away.

"Dr. Oliver, let him finish. I don't think he killed anyone. I just need the information."

"I called the other board members and got them to rally behind me. He was the only one I couldn't convince. I was going to take my chances. I still owned the building and the land outright. They would have to buy me out or resign. I could get a new board if it came to that." Oscar was now standing and walking to the bar for another napkin. "It's all going to shit, and I can't stop it. If my father were here, he would find a way to fix it. He always knew about these things."

"You mean murder?" Detective Oaks was now writing furiously, but his attention was keenly focused on the sobbing man laying out the details.

"No! He just had a way with people. He would have been able to smooth the board over in a matter of hours. None of this would have happened." Oscar was freewheeling his words without any thought of the consequences.

"That's enough, Oscar. You're blubbering nonsense." Marissa was now demanding silence from him.

Detective Oaks turned to face Marissa more directly. He then asked her if she pronounced the death of all the residents at the facilities. The doorbell rang again. Oscar interjected that they had ordered room service. He got up and asked the waiter to leave the cart in the foyer. He tipped the waiter well and showed him out. Oscar returned to the living room, having managed to compose himself again. Marissa had yet to give her answer.

The detective restated his question, this time putting much more emphasis on her name. This made Dr. Oliver more nervous, a fact she was still managing to hide well. She replied that she personally pronounced only those residents who had not been authorized for a nurse to pronounce. Detective Oaks asked if she did eventually sign all of the certificates.

Marissa added that the director of nursing from each facility would put the certificates tagged "nurse may pronounce" in her box at that facility so they could be countersigned by her. He then asked Marissa if she had noticed an increase in the number of deaths recently. She told him that in her line of work, death was a common factor, and you stop counting to keep sane.

Detective Oaks stood up, thanked them for their time, and told them to enjoy their evening. He let himself out. In the hallway, he made several more notes. He was a veteran detective; he asked questions he already knew the answers to only to see if lies were told and to watch reactions. The rest was a game he played well. As he boarded the elevator, he concluded that Oscar was harmless, but the doctor was hiding something.

They sat on the couch in silence for a long time before Oscar blurted out, "I'm scared!" He asked Marissa how the detective could think they were involved.

"He's just being thorough. You heard him. We're not the killers." Marissa was well aware that the detective stated that Oscar was not a killer. He made no mention of her. He was getting close, too close. She couldn't leave again, so she pretended to have to use the bathroom. She told Oscar to set up the food. Neither of them had any desire to eat.

Marissa sent multiple texts detailing her encounter with the detective and her concerns. She received no response. After five minutes of waiting, she flushed the toilet and returned to the living room. Oscar was still sitting on the couch, frozen in time. Marissa sat on his lap and assured him they were fine. She looked in his eyes and asked him what happened to the food. Oscar moved her to the couch to get up and retrieve the food. His emotional ride had worn him down. He had no will to fight her or even challenge any of what he earlier played back in his mind about their entire relationship.

48

It had been a long night sleeping in a chair, but Cathy was ready to get to work. She needed to get a hold of Lenny. She dialed the main number to Green Haven on the burner phone. The receptionist answered. Cathy disguised her voice while asking for Lenny. The receptionist asked if she could tell him what the call was in reference to. Cathy said she was from an IT lecturing service that needed a guest speaker on short notice. She knew Lenny wouldn't be able to resist the call.

Lenny came on the phone. Cathy could almost see the wide expression of excitement on his face. Her guilt grew, but she had no choice.

"Hello. This is Leonard. How can I help you?" An air of professionalism carried with his words.

"Lenny, don't freak, it's Cathy Arden."

"You do know you're wanted by the FBI?" His voice was as condescending as it was surprised.

"I know."

"Why are you calling me?" Lenny seemed to be cowering in his own office.

"Lenny, you know me. Do you think I'm a killer?" Cathy was desperate, and she didn't hide it.

"It doesn't matter what I think!"

"Lenny, I need your help. I need your computer skills."

"No, no way!" Lenny was not the type to get involved. His fear alarm had just reached a new level. His feet were almost marching in place from the anxiety.

"Lenny, calm down and hear me out, okay? You and I are friends. We're better than friends. We get each other." She hated herself. She almost wished that Lenny would hang up just so she wouldn't have to use him.

"Fine, what are you thinking?" Lenny took the bait. Cathy felt worse.

"I'm being framed. I know the answer is in that computer system. You can help me find it." She held her breath waiting for his response.

"What would we be looking for?" His voice had returned to its normal pitch. Lenny was now seated at his computer screen awaiting further instruction.

"I need to know if anyone has been checking the system for death certificates besides Kyle or me. Also, has anyone been tracking charts that have 'nurse may pronounce' on them? Again, besides Kyle or myself."

"Wait, were you and Kyle working together? No one will buy that. He hated you."

"You're right, until a few days before he was killed. Lenny, please focus."

"Sorry. Okay. I'll look. Call me back in a few hours." His fingers were already banging on the keys, causing code to leap across the screen.

"Lenny, be careful. Use all your tricks to cover yourself." Cathy regretted the call even more as she realized the danger she may have just put Lenny in.

"Bye." Lenny was totally engrossed in the world he loved and adding a spy-like twist made it that much better.

Cathy hoped that Lenny heard her. She couldn't deal with someone else turning up dead. She hated herself just a bit more for using Lenny's boyish crush to her advantage, but these were desperate times, and Lenny would survive. Her next move was to call Detective Oaks to help send him in the right direction. She would call him anonymously to tip him off about Green Haven's money problems. She would tell him to look at the contracts and set payments.

She called the police station and asked for Detective Oaks. He picked up the line a few minutes later and asked who he was speaking with. Cathy told him she had to remain anonymous for her own safety. She quickly started in before the detective could say anything. He stopped her when she mentioned the name Green Haven. He informed her that he was officially off the case and couldn't talk about an active investigation with someone unwilling to identify themselves. Cathy didn't realize that when the FBI took over the local police were shoved aside.

Detective Oaks suspected it was Cathy Arden on the phone. He told her that it was nearly lunchtime and today there was a special at Louie's on Fifth Street that he loved. He hung up the phone. Cathy looked at her phone; it was 10:15 am. She got the hint, but she was still wary. What if it was a setup? She decided to get there an hour early and watch to see if anything was going on.

Cathy hopped in a cab and arrived on Fifth Street. She went into Louie's and had a conversation with the waitress. She left quickly, walking across the street to a coffee shop where she ordered a cup of coffee and watched. At 12:05 pm, she saw the Detective enter Louie's. Cathy watched as the waitress came over to him then handed him a note. After reading it, he stood, exited the shop, and crossed the street to the coffee shop. She could see the smile on the grouchy detective's face. She took this as a good sign. He came in and sat down at a table as the note directed him to. Cathy watched to see if anyone followed him in. No one did. Cathy approached him and sat down at the table.

"I like what you've done with your hair." A sarcastic remark at best by the detective.

"I'm putting a lot of trust in you." Cathy had the same look in her eye as she did during their other encounters. She couldn't back down. The rest of her life depended on it.

"Calm down. If I were going to arrest you, I would have already done it. By the way, nice switch." He looked around at the coffee shop, still wearing the smile.

"I used to watch a lot of cop shows."

"I think you're being framed. Just to keep in line with the cop shows." The smile was now gone and the grumpiness had returned.

"Thanks, but why the FBI?" She was sitting back in her chair and holding her coffee in her left hand. The right one still hurt, although not as much.

"Not my call. Whoever is framing you has connections."

"Whom."

"What. Are you kidding? You too? Can we stay focused here? And I don't think you're right in this case." He almost growled the words at her.

"Sorry. I have someone on the inside digging up information as we speak." She was leaning in again and speaking softly so no one else could hear.

"This isn't one of your detective show storylines! People are getting killed. Who do you have doing what, exactly?" He grabbed onto the edge of the table as though he could throw it at any moment.

"Lenny the IT guy is looking to see who's been searching death certificates and charts with 'nurse may pronounce' on them. Wait, do you know that the number of resident deaths has almost tripled at Green Haven?" Cathy pushed back from the table.

"Sorry, this case has me crazy. How do you know? And it's actually at all three facilities." He didn't need his notepad. The information had become engraved in his mind.

"That's what Kyle and I were working on together in the end. At first, we both were putting it together separately without each other knowing.

In fact, he suspected me and I suspected him." She moved closer to the table and leaned in again

"What about the argument days before he died?" Detective Oaks' growl had softened.

"I was calling him out. I told him I would prove he was the killer. By the end of the conversation, we were on the same team." The detective was once again impressed by the coolness Cathy portrayed.

Detective Oaks smiled again at this news. He was right; his detective instinct had been right. "That's why you met him at the diner. No one knows I'm still looking into this, and no one knows about the resident deaths, so keep it quiet."

"No, we went to the diner just to eat. We met at the library to go over everything. And, who am I going to tell?" Cathy looked around the coffee shop as if they were the only ones there.

Detective Oaks got up from the table, leaving a card with his private cell number on it. He whispered to Cathy to call as soon as she heard from Lenny.

"We're not done yet," she said with a bit of frustration.

"I have to follow up on a hunch before it's too late. Get your boy to come through and call me." He walked away, once again getting in the last word.

Cathy left the coffee shop, making sure no one was following her. She headed back to the motel, crossing back and forth along the streets then stopping at an occasional shop to check again if anyone was following her. When she came to a fast food place, she went in one door and left through another on the opposite side of the building. She smiled, thinking that the detective shows did have some worth.

She finally made it back to the motel tired from all the backtracking and misdirection. The cab ride that had taken less than ten minutes took her over an hour to walk. Once inside the room, she called Lenny, this time using the direct line he had given her.

"What took you so long?" Lenny had been sitting at his desk playing rounds of solitaire on his computer, waiting for her to call.

"You did tell me to wait a few hours."

"I was done in less than an hour."

"Never mind, what did you find?"

"Well, first I searched through all last week's data to see if anyone had looked for the information. You know, since you and Kyle had been gone. Then I searched for anything in the past year. Then I decided . . ."

"Lenny, get to the point. No, wait, let me get something to write with first." She dug the pen out of her purse and grabbed the envelope from the safe.

"Don't bother, I put it all in a file that I can text to you and no one will know where it came from." Lenny was imagining himself as a superhero, with his sunken chest all muscled and wearing a navy onesie that outlined all of his chiseled features.

"Okay, I need you to text it to two numbers. Lenny? Lenny! Are you still there?"

"What? Uh, sure. Wait, who else knows I'm doing this? I could get fired." Lenny's superhero vanished.

"Lenny, getting fired is the least of your worries. I'm giving you two numbers because, in case I have to ditch one phone, I'll need it on a second phone. I don't have anywhere to print it out, and I want you to destroy it as soon as you send it. Got it?" Cathy thought lying was getting way too easy.

"Yes."

She gave Lenny the detective's private number. Then she asked Lenny to provide her with a quick rundown on what he found. She told him to skip the showboating and get to the findings. Lenny explained that he found three people looking at the information she asked about: her, Kyle, and Dr. Oliver. Cathy almost dropped the phone. He continued, telling her that if he excluded the residents who didn't have the "nurse may pronounce" anywhere in their files, Dr. Oliver had her electronic fingerprint on every one of the other files. She had searched and opened each file in the past two years.

Cathy was trying to think of any logical reason that Dr. Oliver might be looking at the same exact residents. "Was she reviewing charts?"

"I traced her steps on most of them, and it's always the same. She was definitely just searching for those words."

"And this has been for the past two years? Not in the past two weeks? Lenny, are you sure that no one will be able to see what you were doing?" Cathy was finding it hard to believe that the medical director was framing her.

"Two years. I'm pretty sure no one can see. Maybe I'll check again." Lenny knew he was good at what he did, but he also knew that there would be someone better.

"Good. Send the file to both numbers, and I'll call you back in a few minutes to let you know you can destroy it on your end."

Before she hung up, she asked Lenny if there had been any more resident deaths with labeled certificates. Lenny said that's what makes it look really bad for her. There had been none since she and Kyle were gone. Cathy could feel her shoulders drop.

She dialed Detective Oaks and told him Lenny had created a file he needed to look at and he'd text it over.

Seconds later the file appeared on her phone. Cathy called Lenny back and told him to destroy the file. Lenny said he would and that his work had been covered. Cathy felt relieved for Lenny, but Dr. Marissa Oliver was a different story.

49

OSCAR WOKE UP to an empty space next to him, again. He didn't know if Marissa had left early that morning or sometime in the middle of the night. The more Oscar thought about it, the more he began to realize her actions were strange. He started to understand she was keeping him at a distance. He felt foolish. She had seduced him, played with his emotions, and benefited from his fondness of her. Oscar didn't want to think of her as a monster, but now his mind was overruling his heart. He had to find out what she was up to.

Oscar got dressed and was heading out of the hotel door when he almost ran right into Detective Oaks.

"Not again." Oscar tried to sidestep the detective.

"I'd like to speak with Dr. Oliver." He placed a hand on Oscar's shoulder, blocking his way.

"Me too!" His anger was overwhelming.

The detective saw an opportunity and asked Oscar if he could buy him breakfast. Oscar accepted, thinking he may need some time to clear his mind.

They sat down in the hotel restaurant. Detective Oaks started in by saying he too had been troubled many times by female friends. Oscar was only half paying attention. The detective continued with the question of how well he knew her. He now had Oscar's full attention. Oscar looked up from his coffee cup and said he had known her for over ten years, and yet he really knew nothing about her—a fact that was more disturbing when said out loud. Detective Oaks sensed Oscar was ready to talk, so he pushed on, asking how they met. Oscar was willing to tell the entire story, from their initial hospital meeting to the lie she told yesterday. The detective was soaking up every detail. He didn't take out his notebook; it might spook Oscar. He was convinced that Dr. Oliver was complicit in some way and poor Oscar was along for the ride. He figured Oscar had no idea what was going on.

Even though he already knew, Detective Oaks asked Oscar to tell him how Green Haven, Inc. came about. He needed to get him talking. The detective understood that people couldn't resist talking about their achievements and that usually got them to loosen up. He asked what made it so special. Oscar explained about his father's last years of life and the life insurance policy, how he wanted to build a luxury place so people could live out their lives in style and how he didn't want to be under the control of the insurance companies.

Oscar bragged about his visionary idea of a once a year payment that covered just about everything. The detective let him finish before asking questions about finances and any difficulties he might have had. Again, questions he already knew the answers to, but Oscar's emotions were raw and Oaks could use this to his advantage.

Oscar explained how he bought the land outright with his father's life insurance money. Oscar didn't mention the money in the safety deposit box. He was unable to get financing for the building, so his uncle gave him some money but made him promise never to tell anyone. The rest he managed to get from a handful of investors. Oscar added that he paid them back ahead of schedule.

The owner of the Green Haven empire stopped suddenly. Detective Oaks told him it was okay; he didn't care about the IRS stuff. The detective followed up by saying, "The IRS needs to do their own work if they wanted to put us good guys away." He thought this was like detective 101 class, bond with, gain trust, lock 'em up. Except he wasn't after Oscar; in fact, he almost felt guilty for being another person to use this guy, almost.

They finished breakfast a while ago, but Oscar was still giving valuable information, so Oaks let him go on. When Oscar was done, he looked at his watch, and the detective took this as a hint that it was time to stop pushing. He had new information and new leads. He paid the check. It was much more than a city employee should be spending on breakfast, but it turned out to be worth it. Detective Oaks stood up and shook Oscar's hand. As he left, Oscar thought the man might be growing into a human with some manners.

Oscar sat there for a few minutes finishing his third cup of coffee, happy to have spent some time not thinking about his dilemma with Marissa. He was now calm about the situation. He still wanted to talk with her, but first he wanted more information about who she was and what kind of life she had growing up, all the things that people in a relationship know about each other. He felt the calm giving way to anger. He knew this wasn't the right time to confront her. He didn't want it to be a big emotional blowout. Not that they ever had one, mostly because he would let things go to avoid the battle.

Detective Oaks got into his unmarked car, which any criminal could mark for miles, and started to drive. He called one of the detectives on his team. "I want everything on Oscar Green's family. In particular, I want to know who his uncle is and how much he's worth. I don't want any loose ends. I want to know how much Oscar Green, Sr.'s estate was worth and how much Junior got from it. I want to know how much Junior paid for the land that Green Haven sits on, and finally, I want to know who invested in it and how much. Get everybody on this now. I'll be back in a few hours.

We'll meet in the main conference room. No, I don't care what it looks like. We're close now. I know it."

After ending the call, the detective saw he had received a text sometime earlier. He pulled the car over to open the file. Reading the file made him call back his team. He added that he wanted everything on Dr. Marissa Oliver from the day she was born until this very second. He was pissed. First, because he didn't follow up on his instincts enough and second, which made him feel odd, because she played Oscar. This made him cringe. He decided he needed to close this case fast.

For a laugh, he called the FBI kid to see how far he had gotten on the case. "I haven't had a chance to work on it yet. I have much bigger cases I'm already working on. I'll get to it soon. Don't worry, Detective."

Detective Oaks was all smiles thinking that answer was better than he thought it would be. This case was now bigger and better, and all his. For a moment he felt sorry for the lesson he was about to teach the rookie. Detective Oaks wondered what was going on with him. He envisioned himself aging into an old hard-nosed detective just like one of Cathy Arden's cop shows. *Damn, now I'm soft and an idiot.*

50

CATHY FELT TRAPPED IN the motel room. The news of Dr. Oliver's betrayal ate away at her. Even though she didn't know her well, she had respected her as a colleague. After an agonizing, almost schizophrenic battle with herself, Cathy decided she was done hiding in a motel; she wanted to be home. The only way to do this was to get Dr. Oliver to admit to the murders. She called a cab and then got dressed in one of the "don't notice me" outfits. She planned to wait in a store near Green Haven for Dr. Oliver to show. She would somehow make the medical director admit to everything. Cathy knew the plan wasn't fully fleshed out, but it would be by the time she arrived.

The cab pulled up to a convenience store that had a good view of Green Haven. Cathy paid cash. She looked toward the parking lot; the medical director's parking space was still empty. She headed into the store and pretended to shop at the shelves near the windows. From there, she could see the driveway entrance. It was nearly 9:15. Cathy knew the doctor was late, but she would be pulling in soon.

Dr. Marissa Oliver's car turned into the parking lot minutes later. Cathy left the store, walking quickly toward the Green Haven parking lot. As she was crossing the street, she felt a hand grab onto her right arm, then another on her left. The men holding her arms flashed badges while telling her they were detectives. Cathy had been caught. They escorted her back to the parking lot of the convenience store and placed her in an unmarked police car. Detective Oaks asked her why she was here in a moderately loud but stern voice. Cathy looked at him puzzled. In her own slightly louder tone, she stated that she thought he was on her side. He proceeded to tell her that they were unable to find Dr. Oliver last night to arrest her. She was out of town, so they're waiting here now.

"Arrest her?" Cathy could feel the nightmare washing away.

"Yes. We actually did some detective work and found that she barely passed her residency. There were multiple questionable incidents in her file from other doctors. Also, and this is all I'll share with you, she may have been working with someone to commit the murders at all three facilities."

"But why?"

"Money for starters. Job security, maybe." Detective Oaks was speaking as a seasoned cop who had seen it all.

"What?"

"Look. Let us get her and question her, then I'll fill you in. You need to get out of here. Remember, the FBI is still looking for you."

"You can tell them to stop. You know I'm innocent." She had that defiant look again.

"You need to work on your attitude. And I will handle the FBI, just not yet. I think there's one more player I need to find first. Go back to the motel and stay there until I come get you. Yes, I know about the motel. I had you followed from the coffee shop." Detective Oaks took delight sharing that bit of information.

He nodded to one of his team members, and the door opened, allowing Cathy to get out of the car. She exited the vehicle amazed and feeling stupid. She thought she was doing an excellent job for a first-time criminal. She had more questions but kept silent as she got into the waiting cab. One of the junior detectives leaned into the cab before closing the door.

"Real detective work is hard, not like on TV." Before Cathy had a chance to respond, he closed the door, and the cab pulled away.

Cathy sat in the chair of the dank motel, staring at the walls, waiting for Detective Oaks to call her. She wanted to leave, but she knew that the detective was watching her. Any attempt to return to her amateur sleuthing might end up with her handcuffed to the motel room's bed, or radiator, or whatever her television view of keeping a person locked up and hidden could conjure.

It dawned on Cathy that her ordeal was almost over. She wouldn't have to hide or stay in crappy motels ever again. She felt a wave of emotion come crashing down on her as one lonely tear ran down her face. "Hold it together. You're almost done." She looked in the broken mirror hanging on the wall. She packed all her belongings, trying to keep busy while she waited. She wouldn't spend one extra minute there.

Detective Oaks and his team entered Green Haven to arrest Dr. Oliver. Their original plan was to confront her in the parking lot and keep a low profile. Unfortunately, Cathy's appearance had allowed that opportunity to pass. Detective Oaks sent in one male and one female member of his team. They quietly walked up to the doctor, showed their badges, and politely helped her out of the building. Detective Oaks didn't want too much noise around this, as the case was still officially in the hands of the FBI.

A very pale-looking Dr. Marissa Oliver exited the building accompanied by the two detectives. The operation had gone smoothly and without much recognition. The detective was counting on Green Haven still being somewhat chaotic from the loss of both its administrator and director of nursing. He was correct. Everyone was so busy that no one noticed the three of them leaving.

Once Dr. Oliver was placed in an unmarked car and headed to the station, Detective Oaks picked up his phone. He was about to call Oscar

Green to tell him he would need a new medical director. He stopped, put the phone on the seat next to him, and rubbed his face with his hands. "I really have gone soft! A rookie mistake, Detective." He quietly continued to berate himself as he drove to the station. "What if Oscar was somehow tied up in this? You would have tipped him off." Detective Oaks was now taking short glances at himself in the rearview mirror. "Just because you felt sorry for the guy? You'd better get control of yourself."

Cathy opened the door of the motel and stood at the railing looking out at really nothing. She didn't ever want to feel that her freedom had been taken away again. As she stood there, she started to understand that her life had become so routine that she had taken her own freedom long before the Green Haven murders began. The realization that in the past few weeks she had purpose, she felt energized, and, as cliché as it sounded in her head, she felt alive again.

Cathy returned to her room and turned on the television, hoping to see breaking news about the arrest of a local doctor for murder, but there was nothing. She looked at the burner phone, wishing it would ring. Nothing. Her mind began to create the story that Dr. Oliver put up a struggle and got away. She escaped to a motel, this motel where Cathy fought and subdued her. Detective Oaks showed up and thanked her for a job well done. She laughed then sat there saddened. She had done all this work but didn't get to catch the bad guy. It felt so anti-climactic. She needed an epic finale, like on the shows. She'd tell the detective that she wanted to testify, to let the world know she and Kyle collected all the information and put the whole thing together. How odd, she thought, that she cared for the man who basically tortured her for years. Cathy surmised he died trying to do the right thing.

51

DR. OLIVER SAT WAITING in an interrogation room while Detective Oaks and his team watched her on a camera feed. When they thought she had sat long enough, Detective Oaks went in.

Marissa asked, "Why am I sitting in this room?" She was defiant and loud.

He looked at her calmly as he sat down across from her. "Murder." He waited for her response; there was none for a long time.

Finally, she broke the silence. "I would like my attorney."

Playing the hunch that she didn't have an attorney, Detective Oaks offered, "Sure, I'd be glad to make the call for you. What's the number?" He was right, again.

Marissa leaned in, staring directly at the detective. "I want to cut a deal."

"Why should I cut a deal? You're the only suspect we're looking at. We know you did the murders." Detective Oaks sat back and waited for the information to sink in.

"I didn't kill anyone!" She pounded her fist on the table in a childish tantrum.

"We know how it went down." Detective Oaks pulled out the notebook; the pen tapping created a barrage of clangs against the metal interrogation room table.

The repetitive clanging of the pen sounded like a heartbeat in tamponade, its quick and erratic pace striking booming blows against Dr. Oliver's hardened exterior. "You don't have the right person! Give me a deal, and I'll tell you everything." Her childlike actions continued as she bargained to get what she wanted.

"You start, then I'll decide." The pen tapping stopped, and silence hit the room. The detective never took his eyes from his notepad; again, he waited for his prey to make the next move.

"I need a lawyer." The childlike behavior subsided, and the fear of prison time was setting in as Dr. Marissa Oliver no longer demanded. She was almost begging.

The detective knew the rules, and since this was really an FBI case, he had better follow them more closely than not. He stood up and told her they'd have an attorney here within a few hours. He left the room.

Oscar panicked, as he had not heard from Marissa after leaving a dozen messages. He worried she might have finally broken off their relationship. Her lying was just the tip of the iceberg. Perhaps there was someone else. A younger man, maybe a doctor she met at the hospital. He decided to go over to Green Haven and find her. To hell with the rules at this point.

As Oscar pulled into Green Haven, he saw her car in the parking lot. He sensed some relief. He walked into the lobby and asked the receptionist if she knew which wing Dr. Oliver was in. The receptionist told him she had left a while ago with a man and woman who looked very official. Oscar thanked her, trying not to look too concerned. He went back to his car and called Detective Oaks.

"Oaks."

"It's Oscar Green. I'm looking for Dr. Oliver. I'm here at Green Haven, and the receptionist just told me that she was escorted out to the building by two people. I think she may have been kidnapped by the killer." His cadence was fast and his breathing faster.

"Oscar, cálm down. She wasn't kidnapped. Those were my people. We arrested her."

Oscar dropped the phone. He was on the car's Bluetooth, so it really didn't matter. Oscar wasn't thinking straight. He asked what she was arrested for. Detective Oaks knew this would come down hard on Oscar, but he wasn't used to sugar coating things. He tried.

"She's only a suspect for some wrongdoings, Oscar. I can't tell you anymore."

"Is it something like stealing medications or writing bad prescriptions? She has been acting odd lately. Is she on drugs?" Oscar was almost pleading with the detective for more information.

"Oscar, that's all I can say. Stop talking, hang up, and go back to the hotel. I'll call you later."

Detective Oaks could hear the stress and desperation in his voice, but now that Dr. Oliver admitted there was another person involved, he didn't want Oscar to know much more. Unfortunately, this didn't help Oscar. The detective knew he wouldn't call him later, at least not until he was absolutely sure Oscar was innocent. He also knew that Oscar would follow his advice and return to the hotel. Detective Oaks wanted to know exactly where he was in case he needed to arrest him.

Attorney Joanna Parkland showed up three hours later. She informed the detective that it was not her turn up, but Attorney Landers, whose turn it was, had a conflict of interest in this matter. Detective Oaks gave a muffled chuckle. She looked at him then asked to see her client.

One of the younger detectives led her back to the room. After about an hour of private consultation with her client, Attorney Parkland said her client had information that would lead to the real mastermind behind the whole case.

"My client will tell you everything, but only if she gets full immunity."

"You understand this is a serial murder case? There is no way she gets full immunity. Nice try." Detective Oaks stood there unimpressed with the request.

"And you know this is an FBI case and you can't make any deals. I'm betting you shouldn't even be working this case." Attorney Parkland was also experienced at these sorts of dealings.

"Okay, okay, wait with your client. I'll see what we can do." The seasoned investigator hated having his back against the wall.

Detective Oaks knew he was about to get a verbal beat down from his captain for taking this case so far without informing the FBI. He had no choice at this point. Attorney Parkland was correct; he didn't have the authority to make the deal. He took a deep breath and entered Captain Finn's office. At these times mutual admiration and friendship was not a factor. Oaks explained the situation to him; Captain Finn didn't say a word. Oaks knew it was much worse when the captain didn't scream or even make a sound. He picked up the phone and called the police commissioner's office, gave a brief overview of the matter, and hung up. He looked at Detective Oaks again while dialing a second number. This time it was the US Attorney's Office. He gave an overview once more, listened for a moment, then hung up. He very calmly looked at the detective, telling him they would discuss this later. Detective Oaks would rather Finn just shoot him where he stood. Captain Finn told him to wait at his desk for the US Attorney's Office's lawyer and the FBI agent.

Detective Oaks returned to his desk. His team came over to ask what the next step would be. He told them all to take a long break. He didn't want any of them near the station for the next four or five hours. They left, but not willingly. The US attorney and an FBI agent, not the rookie, showed up at the same time. For all Detective Oaks knew, they could've ridden over together fueling each other up. After introducing themselves, they asked if they could go to a more private space to speak. Captain Finn joined them. They asked the detective to tell them everything from the beginning. He filled them in on everything, including the phone call to the rookie agent and his answer that he was too busy to work the case. To Detective Oaks' happy confusion, they had mixed feelings about his pursuit of the case after it was handed to the FBI. They had to admit he may have stopped a serial killer. He took this as a plus.

The US attorney agreed to a much lower sentence for Dr. Oliver in exchange for her cooperation. Marissa, at the advice of her attorney, took the deal. Attorney Parkland added stipulations of relocation to an out-of-state prison and a new out-of-state identity. She was afraid of the murderer's reach. The US attorney agreed as long as she would testify. Dr. Oliver agreed.

Marissa described being contacted by Bishop Anthony Green just about a year after her residency program ended. She met with him several times before he told her she would soon receive a call from an Oscar Green who had a new business venture for her. She was to accept the deal. He promised to enhance the agreement, including payment of her student loans. He told her if she didn't take the deal, her practice of medicine might be a long and difficult road. Marissa detailed she was going to say no, but after the first meeting with the bishop, some of the patients she had already booked were canceling their appointments. By the third meeting, most of her patients had canceled. Even those she had seen multiple times were now missing their appointments. When Oscar called to set up their first meeting, she pretended not to remember him because Bishop Anthony didn't want her to make it too easy. Marissa explained that she already missed three student loan payments and her patient load was now almost zero. She became desperate at the hands of Bishop Anthony. Once she took the job, her student loans were all paid ahead, with some of the undergraduate loans being paid off in a single payment. Marissa explained the original arrangement called for her to watch over Green Haven and inform the bishop of anything that looked bad or out of control. Then it turned into feeding him information on the board meetings.

Marissa tried desperately to recount all the events in chronological order, but her mind was racing as she struggled with the thought of prison. She backtracked to receiving a call from the bishop, just before accepting the position, telling her that Oscar needed watching over and she was to be, as Bishop Antony put it, "Oscar's special friend." She told him she liked Oscar but not in that way. Marissa told the people in the interrogation room that as time went on, the bishop threatened to completely remove her from the situation if she continued to object. Bishop Anthony told her she could go back to private practice, perhaps in another state or even another country. She admitted he had full financial power over her.

Through tears and long deep breaths, Marissa continued to lay out the events. She explained that for the past two years, at the command of Bishop Anthony, she was forced to collect information on the residents of all three Green Haven, Inc. facilities. She was to find those long-standing residents who the directors of nursing at each facility could pronounce dead. Marissa refused at first, but the bishop had ways of making people do what he wanted. She stated everything was going along as the bishop wanted until Cathy started digging around, then the bishop took it to the next level. Dr. Oliver told them she had tried to get out several times, but the bishop was too powerful. She described being afraid for her life; that the bishop could get to her at any time he wanted.

Detective Oaks wasn't allowed in the interrogation, so he watched the video feed from the next room. He wasn't buying the victim act one bit. He called the captain's cell phone. Another move he knew he'd pay for later. Captain Finn looked up at the camera. The phone rang again. The captain left the interrogation room and stormed into the room where Detective Oaks was watching.

"This better be worth it, or you can quit now!"

"I wanted you to know that the hospital file on her repeatedly says she was unable to take responsibility for mishaps and usually blamed an innocent victim. She's a terrible person, and what she's saying may be partly true, but most of it's an act."

"Okay. I'll ask that we take a break, and then you better do a damn good job of selling this to the US attorney. Understand?"

"Yes, sir." Detective Oaks stood at attention.

"I don't need you to be a smartass now." He flipped Oaks the bird.

Captain Finn went back into the room and requested a break. Everyone, including Marissa, understood this meant the police must have something new to discuss before they go any further. He asked Attorney Parkland if she or her client needed anything before leaving the room. He told the uniformed policeman outside the door to get them whatever they needed.

They all met in the same conference room as earlier, and the detective started reading the file on Dr. Oliver. This time he added the details of specific incidents with staff members and patients. In the end, he added that he had interviewed Dr. Oliver a couple of times, including a phone conversation, and she was always calm and cool, even a bit evasive. Captain Finn looked at him with an impressed expression. He shot a look back suggesting, "Yes, I know how to use fancy words too." Their exchange went unnoticed by the others. As they were leaving the conference room, Detective Oaks gave his opinion that Dr. Oliver was cold and definitely not a victim here. The US attorney turned to the detective and told him to pick up Bishop Anthony Green, now.

52

DETECTIVE OAKS THOUGHT ABOUT sending some of his team over to arrest Bishop Anthony, but if this was to be his last case, he wanted the pleasure of closing it himself.

The detective didn't knock on the door. He wanted to feel the full rush and the thrill of getting his man. He didn't even check to see if the door was unlocked; he just kicked it open. One last hoorah, he thought. He was confident this move would be the last.

Bishop Anthony was sitting in the living room sipping Scotch when the sound of the exploding door jam startled him. His drink spilled down the front of his shirt.

"What is the matter with you! This is uncalled for! Do you know who I am and what I can do to you?"

"Stand up, your unholiness. You're under arrest!"

Both men were now yelling loudly. Neither was going to allow the other to be the alpha in the room. The bishop stared at the detective. His eyes blazed with rage at the total disrespect for the position he held in the community.

Detective Oaks held the handcuffs high in front of the bishop, daring him to take any kind of physical action.

"Go ahead, please. I would love the chance to add resisting arrest to your case."

"Violence is not in my nature. I am a man of God. The Lord takes care of what is needed to be done." Bishop Anthony moved closer to the handcuffs. They were now inches from his face.

"It wasn't the Lord's words that ordered the death of innocent people; it was your words." Detective Oaks' voice was low and gravelly as he spoke.

"You think that your actions here are going to go unpunished, but you're sadly mistaken. The Lord has granted me power in places you can only imagine." Bishop Anthony placed his hands together in front of the detective. His eyes still locked on to the detective's eyes.

"It's you who are going to be punished for everything you've done. You are under arrest for multiple murders, conspiracy to commit murder, and any other damn thing I can think of while I'm filling out the paperwork." Detective Oaks now smiled as he placed the handcuffs on Bishop Anthony.

Detective Oaks was playing the rest of the arrest by the books. He read the bishop his Miranda rights as he politely escorted him to his unmarked vehicle. This may be his last case, but he was going to make sure that the bishop had no room to wiggle free.

The drive to the police station was in total silence. Both men refused to yield. Their eyes fixed on each other through the rearview mirror of the car.

Detective Oaks decided to walk the bishop right through the front door for added effect. A point that did not go well for him later on at his review, but it was worth it. Both the upper brass and the FBI were not pleased with his overt display of conquest. Captain Finn secretly enjoyed the show. A fact that he only admitted to Detective Oaks after several beers in a very loud and crowded bar weeks later and entirely off the record, of course.

53

THE INVESTIGATION WAS OVER. Detective Oaks had pressured the FBI, through Captain Finn and the US Attorney's Office, to issue a public statement clearing Cathy Arden of any involvement in the murders in and around Green Haven, Inc.

The trial of Bishop Anthony Green was set. Cathy testified she and Kyle had figured out that the resident deaths were increasing and that they were not random. She explained her spreadsheets in great detail and how they would eventually lead to Dr. Oliver. Cathy left out the part about Lenny. She promised to keep him out of it, and she kept her word. She had lied to more people in the past few weeks than she wanted to remember. Cathy admitted that her own situation prevented her from finding out the complete story. She finished her testimony by thanking Detective Oaks for being better than the detectives you see on television. She knew he'd like that.

Dr. Oliver's testimony filled in all the blanks missing from Cathy's account. Marissa painted a chilling picture of an evil man cloaked in holy garb. She gave times and details of meetings with Bishop Anthony. She explained emails and texts sent between her and the bishop, including how he manipulated her, Father Brendan, and Sister Diane. She articulated how he blackmailed her by threatening to expose her to Oscar. Marissa conveyed how her relationship with Oscar started with a lie, one she had to keep going because she had grown to care for him.

Cathy testified because she insisted on it, while Marissa Oliver did it as part of her deal. For her role in passing on information about the residents of Green Haven, Inc. that eventually led to their deaths and by extension the deaths of John Perkins, Kyle Strong, Father Brendan, and Sister Diane, and lastly for helping frame Cathy Arden, Dr. Oliver would have been sentenced to two life sentences eligible for parole in twenty-five years. Because of the plea deal, she would serve only five years.

On the last day of the trial, after many character witnesses and his attorney painting Dr. Oliver as mentally ill, Bishop Anthony took the stand, against the advice of his counsel.

"Bishop Anthony, how could a man of God be in league with the devil?" the prosecutor lashed out quickly.

"You are not my judge. Only the Lord will judge me, and He knows I have only done good deeds." He pointed to Heaven as he sat straight and proud in the witness chair.

"Is it true that you're Oscar Green Sr.'s brother? A fact you hid from the world because your brother was a small-time mobster? Wasn't it his money you used to help out Oscar Jr., your nephew?" The prosecutor was standing directly in front of the bishop but addressed the jury for dramatic flair.

"My brother was a good man, and I didn't hide anything."

"When Oscar, Sr. was alive, you were just his puppet. You did the behind-the-scenes grunt work so he could get his way. Didn't he force you to become a priest and then further your career all the way to bishop by pulling strings for you? He knew you could never amount to anything on your own, right?" The prosecutor was taunting him. He knew that the bishop thought of himself as strong and powerful.

"My brother and I were a team. We ran this town together. No one could spit on the sidewalk if we didn't say it was all right. Then just after God called him home, he made me promise to take care of my wannabe millionaire contractor, idiot of a nephew. If he only knew who his father really was and how many people bought those stupid houses he built, just to repay a favor they owed to his father. He never figured it out. He still has no clue. I found that priest. I put him in place. I convinced him to kill those poor souls who hung on for no good reason. I gave him and that mouse of a sister a purpose in life. I told them they were showing peaceful mercy to the forgotten. I showed them what it meant to be in real service. You think this is an easy job? I taught them to put their own opinion aside to create a better world. I told them who to send to Heaven and how to do it. Then that administrator started poking around; thank God the priest had enough sense to call me and tell me about it. With the help of the All Mighty, I was the one who orchestrated it all. I had all the messes my nephew made cleaned up. I did it all for the honor of my brother and all in the name of the Lord. Why? Because my brother's son, my nephew, couldn't hold onto the empire given to him, from beyond the grave, by his father. And, because I swore an oath to my brother and to God." The bishop was almost foaming at the mouth. "How dare anyone question me in this manner" he shouted with every cell in his body.

"Do you wonder where you will go when you die?" The question was asked with calm and in a low tone, just loud enough to tell the jury the prosecutor had gotten his man.

"I will be rewarded well for my deeds. If not, then I'll be with my brother in hell. It's a win-win." His words still carried the fury.

"No more questions."

Oscar sat in the back of the courtroom, in a baseball cap, hiding his face throughout the entire trial. He fought back the tears with anger. His heart had broken as he absorbed every word of Marissa's testimony. During her testimony, she stated that she had come to care for him, but she never said she loved him. A fact that Oscar had noticed at once and that ate at his soul. The confession of his uncle hit Oscar hard. Both his father and the bishop thought so little of him, a realization that Oscar could barely keep quiet with while sitting there in the courtroom.

The jury took only two hours to convict Bishop Anthony Green. When it was over, Oscar left the building without being seen. The newspapers raged for weeks condemning Green Haven, the medical society, and the Church. No one was left untouched.

EPILOGUE

BISHOP ANTHONY WAS BANISHED from the Catholic Church. He currently sits on death row awaiting his third appeal. His attorneys are not hopeful. The attorneys for the Church settled any and all suits for undisclosed amounts. Each settlement included an agreement stating Bishop Anthony, Father Brendan, and Sister Diane acted on their own, without any knowledge or orders from the Church. Now just Anthony Green still maintains he's righteous and still loathes his nephew.

Father Timothy was taken out of his forced retirement and promoted to bishop. He promised he would see that every family wronged by the renounced bishop would receive as much counseling as they needed. None was ever requested.

After leaving the courtroom, Oscar stopped at a hardware store where he bought a sledgehammer. He then drove to each facility, and with all the strength he had, destroyed the cornerstone of each building. Green Haven, Inc. had become a pariah in the industry. In each facility, residents moved out as their yearly contracts ended. Oscar quickly sold each property for much less than they were worth. He had no desire to be part of the dream that became a terrible nightmare. Oscar Green's whereabouts are unknown; he is the better off for it.

Dr. Marissa Oliver writes unanswered letters to Oscar from a prison somewhere. She hopes that one day soon, Anthony Green will meet his maker. She plans to find Oscar when she's released.

Detective Oaks had an official reprimand placed in his permanent file along with a two-week suspension, with pay. He enjoyed visiting Hawaii and plans to move there when he retires in three years. He gets a postcard from Cathy Arden every six months.

Several weeks after the end of the trial, Cathy was asked to return to her old position as director of nursing; she turned it down. As one of Green Haven, Inc.'s last official duties, the board offered Cathy a huge severance check. The check was being drawn from a much more substantial amount of money that Green Haven, Inc. received from the Church in a settlement package. All parties had to sign documentation holding the Church harmless, agree not to sue, and to keep quiet. Cathy took the deal. She added one caveat to the agreement. Since Kyle Strong had no family, the Green Haven, Inc. board would give him a proper burial and donate a large sum of money to a charity in his name. As Cathy attended the funeral, she found it strange that she missed the man who caused her so much angst.

Cathy sat in her apartment looking around and began to cry heavily. These were not tears of joy or relief; they were tears of profound sadness. They came with the realization that she had let her life stray so far from her dreams. These were the same tears that poured from her earlier as she looked at the loneliness her apartment depicted. She understood that staying meant dying, but this time she wouldn't be oblivious. This time it would be painfully slow and with great awareness.

Each box she packed reminded her of the emptiness that her life had become. Most people pack moving boxes filled with memories. Cathy's tears fell harder as she recognized that she was packing nothing but items that collected dust in her world. She sat back down on the couch, a place she had sat countless times in her life, and for the first time, she could feel the cold against her body. Cathy stared at the walls and shelves, now bare, and concluded that they had always been bare; she just never saw it before. There were no family photos, no vacation trinkets, no frozen moments in time with friends. Just a diary of a life lived going through the motions.

Cathy walked into the bedroom and looked in the mirror at the short hair she had now adopted. She knew she could never return to her old life. She removed the dress she had been wearing to reveal mismatched undergarments, and smiled. Cathy walked into her closet and found the bag containing the jeans and T-shirt she bought at the thrift store. She put them on and then slid into the sneakers. She packed only an overnight bag; she wanted nothing except freedom. Freedom from the mundane lifeless world she had created. Cathy put on a denim jacket, grabbed her checkbook, and never looked back.